SPACE ROGUES 2

BIG SHIP, LOTS OF GUNS

JOHN WILKER

Cover art by Antonio Holguin & Greg Bahlmann

ISBN: 978-0-692-14148-9

V 3.2

�֎ Created with Vellum

To my wife, Nicole, who never stops believing in me.

You're about to embark on another fun adventure!
The crew of the *Ghost* is at it again!

When you're done reading, I hope you'll take a minute to leave a review!

OH YEAH!

Coming Christmas 2019!

Space Rogues 5: So This is Earth?

Visit me online at
johnwilker.com
Facebook
Goodreads

Want to be notified when I publish new stuff? Want to get sneak peeks and exclusive short stories?

PART ONE

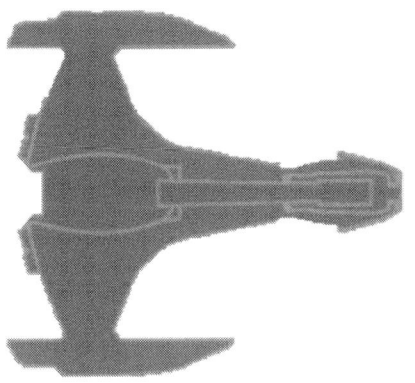

CHAPTER 1

PRIVATEERING

"OKAY, you know what, that was a lot of fun!" Bennie exclaims, a grin splitting his green face, entering the bridge of the *Ghost*. Behind him, Wil and Zephyr follow, both exhibiting a little bounce in their step. Zephyr is also smiling broadly.

Wil drops into his command chair in the center of the room, running a hand through his light brown hair. *Might be time for a haircut.* "No argument there. Those idiots got in way over their heads," he says, tapping a few commands into the control on the arm of his chair. "Between the reward and what we got from their hold," he looks down at the ship's account balance, "we should be able to pay off the bounty the Consortium put on our heads in no time."

Bennie cackles, and in a mocking voice says, "The Xenetan pirates are known throughout this sector, blah blah blah." He drops to the ground, kneeling, and cries out, "Don't hurt us! Please! Mercy!" Then he doubles over, laughing.

Zephyr takes her seat, bringing her own console to life. "I'll admit, getting a letter of Marque from the Harrith government has proven to be less of a terrible idea than I first assumed. There is something satisfying in kicking pirate ass, as Wil would say." She reaches up and releases her hair from the ponytail she prefers to use when in combat.

Wil beams. "So I was right? I'll take it." He leans back and puts his boots on the pilot station in front of him. "Bennie, what's up next?"

The small Brailack gets up from the floor and hurries to his console. He swipes the screen a few times. "We've got a few options. There's a mining colony that's been harassed by pirates a few times, so they're asking for help. There's an agricultural settlement that's offering a pretty credit for some livestock transfer. There's a freighter convoy looking for some protection out in the badlands, and a few other things on the network." A few more swipes. "The livestock job actually has the highest guaranteed pay-out."

The hatch to the bridge opens, and Maxim walks in. "I've secured the last of the crates we took on, what's next?"

Before Wil can answer, Zephyr does: "Livestock."

Without another word, Maxim turns and leaves the bridge.

"I know what he means," Zephyr says, looking from Bennie to Wil. "Livestock jobs suck."

Wil nods. "No argument here. Maybe that mining colony?"

Inclining her head, "Probably a good one. If it's pirates, we get to claim whatever is in their hold, plus fees." She smiles. "And their ship, those always fetch a good price."

Nodding, Wil says, "Yeah. Okay, Bennie, take the mining colony gig."

The Brailack nods. "Roger that." A few taps and then, "Okay, I'm sending the nav plot to your station. The colony is about three days from here, a small system called... well it doesn't appear to have a name, just a registration number. 'P3X-984', how poetic."

Wil nods. He flips a few switches and a low rumble begins to build from deep within the ship. Moments later, the *Ghost* is on its way. The station they have been docked at, in orbit over the outermost planet in the Harrith system, quickly recedes from view on the main screen. "We can go FTL in twenty minutes." He turns to Bennie, "Why don't you go down and set the table? We'll get dinner going as soon as we hit FTL, and if I recall, it's your turn."

"It was my turn last night!" the small Brailack protests

"No, it wasn't. It was mine, and you know it," Zephyr says from her station, then sticks her tongue out at him, while pulling one eyelid down with her finger. The small alien mutters something under his breath as he leaves the bridge.

As the *Ghost* clears the station, and the gravity well of the planet it's orbiting, the large FTL nacelles at the end of its wings power up. At the rear of each a red glow begins to form, then with a flash the *Ghost* jumps to FTL. Wil and Zephyr have worked in companionable silence, getting the ship ready for their next mission and filing the appropriate paperwork to close out their most recent adventure in privateering. The letter of Marque might be lucrative, but the paperwork is monstrous. They stand to leave the bridge and join the others in the lounge. Before they reach the hatch, Zephyr turns to Wil.

"You know we can't keep this up forever. Right?"

Wil sighs. "I know, but that dickhead Xarrix burned us good. The Consortium still has its members and their bounty hunters out for our heads, and the only thing keeping them at bay, even a little, is the Harrith government and our arrangement with them. We leave this region of space, and it's a free for all. Believe me, as soon as we have enough to pay the bounty, we'll pay it."

He continues: "Stealing Gabe from the gangster storage facility was still the right thing to do."

Zephyr nods. This isn't the first time the two of them—she acting in her mostly-official role as first officer—have had this conversation. When they had agreed to raid a secret space station for Xarrix, they hadn't known that a Peacekeeper Engineering bot would be aboard. It turned out that GBE-102002—Gabe—was carrying important data, proving that the Peacekeepers were conspiring to create a war in order to force several non-member systems to join the Galactic Commonwealth. The *Ghost*'s decision to expose this plot had kicked off what GNO were now dubbing the "Harrith Incident," a shoot-out that had eventually involved several major systems, the Peacekeepers and the rebels and which was still having significant repercussions throughout the galaxy.

"I know it was the right thing, Wil," Zephyr says. "And the crew does too, but that doesn't mean they're not getting restless. The other day I caught Bennie hacking the voting system on Galatea—for the 'fun of it' he said, but I suspect he's been taking on side work."

"That little..." Wil starts then takes a deep breath. "Yeah, I can't blame him, I guess. Fucking Xarrix, it's not our fault whatever deal he had set up for Gabe and the data he contained fell apart."

"It sort of is," she smiles.

"Well, yeah, but it's not like we could have just walked away. I mean I wanted to and all..." he trails off, then resumes. "You and Max's reputations and lives were on the line. Not to mention everyone back there on Harrith." He shrugs. "I wonder what he even had planned—it's not like what Gabe had was all that lucrative. Outside of maybe the GC and Peacekeepers paying to keep a lid on it."

"Don't underestimate how much they would have paid to do just that." She sighs. "Well, just keep this in mind: something is going to have to change sooner rather than later if you want to keep this crew together." She turns and opens the hatch leading off the bridge.

NEWSCAST

"GOOD MORNING from GNO stage fifty-nine on Artrax Three, I'm Mon-El Furash. The long-awaited closing arguments of the trial against the Galactic Commonwealth and the Peacekeepers has begun. It's been several months since this historic trial kicked off, following the incident at Harrith Prime that led to several member worlds of the Galactic Commonwealth filing a suit against the GC Governing Council as well as the top levels of Peacekeeper Command." The newscaster touches her large elephant-like ear, listening to someone. "That's correct, this trial has moved so slowly due to the sheer number of witnesses called and the time it has taken to assemble them—all while trying to ensure continuity of government here. It's been a long back and forth, and the outcome is still far from certain, but we'll all find out soon enough what the judges decide."

DINNER, INTERRUPTED

IN THE CREW LOUNGE, the rest of the team is either lounging in one of the comfortable chairs in the center of the room or sitting to one side, at the small kitchen table set against the wall. Bennie is puttering around the kitchenette area, singing something that sounds to Wil oddly like "Manic Monday" by the Bangles.

Gabe is the only one standing, his yellow optical sensors spinning and focusing, his smaller fine manipulator arms are tucked up against his torso where Wil has noticed he keeps them to be out of the way. In his seat nearby, Maxim has a bottle of grum and is flipping through news feeds on the main room display.

"So, what's for dinner?" Wil asks, grabbing two more grum from the fridge. He hands one to Zephyr before she walks over and takes a seat next to Maxim, her free hand finding his.

Bennie turns around, holding a large pan with something sizzling in it in his hands. "Fried melba fish." His face scrunches up. "Wait, no that's not it—tahlo! Tahlo fish, that's it."

Zephyr, Wil, and Maxim exchange a look from across the room. Maxim asks, "What's a tahlo fish?"

"I picked some up on Harrith Prime when we were there last. The merchant said it was a delicacy. Something about the lake they live in, chemicals and such. Somewhere in the northern reaches," he shrugs. "After that, I kind of tuned him out until I paid." He raises a hand just as Wil opens his mouth. "But. I had him send me a recipe with my receipt."

This mollifies Wil. At least with a recipe, Bennie isn't winging it, which is usually when things go wrong in the kitchen—typically with fire involved. Followed by intestinal distress for one or more members of the crew.

Since the "Harrith Incident," as GNO has dubbed it, the crew have enjoyed a reasonably comfortable life as privateers for the government of Harrith. The battle had severely reduced the size and power of the Harrith fleet, and the Quilant and Zengar fleets had suffered similarly. As a result, piracy and general lawlessness became the order of the day in the Harrith system and its outlying territories, as well as several smaller systems nearby. Opportunists from all over the quadrant had started setting up shop: raiding small colonies, attacking shipping routes, and more.

That was when the governments of the major systems in the region began offering letters of Marque to any ship that could show sufficient firepower to act in that system's interests. The *Ghost* was more than suited for this type of work, and the work itself resonated with the crew. For the last seven standard months, the *Ghost* has been crisscrossing the sectors of space around the Harrith system: protecting trade convoys and ore shipments, and even occasionally running freight, when the load (and payout) is right.

All told, there are several hundred small- to mid-size ships roaming the area, acting for one government or another. While law and order are not fully restored, the last few months have seen a drastic decrease in overall crime in the area. According to the local news outlets, it'll be several cycles before any of the major powers get back to full military strength. Despite the losses, Harrith and its unaffiliated neighbors have flat-out refused the aid of the Galactic Commonwealth.

Luckily, all that balances out the other issue facing the crew. After the "Harrith Incident" and their theft of Gabe from the secret space station, the Consortium that owned station had somehow been clued in as to why they had been robbed and who set the job up. Xarrix had one shot to escape the blame and quickly took it, burning Wil and the crew of the *Ghost* without a second thought. Bounty hunters from all over the quadrant were now looking for the *Ghost*, and while it was no secret where they were, the Harrith government and Navy had made it clear that the *Ghost* was still quite popular and would remain wholly protected while in service to the people of Harrith Prime.

Wil watches Gabe, who has moved to the kitchenette to talk to Bennie. The two-meter-high droid deploys his smaller arms and begins taking dishes and returning them to their storage cabinets. He finishes the task quickly, four arms helps. He has a wash cloth draped over his left primary arm.

Suddenly, Gabe pauses. "Captain, we're receiving a distress call. Wideband." Everyone else immediately stops what they're doing.

Wil gets up and heads for the bridge, Zephyr, and Maxim on his heels. As they go, Gabe offers, "I've instructed the ship to alter course." The hatch out of the common space closes.

Bennie looks up at his mechanical friend. "Guess we're clearing the table," he says.

Gabe picks up the tray with the fish on it. "It would appear so. Is tahlo fish good reheated?"

CRIME DOESN'T PAY

As Wil approaches the bridge, the hatch opens automatically. The main screen is already displaying a tactical plot showing the source of the distress call and the *Ghost's* relative position and speed. Taking his seat at the command/pilot station, he announces, "We're on course." Zephyr and Maxim quickly take their places.

Zephyr taps out a few commands and is murmuring into the mic at her station—likely talking to the source of the distress call, Wil assumes. She looks over at him and nods, and the overhead speaker comes to life. "Please repeat last," She says louder than before.

"This is freighter Sartomo. *We're under attack, there are three freighters in our convoy. We're under attack! Help us!"*

Wil tilts his head up slightly—a habit he's never been able to shake, despite it being completely unnecessary, as the computer will pick up his voice no matter what he does with his head. "This is Captain Wil Calder of the *Ghost.* We're on our way, but we're..." he looks over to Zephyr, who shows the count by flashing both hands four times—luckily, Palorians have five fingers, or more accurately, three fingers and two thumbs. "...forty centocks out. Can you hold them off?"

Static fills the speakers momentarily, "*I think so—all three of us have defenses, but we won't last forever. Please hurry!*"

"We're on our way. I promise. Just hang in there." There's a soft beep, indicating that the channel is closed. Wil taps on an icon set into the arm of his chair, and says quickly, "Gabe, are you in engineering? I need more speed. Ramp up the reactor to one-twenty."

"I am, Captain," the droid's voice informs him. "But the reactor and the engines will not be able to sustain that level of power for long."

"They only need to last less than forty centocks. Do it."

The ship shudders, and even with the inertia compensators everyone feels a slight lurch and pressure pushing them back against their seats. "Acknowledged," says Gabe's voice. There is another soft beep—the channel closing.

Zephyr looks up from her station. "New ETA, twenty-five centocks."

Wil nods. "Max, get ready. I'll drop us out of FTL as close to on top of them as I can. You'll have to lock on and open fire as fast as you can. Zee, did the Captain of the *Sartomo* say how many attackers there were?"

She nods. "Yes. Four."

Wil whistles. "Tough odds. For them." He grins at Maxim, who grins back.

The next twenty-odd minutes drag on, everyone waiting tensely in their seats. At fifteen minutes out, the long-range sensors are able to start telling them what's going on up ahead: two, not three, icons representing freighters are clustered together, with three red triangles orbiting them, occasionally swooping in close then back out again. *Looks like the situation has changed quite a bit*, Wil thinks. He assumes that one of the freighters is out of commission, either destroyed or at least disabled enough to not register on the long-range scopes.

From the overhead speakers, Gabe's voice comes again: "Captain, the heat shielding on the reactor is becoming unstable. We have, at most, five more centocks before I have to bring the reactor back down below one hundred percent. Ideally closer to eighty percent. Beyond that, the reactor will scram, and we will be on emergency power." The level of detail is, as usual, perfect—Gabe takes his role as ship's engineer seriously, and Wil appreciates it.

"Acknowledged. Push it as far as you can, as long as you can, then dial it back. Just remember, we're going into combat, so we're going to need more, not less, power."

There is what sounds like a sigh. "Very well." A soft beep as the connection is closed.

Bennie, who had joined them on the bridge mid-way during the flight towards the battle, finally chimes in. "I'm picking up narrowband comms, likely the pirates talking to each other. They're encrypted, of course."

Wil turns to the station Bennie has called home for almost a year. "Can you crack them?"

"Of course I can, but do we care what they're saying? It'll be easier to just jam their comms." He rubs his small hands together.

"Fine, do that, I really don't care as long as they're off balance." Wil taps a few controls and the display switches to the view directly ahead of the ship: currently the stretched-out stars of FTL travel.

"Two minutes. Zee, hail the *Sartomo*."

She nods and taps a few things on her console, then nods again. Wil speaks loudly towards the ceiling, "Hang in there, we're here." He motions to her with a slashing gesture of his hand, and hears the soft beep of a closed comms channel.

A slight lurch forward tells them that Gabe has reduced the power output of the main reactor significantly. A minute later, Wil slides the FTL control back to "sub-light," and the *Ghost* is immediately in the middle of the fray. Directly ahead and to port are the two remaining freighters, one venting drive plasma from a wound near its main engines. Slightly further ahead and to starboard are two of the three attackers. They're small combat craft, about half as big as the *Ghost*, but well armed—cutter class at best, Wil decides. Likely a crew of two or three, the rest of the ship probably just cargo hold and engines.

Maxim unleashes the forward weapons on the two craft. The turrets below and beside the bridge roar to life.

Wil nods to Zephyr. "Hail them."

On the screen in front of them, the plasma cannons mounted on the main engine pods stream lethal bolts of energy at the furthest pirate, while the forward weapons, mounted under the forward section of the ship, spit almost equally deadly fire at the nearer pirate.

Zephyr nods back. "Attacking craft," she says, her voice all business, despite the battle raging outside, "this is your only warning. Power down your engines and weapons, or be destroyed." Then there is the familiar soft beep, telling Wil the channel has been closed. "Bennie?" Zephyr asks.

"Their comms are jammed. If they want to talk to each other, they'll have to do it in the open, until they settle on a new frequency... that we'd hear them agree to and I could jam again." He grins.

A pair of missiles streaks out from the launchers on the *Ghost*'s underside. They fly from the bottom of the view screen, splitting up and heading towards two of the pirates. The two attackers directly ahead explode. Maxim is grinning from ear to ear.

"Well done, Max!" Wil shouts.

THE PAST

"Well as jobs go, this one sucked," Wil says plopping down into the command chair on the bridge. From the hold comes a screeching moo-type sound, and Wil winces. "Computer, is there a way to dampen the sound from the cargo hold?"

"*Negative.*" The infuriatingly calm male voice replies.

"Shit." He pulls up the pre-flight checklist and starts getting ready to leave whatever this planet is called. "Computer, open a channel to Xarrix."

A soft beep announces the channel is open. A few seconds later comes a familiar raspy voice. "You have them?"

"Yeah, I got 'em. Whatever the hell 'they' are."

"They're expensive, that's what they are. You don't need to know more. How soon can you be here?"

Wil looks at his console. "Eight hours—er, uh, long ticks? No. Eight tocks. Yeah, tocks."

There's a loud, hissing sigh. "Fine."

The soft beep announces the connection has closed.

"Asshole," Wil says.

The *Ghost* lifts off the planet and accelerates out of the atmosphere. It's powerful atmospheric engines roar, pushing it away from the planet. The smuggler that met Wil with the creatures covers his face and swears.

Once the ship's course is underway, Wil heads back to the hold. As soon as the personnel hatch opens, he's assaulted by a smell so bad he makes a gagging sound and almost pukes. The creatures below look up and let out a screeching *moo* sound. He shudders and walks down to the hold. Whatever these things are called, they're ugly: six stubby legs sprouting from a tubby tube-shaped body, covered in slightly sticky leathery skin. Three tails swish back and forth lazily. To Wil, the worst thing about them is their faces—four beady eyes set wide apart on a big, flat skull, above a completely toothless mouth.

Wil pushes through the shuffling animals to the port side of the hold, where he grabs some of the feed Xarrix's henchman gave him. He scoops it up and tosses it to the floor. The salamander-cows, as Wil has decided to call them, shuffle around. Long, prehensile tongues loll out and writhe on the floor looking for the pellets.

"That's disgusting!" Wil shouts, edging back to the hatch while trying to avoid salamander-cow saliva. He shuts the hatch and heads back to the lounge with a shudder.

Wil drops into one of the large chairs in the crew lounge, a grum in one hand, something like beef jerky in the other. "Computer, update on search routine, 'find Wil friends'?" He looks at the ceiling, waiting.

"*No results.*"

"Really?"

"*No humans have been reported within the sphere of the Galactic Commonwealth.*"

"Man! Why hasn't someone kidnapped anyone else from Earth? How can I be the only one?"

"*Unable to answer.*" Wil imagines a smug, beach tanned face smirking.

"Shut up!"

With six hours to go, he looks around the lounge. "Mr. Sulu, are we still on course?" He nods slowly a few times. "Good, good." He looks over to the couch-thing, also empty. "Commander Worf, weapons status?" More nodding, then Wil sighs, and says, "Good. Hope we won't need weapons to transport salamander-cows."

CHAPTER 2

YOU CAN RUN

THE THIRD ATTACK CRAFT, currently on the other side of the two remaining freighters, immediately turns away from them and accelerates to what Wil assumes is its maximum sub-light speed.

"Hail the freighters." He is looking at the tactical plot on a sub monitor of his station, watching the remaining pirate flee. The channel opens with a crackle.

"*Thank you! Thank you so much—we thought you wouldn't make it in time.*"

"Are your ships intact?" The third freighter that had no longer been showing on the long-range scans is in fact just heavily damaged and adrift, no power readings. There's a large hole in it's side, likely where the reactor used to be. The crew is lucky the reactor scrammed versus exploded, Wil thinks. The other two freighters are in slightly better shape.

"*We are, yes. The* Lothal *is on back up power, but her crew is alive. We can transfer them and their cargo to our ships. The* Tarkin *can be repaired on site.*"

Wil nods to himself and brings the *Ghost* around and under the freighters, on a course to pursue the last pirate. "Good, we'll be back. We've got one left to engage."

Over the speaker, the voice is clearly smiling. *"Good. Destroy them. Those krebnacks deserve no less."* The channel closes.

Wil smiles. "I like that guy. Zee you still have eyes on that ship? Bennie, see if you can keep tabs on his comms."

"I'll try, he picked up a good lead," Zephyr replies from her station.

"Just don't lose him, they must have a mothership or base somewhere nearby. I don't think that little cutter can go FTL."

Max looks up from his station. "Confirmed. I was able to scan the other two before I destroyed them. They were not FTL-capable vessels, nor is the remaining ship."

Wil pushes the sub-light throttle all the way forward. "Let's go hunting, then."

Only a few minutes later, the sensors pick up several asteroids —presumably part of this system's asteroid belt, which Wil knows is nearby. He slides the throttle back, letting the small ship leave them behind.

"Keep an eye on them, let's wait until they get to their base. Maxim, Zee, go get dressed."

As both ex-Peacekeepers stand up and leave the bridge, heading for the small armory that sits behind the bridge between the port and starboard airlocks, Wil brings the *Ghost* about and accelerates away from the pirates. "Bennie, engage full stealth systems. Let's let them think we're heading back to protect those freighters."

The *Ghost* is now for all intents and purposes invisible. Not cloaked—that technology on the scale of a starship is still next to impossible—but the pirates most definitely can't see them.

"They're slowing down," Bennie reports. He has added Zephyr's station's capabilities to his, so as to monitor the long-range scanners. The main screen zooms in on a particularly lumpy-looking asteroid, roughly a kilometer wide and two long. There are a few habitat modules and other pieces of equipment visible on its surface, as well as a large bay door leading down inside the asteroid. The small attack craft has vanished down that rabbit hole. There are also several visible weapons emplacements on the surface, to protect the bay doors. "It looks like they don't close that bay door all the time," Bennie says. "So as long as their guns don't pick us up and shred us, we can fly right down their throat."

Wil shudders. "Dude, that's a really weird and off-putting mixed metaphor." He slides the throttle forward a bit, to the max speed that the stealth system can keep them hidden, and brings the *Ghost* back around on her original heading.

"What? I'm trying to work in more humanisms." The small being shrugs.

"That's not... never mind." Wil turns back to face the screen. It takes a lengthy temple rubbing to remove, *humanisms* from his mind, until finally he reduces the *Ghosts* speed sliding past the sentry gun emplacements and into the entrance to the launch bay that has been carved into the asteroid.

"Bennie, find me an airlock or something." Wil stands up. "Gabe—to the bridge." The computer picks up that this was directed at Gabe, and routes the request to engineering.

Less than two minutes later, Gabe enters. "Take the controls," Wil says, "and dock us where Bennie says. I'm going to change. You're in command."

"Why is he in charge?" Bennie groans, as Wil heads off the bridge to join Zephyr and Maxim.

"Because he has never accidentally crashed the ship into anything."

"That was one time," Bennie says, almost under his breath. Gabe turns to look at Bennie, then takes his seat.

In the armory between the port and starboard airlocks, Wil sheds his basic flight suit for a more form-fitting armored suit. He looks at himself in the mirror *Maybe more sparring with Max and*

Zee, he thinks, putting a hand on his stomach. *Or less grum. Overall not bad for thirty-six though.* He turns once to look himself over, then notices Zephyr watching him. Blushing, he adds armor plates to the hard points on his torso and limbs. Once connected, each piece signals the suit computer that they're active. Then he grabs the long brown coat that he had specially made a few years ago—it hangs just like a trench coat, but can absorb several direct hits from energy weapons and will even stiffen on contact with projectiles. Once done with that, Wil grabs two blasters and adds them to hip holsters built into his armor, and then grabs two armored gauntlets. One has a space where his wrist comms integrates into the material. Turning his palms over, small circles on each begin to glow.

Over the intercom, Gabe announces, "We are in position. We have attached to a service airlock. It's on our port side. Bennie is attempting to hack the computer so that they do not see our connection. The docking tube is extended."

Wil finishes attaching a few last shield emitters and other pieces of equipment to his armor and trench coat, then activates the helmet that retracts into his armor when not in use. His armor isn't as advanced or as powerful as the Peacekeeper combat armor Zephyr and Maxim wear, even outdated as those suits are, but it's served him well so far, and the lighter, modular design allows him to upgrade and replace pieces as needed. It's the same armor he wore, always under his long brown duster, when he rescued his two friends from the Partherians after they had been set up by the Peacekeepers and captured, all that time ago.

BREAKING AND ENTERING

THE *GHOST*'S AIRLOCK OPENS, and fifty meters away Wil can make out the faint outline of another airlock. Apparently, this one doesn't get used often—several of the light-strips outlining it are burnt out. The lights in the ship's docking umbilical are dimmed, which is smart thinking on Gabe's part.

Wil leaves the *Ghost* and drifts through the tunnel connecting the ship to the airlock, Maxim following behind him and Zephyr bringing up the rear.

"Secure Comm, channel nine," Wil says, and the limited AI in the suit activates the channel and communicates the change with the rest of the team's suits. "Check in, Ghost one."

"Ghost two," Zephyr says.

"Ghost three," Maxim adds.

"Ghost base," Gabe says from the bridge.

Wil reaches the airlock. "Ghost base, we're at the airlock, open her up."

"Ghost one, open who up?"

Wil sighs. "It's an expression... just open the airlock. Please."

"Huh, dumb expression. Wait one," Bennie replies. A moment

later, the outer door of the airlock slides open. There's enough room for all three to enter.

Maxim, the last to get in, places a small device on the surface of the asteroid. "Booster planted, relay active."

"Confirmed," Gabe replies.

Zephyr looks at Wil. "We seem to be getting better at this."

He nods. "Don't jinx it."

The outer door slowly shuts. The airlock takes an agonizingly long time, to pressurize, at least to Wil. Finally, the inner door opens—Wil steps immediately right and takes a knee, while Zephyr goes left and takes a knee as well. "Clear." They say in unison. Maxim steps out, pulse rifle up, and quickly pans left and right. Then he reaches back and presses a button on the control panel for the airlock, the inner door closes.

"Passive scanners can only pick up so much, but looks like you've got about twenty or thirty bad guys throughout the rock," Bennie reports over the comms. "I've got control of some of their systems. I'm working on the rest, but for now, they're at least blind to our presence out here."

The corridors of the base are all cut right from the rock of the asteroid: rough walls lined with pipes and conduits, floors worn smooth and shiny from countless boots.

Up ahead, just before a large blast door, the corridor forms a "T"—and two pirates emerge from the right avenue. They turn and stop, staring blankly at the three armored intruders. Before the dumbstruck pirates can move, let alone sound any type of alarm, Zephyr shoots past Wil, arm-mounted blasters opened fully up, ripping both pirates to shreds. Wil and Maxim quickly move in to drag the bodies around a corner.

"Ghost base, any alarms sounding?" Wil asks.

"Negative."

Wil nods and looks around. "Those two were coming from that direction," he says, pointing down the corridor the two pirates had come from. "Let's go up there, see where they were coming from. Maybe a command center or vault." He heads off down the corridor.

Ten minutes and nearly half a kilometer later, the boarding team is standing in front of another large blast door, this one locked. Wil steps in front of the door. Maxim and Zephyr stay a few meters back, keeping watch down the corridor. "Bennie, can you crack this lock?"

The cough Wil hears tells him the answer before the testy Brailack can answer. "Of course. Put the remote key next to the control panel." Wil does, While the device works, he flips through screens on his wristcomm, *Hey there are games*. Finally, the large blast door opens. Inside is a cavern cut from the asteroid, just like the rest of the facility, yet much rougher—the walls here are more ragged, the ceiling is jagged and uneven, the lights mounted haphazardly. The floor isn't as worn or even flat as the corridors, but it is covered with crates, many of them overflowing with ingots of various metals. There are jewels, works of art, pieces of expensive looking technology, and more, lying all over the place.

Over the comms, Bennie's voice interrupts them. "Uh, Ghost One. I think they noticed my intrusion." As he speaks, the lights in the chamber, and the corridor outside it, all dim and change to a deep red. A warning klaxon blares.

"Ya think?" Wil turns to his two teammates, their matte-black armor menacing as ever in the red glow. "Okay, let's finish this, and claim this stuff." He waves his hand around the room. The two former Peacekeepers waver, then fade away, their body armor shifting the light around them, rendering them next to invisible.

Wil turns and leaves the treasure chamber, where he runs right into three pirates.

MESS WITH THE BULL

"WAIT! WAIT!" Wil shouts at the three pirates, all currently leveling blaster rifles at him. They pause, looking at each and then back at Wil, then each takes a blaster shot to the head, dropping to the ground. Wil nods, already heading down the corridor. "Thanks, you two! Ghost base, can you pinpoint their command center?"

"They activated scramblers the moment they realized you were there," Bennie replies, "but our last passive scan showed that what looks like the command center, based on power consumption, is five levels above you."

"Wil, you head up to the command center, we'll clear these levels," Zephyr says. Wil only knows where she is because her suit computer is talking to his and relaying her position to his HUD as a faint green outline.

He quickly turns and runs down the corridor, following Bennie's instructions to the nearest lift.

Behind him, he hears Zephyr turns to Maxim: "Ready to do this?" Then footsteps, and they are gone, in the opposite direction.

As Wil turns a corner, he sees the lift. It's guarded by two pirates, rifles leaning on their shoulders. Thinking quickly, he steps around the corner and walks right up to the two guards. "What're you two doing here?" he asks.

The two pirates look at each other, then the taller one turns to Wil. "Who the wurrin are you? I've never seen you before." His rifle lowers to aim right at Wil, and the other guard follows his lead.

Wil raises both hands. "Hey, hey! What're you talking about? I sat with you at lunch, what—last week? What the wurrin dude! We talked about the Breakfast Club!" The taller guard glances at the other one, then back to Wil. Wil smiles, then glances at the other guard.

The taller guard glances back to the shorter. "What 'breakfast club'? I don't even eat breakfast."

Wil drops both hands and fires two plasma blasts from the blasters built into each palm of his armor. The glowing plasma emitters steam slightly as they cool down after firing.

Wil steps over the two bodies and pushes the button next to the lift. "Eat your heart out Tony Stark," he says, grinning.

As the lift doors open, his comms crackle. "I've still got a little control," Bennie reports. "No primary systems, but plenty of subsystems."

Wil steps into the lift. As the doors close, he tells Bennie, "Kill the lights."

"On it."

The lights in the lift immediately go out, and so does its upward motion.

"Just the lights, you dummy!" Wil says from his now motionless lift. "Now I'm stuck in here."

"Dren, sorry. Hold on."

"Not going anywhere, take your time." A beat later the lift gets moving again. "Thanks, Bennie."

The doors open onto a large receiving area, a massive blast

door standing directly opposite the lift. Between Wil and the entrance to the command center are several pirates.

"You guys!" Wil pants, and drops his hands to his knees. "They're a level below! I barely got on the lift before they over-ran us."

One of the pirates, who actually has a peg-leg, comes forward suspiciously. "You don't look like you just fought anyone."

"How many are there?" a different pirate shouts from the other side of the large room.

Peg-leg raises its rifle, aiming at Wil. "Shut up Merkle! He could be one of them! I don't recognize him."

Wil looks around the room. "Well I don't recognize..." and he thrusts his finger at a random pirate, "this guy!"

"I'm female, you krebnack!"

"Oh..."

All the rifles in the room are up and aimed at Wil now.

"Hey, Wil, you need some help or something?" Bennie asks from the *Ghost*.

"Lights out," Wil says and dives to one side, just as pulse blasts begin tearing the back of the lift apart.

"What?" Bennie asks.

"The lights, asshole! Turn the lights out on this level! They're shooting at me!" Wil has his back to the side of the lift and is stretching one hand forward, palm out to fire plasma blasts from his palm emitter.

"Oh, well you should have told me the plan first, then!"

"Goddamnit Bennie!" A shot hits Wil's glove, destroying the plasma emitter.

At that moment, the lights go out. There's a fair bit of shouting. Wil grabs his pistols and scoots across the floor of the lift. His armor helmet engages and switches to light amplification.

"Where is he?"

"He has to be in the lift still. Move forward!"

"What do you mean you can't turn the lights on?" another pirate yells into its comms.

Wil leans out, and unleashes pulse pistol hell on the three pirates that are now less than a meter from the lift. Before the remaining pirates can react, he rolls to the opposite side of the elevator, then immediately leans out again, just in time to see two more pirates creeping towards the lift. One after the other, he drops them with his pistol, then crawls out of the lift, keeping to the edge of the room.

Peg-leg and the female pirate are backed up against the door to the command center, with one other remaining pirate.

"Shit," Wil mutters.

"What's wrong?" Bennie asks.

"Shut up."

The remaining pirates are looking this way and that, trying to listen. The weapons fire has stopped, and the room is silent now. Wil slowly reaches over to the body of one of the pirates and grabs a piece of tech off the being's shoulder—then tosses it across the room.

Peg-leg and girl-pirate spin and fire at the source of the sound, stepping towards it and away from the door. Wil jumps up and dives for the lone pirate, slamming the butt of one of his pistols into the creature's temple—at least, he thinks it's the thing's temple. The last two pirates spin around at the sound of the fight, just in time to take a pulse pistol blast each to the face.

"Sorry, girl alien," Wil says. "Mess with the bull, you get the horns. Bennie, I'm outside the command center." He turns back to the pirate he hit with his pistol, firing once more. "Sorry dude."

"Finally. Zephyr and Maxim are having a hard time."

"What? Are you kidding me!?" He turns and runs down the corridor, following Bennie's instructions to the nearest working lift.

THE PAST

"TEN THOUSAND CREDITS. AS PROMISED." Xarrix nods to Wil as his wristcomm beeps, signaling that the transaction is complete.

"Yeah. Thanks," Wil says, looking past his sometimes-employer. They're in Xarrix's customary booth, at the same bar where Wil first met him on Fury, close to the spaceport.

"You seem... I don't know, weirder than usual. What's wrong with you?" Xarrix is idly tapping a few commands into his wrist-comm. He pauses and looks up at Wil, his reptilian face tilting like a Labrador when it's listening to its human. His big eyes blink three times quickly.

"I'm touched. I'm fine though." Wil looks down at his hands, and sighs. "I guess I'm just lonely." Before Xarrix can cut him off, he continues, "I mean, as far as I know, I'm the only human out here. Everywhere I go, everywhere I look, I never see another face like mine."

"Multonae look a lot like you..." Xarrix offers, "pink, mostly hairless..."

Wil doesn't even acknowledge the comment. "I guess it's starting to weigh on me. I don't really have anyone out here. I'm alone on the ship..."

"I'll buy the ship from you." Xarrix is looking directly at Wil now.

Again, Wil ignores him. "I drink alone between projects for you. I haven't had sex in..." He starts ticking off his fingers. "... two and a half years! Oh god! Can you even imagine that? Over two years, no sex?" Finally, he looks up at Xarrix.

"My people mate once a year, in a collective orgy that fills a space the size of a stadium. Our women carry their young for three years, so they skip every two ruts if they're with brood. The competition is fierce, many go — unfulfilled."

Wil blinks a few times. "Uh yeah. My people mate considerably more frequently, though usually much more privately. A stadium, really?" He shakes his head and mumbles again, "Three years!"

Xarrix stands up. "Yes, well, this has been... it's been something. I hope to never do it again. I'll be in touch when I have work for you." Awkwardly, he puts a clawed hand on Wil's shoulder, before walking away into the crowd.

"Great. Thanks, I'll wait for your call. Nothing else to do." Wil looks around and spots a server, flagging him—he thinks it's a him —down. "What's stronger than grum?"

CHAPTER 3

WHY IS IT NEVER EASY?

As WIL DISAPPEARS AHEAD of them, Zephyr turns to Maxim. "Ready to do this?"

"I'd follow you anywhere."

"Flirt."

"Ghost base, any idea what's down this corridor?" Maxim asks, as the two of them head in the opposite direction to Wil.

"Unfortunately, no," Gabe replies. "Our passive scans registered a few chambers and a cross corridor that leads to a stairwell. I suggest you head towards that and begin clearing the levels."

"Roger that," Zephyr says, as the two Palorians increase their pace to a light jog, doing their best to mix speed and stealth.

Bennie chimes in over the comms. "I can open all the access hatches on the stairwell. They won't know where you are, and as long as there are no environmental emergencies, the computer won't force them closed."

The stairwell hatch is indeed open when they arrive, having secured the two chambers they came across on their way there. As they reach the next level, they see a small group of pirates standing not too far from the door to the stairwell.

"Glad he opened all the doors," Maxim whispers, as they slip out into the corridor.

The pirates are a mixed bag of races—some they recognize, some they don't. There are two Ruknaks, though. "This could be a problem," Maxim mutters, watching the group. Ruknaks are from a high-gravity world, and as a result, their typically five-foot frame is entirely muscle. Their skin is thick, almost rock-like, and it does a good job of absorbing energy-weapons fire. The Tarsi attempted to add the Ruknak to their Peacekeeper legions, until they realized that as a race the Ruknak aren't much smarter than a garden pail. If it weren't for their neighbors, the Sylban, they wouldn't even have space travel.

The group is talking amongst themselves, apparently trying to coordinate with someone somewhere for the defense of the station. "Should we just kill them?" Maxim asks.

"I don't know if we can take those Ruknak down fast enough," Zephyr answers. "Let's see what they do."

The pirates start walking down the corridor. Either they came from the level above or the one below—most likely above, as otherwise Zephyr and Maxim would probably have heard them before now. Twenty meters down the corridor, the group turns a corner and runs into another group of pirates, who are escorting some kind of a technician with scanning equipment.

"Uh oh," Maxim says, right as the technician looks up from her hand terminal at the other group of pirates, and directly at Maxim and Zephyr two meters behind them.

"Watch out!" is all the startled tech has time to say, before Maxim and Zephyr open fire on the confused group. The pirates of the new group were furthest from the two ex-Peacekeepers, and have time to drop to the ground and open fire. Blaster bolts strike them both, glancing off their armor, causing the prismatic shielding to waver and fade in places. The nearest group of pirates are mostly lying on the ground, plasma blasts smoking—except for the two Ruknak, who have slowly turned to face the now very visible invaders.

"Dren," Zephyr hisses as the two walking piles of rock start to advance. Ruknak only have two large fingers and a thumb, so most weapons don't suit them, but clubs are made to be held by any hand, and each Ruknak has one.

"Fall back!" Maxim orders, his HUD showing red warning icons on several parts of his armor. With his hand on Zephyr's shoulder, the two backtrack down the corridor, towards the stairwell.

"Ghost base, we're taking heavy fire, and our armor is compromised," Maxim shouts, as they try to keep up a steady rate of fire to keep the advancing pirates back. Unfortunately, the two Ruknak are providing an excellent walking barrier to fire from.

"Get to the stairwell, and go up," Bennie orders.

The moment they enter the stairwell the hatch slams shut. "You have thirty microtocks to get to the next door," Bennie tells them.

Their armor may no longer be able to provide stealth, but its power enhancement capabilities allows them both to dash up the stairs three or four at a time, clearing the threshold of the next level's hatch with microtocks to spare.

"What's on this level?" Zephyr asks, as the hatch closes behind them. A light on the panel next to the hatch lights up, indicating that the hatch is sealed.

"Well, for one thing, less bad guys," Bennie says. Before she can snap at him, he continues, "From our limited sensor data, it also looks like this level is mostly crew bunks. I don't have full control of their systems. They've got a good hacker somewhere who's keeping me from taking over entirely, but I can keep that stairwell locked up for at least a few more centocks."

"Acknowledged," Zephyr replies, as she and Maxim head down the corridor, poking their heads into each room they come across to ensure no one has slept through the alarm and is still in their bunk.

A few minutes later they reach the lift. Maxim reports in: "Ghost base, this level is clear."

The next level, however, is not.

OKAY, THIS IS GETTING OLD

THE LIFT DOORS open on the level Zephyr calculates is two below the command center—a level with a few dozen pirates assembled on it, currently. They are looking at what appears to be large training room, which the pirates were using as a staging post before they assaulted the command level.

"Oh, dren!" Zephyr exclaims, palming the lift control as the mass of pirates turns to face the lift. Maxim pushes her out of the way as several plasma blasts rip the back of the lift car to pieces—along with several pieces of Maxim's armor.

The car shakes and the light panels inside explode, as plasma rips them to shreds.

"Bennie, we're taking fire! We need help!" Maxim shouts into the comms in his helmet. Pieces of his armor are sparking as plasma blasts make contact.

The lift doors start to close, but are quickly damaged under the barrage of weapons fire, until they stop moving, a foot apart from each other. "Oh Grolack!" Bennie says, over the comms. "Their hacker is good—he's keeping me out of most of the station's systems."

Zephyr is leaning against the right door, Maxim against the

left. Each is taking turns to lean out and fire their plasma rifles into the room.

Bennie is back: "I'm trying to talk Wil through hacking his way into the command center. How his people ever got into orbit, I'll never know," the Brailack scoffs.

"Bennie! You little krebnack! We're taking fire! This lift is compromised, and we're going to die!" Maxim shouts.

"I'm working as fast as I can! Wil isn't that bright!"

"I can hear you, you asshole!" Wil shouts back, over the open comms channel.

A plasma blast strikes Zephyr, just as she leans out to fire. She falls back with a cry, her shoulder smoking, the armor melted and deformed.

"We're working on it! Hold on!" A few seconds pass, then Bennie is back: "Are both of your armors intact?"

Maxim glances at his HUD: lots of green, a lot more yellow, but no red. He glances at Zephyr and nods. "Seals intact. Why?"

Suddenly there's a loud roaring, as the lift car lurches and drops a few inches. It shakes with the force of the air rushing past it. The lights in the room beyond the lift turn orange—if there were lights left the lift car, Zephyr assumes they'd be orange too, signaling a breach. The doors would be also snapping shut, if they still could.

Over the roar, they hear Bennie's voice. "Wil was able—"

Wil cuts in: "I can speak for myself, you green turd. I couldn't get much control, but wherever their pet hacker is, he's likely either sealed in a room or dead." He sounds like he's out of breath. "I was able to get access to enough systems to blow a few hatches and keep the emergency bulkheads from closing."

Outside the lift car, Maxim can see the pirates collapsing. He lifts his rifle and shoots one smart enough to wear a vac suit dead center in the chest. Not an armored vac suit though, he sees with satisfaction.

As the roar of escaping air starts to die down, Maxim helps Zephyr stand up; her armor is severely damaged in several places, and it's a minor miracle it hasn't been compromised. He looks around the room—nearly two dozen bodies are bathed in the orange light of the decompression alarms.

"Are you guys okay?" Bennie asks, over the comms.

"We're fine," Zephyr answers. "But we're going to need a different way to the command center."

"Or back to the ship, whichever," Maxim amends.

"I'm locking down the station; there are a few last pirates scattered around the base. Looks like the smart ones that had vac suits on," Wil says, over the common channel.

"They'll be dead by the time the Harrith Authorities arrive, and we can cash our credits in," Bennie replies. There is a disturbing amount of glee in his voice.

"You're a dark little fella; you know that?" Wil answers back.

"Whatever," the Brailack answers. Then, "Gabe says he's called in the Harrith. Nearest cruiser is five tocks out."

"Wil, meet us down here and we can walk back to the ship," Zephyr says, as she and Maxim pick their way through the corpses of the pirates.

"I'll be down in a second; Bennie has me installing something or other."

"It's a remote... never mind," the hacker grumbles.

By the time the team has explored and secured every level and room of the asteroid base, the Harrith Navy Cruiser *Sword of Justice* arrives and takes custody of the base. The team files their claim against the contents of the base before heading off into space, while the Harrith navy begins to go over the place with a fine-toothed comb.

As the *Ghost* speeds away, its cargo hold packed with what the team could carry off before the Harrith arrived, Zephyr says to Wil, "You know. I might have an opportunity for us."

LOG ENTRY: WE'VE FOUND SOMETHING

"LOG ENTRY. *Farsight Corporation. Capralla Research Station, Chief Scientist.*" A breath. Followed by another, deeper. "*We've discovered something. Something big. One of our long-range probes was exploring the Sargul Nebula and came across it. I hesitate to say what it is. Honestly, I don't know what it is. Dren! The implications are astounding. If it is what I think it is, this will have repercussions throughout the GC.*"

The sound of pacing back and forth. "*It's a ship, I think. It's bigger than any I've ever seen. Bigger than any that exists in the GC as far as I know. The others have started calling it 'the beast'—that seems fitting, but implies it has a military intent. Does it? We don't know. It certainly has a lot of weapons. The probe went offline after scanning the ship, the object. It's a ship.*

"*What does this mean? For the GC? For civilization in this part of the galaxy? Who do we tell?*"

PART TWO

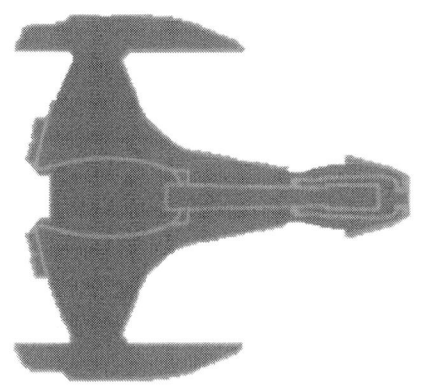

CHAPTER 4

"You're right, Belzar; the guilty verdict will have long-lasting and quite far-reaching implications throughout the GC. Peace-keeper Supreme Commander Larin has resigned, as has GC senior council member Qua'trall, both in disgrace. As you may recall, it was revealed during the trail that Qua'trall was pushing the GC Security Council to focus it's attention elsewhere, while the Peacekeeper operatives did their dirty work in the Harrith system. It remains to be seen what the rest of the GC council will do—whether it's emergency open elections or promoting one of the remaining council members. As we know, power abhors a vacuum, so I'm sure we'll have an answer to that question soon." Mon-El Furash stops, nodding a few times. "Yes, that's true, Bruul, Peacekeeper command has gone on record as saying that their highest office will go unfilled, while the Admiralty decides on the best course of action and does a thorough review of all its members." She gives another nod. "Yes, and thank you both. Back to you."

WORK IS WORK

WIL STEPS TO THE FRIDGE—OR what he calls the fridge—and grabs a grum, before walking back to the lounge area. Grabbing a seat next to Maxim, he looks over at Zephyr. "You mentioned, a job?" He waves his hand in an expansive "after you" type motion.

She clears her throat and stands up, looking each crew member in the eye, before finally stopping at Wil. "I've been approached by someone who has paying work. Work that doesn't go against our common moral grain." She looks over at Bennie, eyes narrowing.

The Brailack hacker looks at her and screeches, "Hey! I have a moral grain! I think!"

"Anyway, I received a message the last time we put down at a spaceport. Someone I know—or rather, used to know—needs our help."

As she pauses to take a breath, Wil raises his hand. "Used to know? Why'd they reach out to you?"

"I'll answer the last part first," Zephyr says. "I assume she reached out to me because of the Harrith thing. Even keeping a low profile while we avoid the consortium's bounty hunters, we're pretty well-known. As for the other part, I haven't seen or spoken to her in tens of cycles. The last time I saw her was my first year in the academy back on Palor."

This time it's Maxim who chimes in. "I've known you since your first posting out the academy, and you've never mentioned anyone from your time there."

Zephyr walks to the fridge and grabs a grum, taking a long swig. "At the time I was following protocol." She looks meaningfully at Maxim. "You know the one: excommunicated Peacekeepers are for all intents and purposes dead to everyone. I know now how stupid that rule is, how hurtful it is—but at the time I didn't, and when she left the service I swore I'd never speak to her or see her again." She takes another long drink, visibly shaken. "She saw, like everyone did, the Harrith incident, and she reached out to me. She needs our help."

Wil looks from her to Maxim, even glancing over to Bennie. "Um, what do you mean, 'excommunicated'? I knew you and Max were framed by Janus, but what's this? It's not related, right?" He looks to Gabe who, as usual, is standing off to the side. The droid shakes his head, remaining silent.

Zephyr drops down on the bench next to Bennie at the kitchen table. "As you know, the Peacekeepers are police, army, and more for the Galactic Commonwealth. Our people take that role and responsibility seriously. There's very little on Palor that doesn't revolve around being a Peacekeeper. Close to ninety-five percent of our population are Peacekeepers, whether frontline troops or some manner of support service. Before the Tarsi came, we were like any other race, with diverse interests; business, arts, science, and so on. But we were always warriors just below the surface. Our people fought war after war after war. Peace never lasted more than a ten-cycle on Palor. Once the Tarsi showed up, they began encouraging our baser tendencies. Over the generations, those other interests became extraneous. Our skills and interests were continually honed by the Tarsi until there wasn't much left to us but fighting." She looks right at Maxim. "Even if being a Peacekeeper isn't what a Palorian child wants, all children enter the academy. Some test out, showing exemplary skills in the few remaining non-military or support jobs. Some wash out and are ostracized by our entire population, and the rest—whether happily or not—serve in the Peacekeepers."

Maxim gets up and goes to the kitchen table, picking up a squirming Bennie without a word and placing him in the lounge chair that's just been vacated. Then Maxim sits down beside Zephyr and takes her hand. Not a single word is said during this movement, except the expletives that spill out of Bennie.

Zephyr continues, "There's nothing for washouts on Palor. The population looks down on them. Their families either publicly shun them or try to hide them from public view. It's so unbearable most take their own lives rather than live with the embarrassment."

Bennie, who's been quiet this whole time—not counting when Maxim picked him up like luggage—finally has something to say. "They kill themselves?" He's incredulous.

"You have to understand; the entire populace wants nothing to do with you. Many shops won't sell to you, the few nonmilitary employers won't hire you. Washing out of the academy is quite literally a death sentence at worst, and at best, as is the case for my friend, a life sentence of exile."

Bennie, still clearly confused, just says, "This is why family is overrated. I haven't been back to Brai since ten cycles after I left the pouch. Don't miss it."

Gabe, who's been silently taking this all in from the corner of the kitchen area, standing like he always does, finally breaks the silence. "Pouch?"

A LITTLE BACKSTORY

AFTER A RATHER LENGTHY and at times stomach-turning explanation of Brailack culture and physiology, the crew grows silent again. This time, Wil breaks the silence. "So, who is this and what's the job?"

Zephyr takes a breath. "Her name is Prathea. She's a chief scientist for one of the big multi-system corporations. Farsight Corp, she said."

Gabe raises his hand. "Farsight Corporation is not just 'one of' the big multi-system corporations." Somewhere along the way he seems to have picked up the rabbit ears gesture of air quotes. "They are in fact the *second largest* corporation in the entire region. Among other things, they are one of the largest research and development firms in the Galactic Commonwealth, holding several high-level contracts with the GC and Peacekeepers."

Maxim leans forward. "I've heard of them. They supply the Peacekeepers with advanced weapons."

Gabe nods. "Weapons research is also one of their larger verticals."

Wil looks at his mechanical friend. "How do you know so much about this company, Farsight Corp?"

Gabe tilts his head. "I was built by Farsight. Another of their key verticals is service droids, primarily engineering and scientific models."

Bennie leans over. "So, they're like your Gods or something?"

Gabe's head swivels to look down at the leering hacker. "I am not religious."

Wil nearly falls over laughing. It takes a few minutes for him to catch his breath. "Okay," he says, "back on track folks. Gabe, will dealing with Farsight be an issue?"

"No Captain. I was merely stating a fact. My loyalties lie with our crew."

"Good to know." He nods to the droid, who nods back.

"As I was saying..." Zephyr pauses and looks around the room before continuing. "She's the chief scientist at some research station. All she said in her first comms was that it's out near the edge of the GC."

Wil stands up. "Okay, go ahead and get in touch with her. Figure out where she is, and see if she'll commit to a number, too." He smiles. "Just so we know. We can set course when we hear from her." He turns toward the hatch that leads to the crew berths. "I'm going to bed now, see y'all later."

Bennie climbs out of the chair Maxim had dropped him in. "I'll be on the bridge. That new personality module I installed on the main computer is annoying even me. Gonna see what I can do with it." He heads back toward the hatch to the long corridor, often called the neck, that connects the body of the ship with the forward section housing the bridge and armory. Without speaking, Gabe turns and follows the hacker out.

Alone in the lounge, Maxim looks over at Zephyr. "You've never mentioned Prathea to me. Even privately, where no one would hear you break protocol." He sounds hurt, the concern is etched on his face.

She reaches up to stroke his cheek before placing her hand on top of his. "Love, before we were framed and saw what the Peace-keepers were all about, I took the rules, even those that hurt, seriously. The morning Prathea was announced as missing, I knew. I knew she'd left, washed out. Our ways are so rigid; it was like a switch. I spared her a moment to wish it had turned out differently and maybe in the back of my mind, wish her well. Then I pushed her from my mind and went to the assembly field for the morning parade."

Palorians don't have tear ducts—their inner set of vertical eyelids handle wetting and debris removal just like tears do for humans. Zephyr closes her eyes now, and Maxim can see that her inner eyelids are working overtime.

THE PAST

WIL IS SITTING at a bar on a world he can't remember the name of. Xarrix has him waiting for a shipment of something from somewhere. Wil asked where, and was told it was none of his business.

He's about six grum into the evening, so far having only eaten what passes for pub mix on this world. Instead of shoving cashews aside as he would be on earth, he's pushing some type of dried bug thing around.

He waves at the barkeep. "Hey!"

The round, four-legged being comes over. The tank-top covering its top half is stained and has a sizable rip in the center. "Yeah?"

"You have tacos?"

The barkeep's face scrunches up; one three-fingered hand comes up to scratch its bald head. Wil has gotten used to beings with anywhere from one eye to twelve or more, but this thing has three enormous eyes in a triangular arrangement, and somewhere around ten more smaller ones scattered around them. Its mouth reminds Wil of... well, a part of the human anatomy he's trying really hard to not picture in more detail.

"Ta' Co?" It leans forward, bringing its face closer to Wil.

"Oh god, don't get so close! Tacos. You know ground meat, tasty, crunchy shell. Shredded lettuce, cheese or something that looks like it." He pantomimes what he assumes he looks like when eating a taco. "Maybe some guac too?"

The quadruped bartender looks at him with every single eye, each blinking seemingly at random intervals. "What is, Kwok? I think maybe you've had enough grum."

Wil slams his glass down, sloshing grum all over the table. "I'll tell you when I've had enough! I just want some fucking tacos!" He pitches his glass over the barkeep's head, shattering it and several bottles of alien liquor in the process.

From behind Wil comes a voice. "Okay, little fella, I think maybe you need to calm down."

Wil spins around, throwing a left hook right into the stomach of one of the bar's bouncers. "Well, I'll be honest—I expected a head to be right there," he says. His fist is still resting against an orange-skinned abdomen. "Why aren't you wearing a shirt?"

The large alien looks down at him, smiles sadly and lifts him by his shirt. "Like I said little guy, time for you to cool off."

Wil smiles. "Thanks!"

The bouncer frowns. "For what?" he asks, just as one of Wil's boots smashes him right in the crotch. He grunts and drops Wil, who lands less gracefully than he had planned. He lurches to his feet as the bouncer turns back toward him. "You little..." There is a pause. "What *are* you—?"

"I think it said it's a Gobot," the bartender offers.

"Human!" Wil screams.

"You know what? I don't care—I can throw you across the room without knowing what planet you come from." The bouncer reaches down for Wil.

"Earth, asshole!" Wil slurs, as he dodges the giant hand by slipping to the side and shoving a recently-vacated barstool between himself and the bouncer.

"What?" the big alien says, stomping after Wil's rapidly scurrying form.

Wil finally gets to his feet and grabs a bottle of something off a nearby table, amid several shouts from the previous owners. "It's where I'm from!" He hurls the bottle at the bouncer, then turns to sprint away into the crowd—or would have, if a giant hand didn't clamp down on his shoulder, spinning him around. "Well," Wil says, "your arms are longer than I anticipated." The bouncer lifts him off the ground again and shakes him. "Oh god, don't do that!"

"Time for you to leave." The bouncer turns toward the door, still jostling Wil around.

"Oh god, I'm gonna…" is all Wil gets out, before the six grum and countless little cups of pub mix come back for a visit.

"Oh man! That's disgusting!" the bouncer shouts, holding Wil as far from his body as he can, spraying an unfortunate bar patron instead, before he gets to the doors and tosses Wil out. Wil doesn't even feel the landing; he's already blacked out.

CHAPTER 5

PHONE TAG

ZEPHYR AND MAXIM are in their quarters—he laying on the bed, browsing something on a large PADD, and she hunched over a terminal. Straightening up, the popping sounds of her vertebrae causes Maxim to look up from what he's doing.

"That doesn't sound good." He stands up and puts his hands on her shoulders.

Reaching up to rest her hand on one of his, she says, "Thanks. Prathea did a really good job routing her comms signal to hide her trail; it's taking me some time to replicate her efforts for my reply." She shakes her head. "What could be so secret that she'd go through all this trouble? Neither she, nor I, are Peacekeepers. She works for a mega-corporation and knows I'm here aboard the *Ghost.*"

He massages her shoulders as she rolls her head side to side, trying to loosen up the muscles in her neck. He shrugs. "Who knows? Like you said, you haven't seen or spoken to her in tens of cycles. A lot can change in that amount of time." He smiles at the joke—so much has changed for the two of them it would make anyone's head spin. He leans down and kisses the top of her head.

She keeps working for a few more minutes, then finally powers down the terminal. "Okay. Sent. I think. Nothing to do but wait for her reply."

The next morning, Wil is sitting in the lounge having breakfast, reading personal ads from Multona, on a PADD. Bennie and Gabe walk in, deep in conversation with one other, and Wil looks up, closing the tab on his PADD. "Bennie, I know I don't know much about your people, other than some truly disgusting breeding habits, thank you very much, but I think you need sleep. Right? You look like microwaved dren."

The weary Brailack hops into the seat opposite Wil, while Gabe stands at one end of the table. "Yeah I know. I'll grab something to eat then smack the sack." He looks at Wil expectantly.

"You know I'm never taking you to Earth, right? You don't have to keep trying to master human colloquialisms. Also, it's *hit the sack*. Why would you think it'd be 'smack' the sack?" Wil shakes his head and smiles.

"Hit, smack... whatever. You Earth people don't sleep in sacks, as far as I know, why do you even say that? Plus, you never know, maybe you'll change your mind. I should be ready."

Wil slowly takes a sip of his coffee—or what he has to drink instead of coffee, since he's run out of the real deal. He looks from Bennie to Gabe. The droid is doing his usual stand-silently-and-watch thing. "I honestly don't know where the saying came from, and how do you know we don't sleep in sacks? You haven't been rummaging around in my quarters have you?" His earlier smile is gone, all of a sudden.

Bennie looks around, shakes his head and in a voice a few octaves higher than usual says, "What? No! Why would I do something like that? I'm insulted! Insulted you'd even ask that."

"Uh, huh." Wil looks to Gabe, who's been slowly moving his

head back and forth like a spectator at a tennis match. "Can you set up a security subroutine for my quarters? Link it to my wrist-comm or something? Maybe DNA?"

"Of course, Captain. It should not take long."

"Good luck," Bennie sniggers, then seeing the look Wil is throwing him, looks down at his lap. "So, uh, how come you don't want to go home? I mean it's not like I want to move back to Brai or anything, but you know, I could visit... if I wanted to. I don't, but still." He looks up at Wil. "Isn't there anyone or anyplace you want to see again?"

Wil slides his plate to the side, which Gabe deftly picks up and takes to the cleaning unit. "I don't know, man." He spreads his arms to encompass the lounge and the ship as a whole. "After experiencing this? After owning my own starship, fighting a fight no one would have expected us to win, let alone survive, saving entire solar systems. After meeting you all, after everything I've been through..." He trails off for a second. Gabe, who's now standing near the dish cleaning unit turns to look at Wil, as he continues, "It'd be so boring. Earth is fifty—okay, probably one hundred years from ever leaving the solar system, let alone making contact with anyone. Assuming they even live that long. When I left, the planet wasn't even unified."

Bennie interrupts. "Not unified? Like separate nations and stuff? How can you all speak the same language but not be unified?"

Wil raises an eyebrow. "We don't all speak the same language."

"Wait, really? How's that work?"

"What do you mean? There are all kinds of human cultures and languages."

"How do you get anything done? You said you didn't have translation software," Bennie says, clearly stymied.

Wil shrugs. "We do it the hard way, learning other languages.

Plus, the first experimental FTL pod my government made left the solar system when I did. Lanksham stripped it down for parts and sold most of it off. What he couldn't sell he dumped on Fury. Oh, and I'd rather not be dissected."

Bennie's face goes a few shades lighter. "Dissected?"

Wil shrugs. "I've been gone a few years, they declared me dead. Showing up back in Denver for brunch one day might raise a few eyebrows. Last time I went for supplies was risky enough. So yeah, I think I'll pass. Earth can get along just fine without me." He looks at his cup of not-quite-coffee, adding, "and, for the most part, I can get along without it."

Gabe raises his hand, indicating a question. "Do you not have familial relations on Earth? People who might want to know that you are indeed not, lost in space? Love ones? Friends?"

This time Wil sighs. "This conversation is a barrel of monkeys. No, not really, Gabe. My parents are dead. My sister has a family who I've only met once or twice in person, and barely more than that over FaceTime. She lives in Rhode Island. I wasn't seeing anyone when I went on my mission, so no girlfriend back in Colorado or anything. I got to say 'goodbye' to my best friend, so, nope, no one is missing me back there." He stands up. "Great chat fellas, next time we can talk about that time when I was eight, and my dog died." He walks off toward the hatch leading to the bridge.

Gabe looks down and says, "Dog?"

Bennie shrugs and hops out of his chair, "Beats me. I'm gonna go smack the, wait no, HIT the sack. See you later." He waves a hand dismissively as he trots off toward the crew quarters.

Gabe's optic sensors spin a few times, then stop. He turns back to the kitchenette area and pause, unmoving, then turns and heads off toward the hatch leading to the engineering space. "Biologicals... Why would anyone microwave dren?"

SEE NEW PLACES

THE PLANET CAPRALLA isn't particularly interesting, except for its location—and even that only makes it interesting to scientists. Located near the edge of explored space, it's the perfect planet for long-range, deep-space scanning. The breathable atmosphere and small population add to its value.

Farsight Corporation has had a primary research facility on Capralla for several dozen cycles. The small local population was employed to help build the planetary facility as well as the launch pad that placed several dozen advanced-scanning satellites in orbit. While not technologically advanced themselves, they know about technology, but simply don't care.

"Welcome to Capralla," Wil announces, as the *Ghost* drops out of FTL. He taps a few controls on his station, bringing the FTL engines to standby mode and powering up the sub-light drive. "Zephyr, call down, get us cleared to land. Does this research station have a landing pad or spaceport, or are we landing near the city?"

Bennie looks up from his station. "From what I can tell, there's a pad just big enough for us at the station."

Zephyr is speaking to someone at her own station, keeping her voice low so as not to interfere with anyone on the bridge. Old training dies hard, Wil thinks to himself, smiling, just as she looks up. "We've got clearance at their pad. They didn't sound super thrilled to hear it was us coming in." She looks back to her station. "Receiving a vector, sending to your station."

"So, about the same as normal then," Wil says, turning his chair to face Maxim at the tactical station. "Max, don't be shy with the scanners, I want every nook and cranny of that station and the surrounding area mapped out."

Maxim nods, and turns to his displays. "Of course." He scratches at the stubble on his cheeks, Wil notices—he must be growing out a beard.

As the *Ghost* nears the planet, Bennie lets out a low whistle. "Would you look at those." He taps a few controls and the main display switches from the view of the approaching planet to a zoomed-in view of one of the Farsight Corporation's deep-space observation satellites.

Zephyr nods toward the screen. "From what I've learned during our trip, they've got a small fleet of those things at various orbits, looking all over deep into the black. Some are even FTL-capable."

Wil switches the display back to the now much closer planet. He taps a control. "Hey, Gabe, everything good down there? Gonna be lighting up the atmo-engines in a few seconds."

Over the speaker comes Gabe's voice. "Acknowledged. The atmospheric flight engines are ready, as are the repulsor lifts."

The repulsor lift generators are immensely up-scaled anti-grav lifters, Wil knows, like those used in grav-sleds. Gabe has explained it to him: ships that can't generate aerodynamic lift need lift generators to keep them from plummeting to the ground when in atmosphere. The *Ghost* has a lift generator in each of its wings, at the forward section of the nacelle that house the FTL engines, providing a balancing point which the atmospheric engines can push against.

"Roger that buddy. Hold on everyone, atmosphere in 15 seconds. Shields set for atmospheric entry," Wil announces, adjusting his position in his seat. The pilot station in front of him shifts appearance for atmospheric flight: pedals lift out of the floor, and a flight yoke disengages from the console and swings into place in front of Wil.

The *Ghost* begins to vibrate—just a little at first, then slowly building in intensity. The main display begins to brighten as superheated plasma builds up along the deflector shields. The shaking starts to diminish as the shields further adjust to the atmosphere, and soon the ship is flying as smoothly as ever, plunging further and further into the atmosphere.

"Atmo-engines in three, two, one." Wil touches a control, and there's a solid boom from the back of the ship as two powerful thrusters engage and begin pushing the ship forward. At the same time the engines erupt into life, the lift-generators begin to thrum, glowing green, providing the not-at-all aerodynamic ship with the lift it needs to keep from falling very fast into the planet below.

Soon, the *Ghost* is gently lowering itself onto the landing pad outside the Farsight Corp research complex.

MEET NEW PEOPLE

As WIL, Zephyr, and Bennie walk down the cargo ramp, a hefty blast door opens in the side of the science facility, and a small group walk towards the ship. Wil whispers, "One of them your friend?"

Zephyr shakes her head once.

"Welcome to Capralla," the leader of the small party says, reaching the bottom of the cargo ramp. "I'm head of security, Murta." He's a tallish Harrith in his mid... well, Wil doesn't know how long Harrith live, but somewhere in his middle years. "I'll escort you to Chief Researcher Prathea." At that, he turns and heads back into the building. His cohorts—security officers, most likely—turn and follow him.

"Friendly," Bennie mumbles, as the trio steps on to the landing pad and follow the security group into the facility.

Wil lifts his wristcomm. "Max, keep an eye on us."

"Acknowledged," comes the response over the comms unit.

As they enter the facility, the blast door closes behind them with a loud clang. The inside of the facility is made of clean, white plasti-steel, and what's likely to be shatter-proof transparent ceramic. The hallways they walk down are lined with what Wil assumes are labs: walls of computer banks, tables covered in tech he's never seen before, rooms with nothing but computer terminals and computer operators.

Wil looks down at Bennie. "You're drooling."

Bennie wipes his mouth and glares at Wil. "This place. It's amazing. We just passed a Quantum Industries YT-1000. A. One. Thousand!" He's practically dancing. "Do you know what I could do with that thing?"

Wil shakes his head. "I don't even want to know, and no touching."

They round a corner and the security entourage breaks off, taking up positions on either side of the door in front of them.

It opens to reveal a lift. Murta turns to them. "The Chief Researcher's office is upstairs." He walks into it, and Wil, Bennie, and Zephyr follow.

The lift takes them to the fifth floor—the top level, if Wil's guess at the size of the building is right—where it opens onto a long hallway with doors on both sides. They walk toward the door at the very end of the hall, which is larger than the rest.

Murta touches a control panel next to the door, then gestures. "Right this way."

The office they enter is the office of a scientist, but also an administrator. Equipment and PADDs are everywhere, including the floor. The woman behind the desk, while a Palorian like Zephyr and Maxim, is quite clearly not a Peacekeeper. She's barely as tall as Wil, while Zephyr is easily a head taller, and Maxim more so. She's also obviously not in the same physical condition as Zephyr, if she ever was. Her black hair is cut short in a pixie-bob style.

The woman behind the desk nods to Murta, then looks at Wil briefly, then at Zephyr. "Zephyr," she says, standing up.

"Prathea." Zephyr nods in welcome. "This is Wil. The little one is Bennie." She nods to each in turn.

The smaller, rounder Palorian dashes around the desk and hugs Zephyr tightly. Zephyr lets out a startled yelp, then Prathea pulls back, still holding on to Zephyr's forearm. "Thank you for coming. I didn't know who else to go to. Then I saw all that footage of what happened at Harrith. I knew you could help me figure this out."

THE PAST

"D*AMAGE TO STARBOARD ENGINE ASSEMBLY. Power output to starboard disruptor dropping,*" the computer reports, as the *Ghost* tilts wildly, sparks erupting from one of the consoles on the bridge.

"Crap!" Wil shouts, to no one in particular. "What'd you get me into, Xarrix?!"

He pulls on the controls, swinging the *Ghost* into a wild arc around the three attack craft chasing him. They've been on his tail ever since the space station where he picked up five large crates for Xarrix.

Wil glances at a display he's set up to view the cargo hold: in the middle of the screen is a stack of crates, lashed down to the deck. "What the hell is in those crates?!" he asks. The *Ghost* shakes and more sparks fly from a different console.

"*Unable to —*" the computer starts.

"Not talking to you!" Something explodes against the aft shields.

"*Warning. Aft shields at thirty-four percent.*"

"Calculate escape jump to FTL!" It's getting smoky on the bridge. "And unseal the bridge hatch, try to clean up the air in here!"

"Escape jump calculated. Please reach minimum FTL distance from nearby gravity wells." The hatch to the bridge opens. *"Increasing power to oxygen scrubbers in the main corrido*r."

Wil slams the controls hard to one side, while pushing the throttle control all the way forward.

"Warning, inertial dampers exceeding maximum capacity."

"Almost..." Wil hasn't taken his eyes off the primary tactical display, showing nearby space. The planet that the space station orbits is a massive gas giant. Its gravity well is enormous, and the *Ghost* is almost to the boundary.

"Almost..." black dots are beginning to swim around the edge of his vision.

"Warning, inertial dampers have exceeded maximum capacity." The *Ghost* shudders again, more sparks erupt, this time from yet another console. Red lights are starting to flash on consoles whose functions Wil has no idea about. "Aft shields at fifteen percent."

A light on the console in front of Wil turns green. "Yes!" He slaps a palm on the console, activating the FTL drive. The *Ghost* lurches, then shoots into FTL space.

Wil slouches back in his chair. "Shit. That was close. Computer, damage report."

"Starboard engine pod sustained damage, currently operating at forty-five percent. Starboard disruptor is offline. Port wing assembly damaged, structural integrity at sixty percent. Port atmospheric engine damaged. Aft shield emitters damaged."

"Well..."

"Main engine, power output at seventy percent."

"Shit," Wil says, reaching for a control on his console.

The computer makes a soft beep, then Xarrix says, "Go ahead."

"Got 'em, but the price went up. The station had way better defenses than you said—defenses that included fighters. Fighters,

Xarrix! You said your girl had the station security forces under her thumb."

"You don't get to raise the price, you hairless poondar."

"You want those crates; you fix my ship. What's a poondar?"

"Are all five intact?"

"Of course they are, I'm a professional." Wil toggles a camera feed from the cargo hold onto the primary display. All five crates are sitting in the middle of the cargo hold, strapped to the deck plating.

"You're anything but a professional, but fine. Get here as fast as you can. I'll have a repair bay waiting. When you contact space control, they'll send you to the right place."

The computer beeps.

Wil gets up and heads to the hatch. "Hate it when he hangs up on me." he grumbles.

CHAPTER 6

LONG TIME, NO SEE

AN HOUR OR SO LATER, the entire team is in Prathea's office. Maxim and Gabe have secured the *Ghost* on the landing pad and joined the rest of the crew.

Bennie is in one corner of the room, touching things that Prathea has already said not to touch, at least twice now, and Gabe is doing his usual stand-in-the-corner-quietly thing.

Wil puts down the cup of something like tea that Prathea has offered him. "So. Prathea, no offense here, but you called us for a reason, and while this visit has been fun, and I'm glad you and Zee have reconnected and all..." He leaves it hanging there, as she lowers her own cup.

She sighs. "I'm afraid I can't tell you a whole lot. What I can tell you is that it's serious and could have big repercussions for the GC."

"Oh, *that* doesn't sound ominous," Wil says.

"One of our long-range probes picked up something," she continues. "Something big. Really big."

Bennie turns around, leaving off poking at something that looks expensive. "This sounds interesting." He comes over and hops on to the arm of the chair Maxim is sitting in. Maxim glares at the small Brailack, then looks over at Zephyr, then Prathea. "A big something, like how big? What is it?"

"A ship."

Wil leans forward in his chair. "A ship? Whose ship? How big are we talking? Peacekeeper-Command-ship big? Where?"

Prathea shakes her head. "Bigger than that. Beyond that, I can't say, not yet." She raises a hand, as Wil opens his mouth to interrupt. "Partly because I don't know the answer, partly because it's too dangerous."

"What do you mean a ship? A big ship? Where? Like a colony ship or something?" Bennie is leaning forward on his perch.

"A few light years beyond the border, at the edge of the Sargul Nebula. We're not sure exactly how big, there's too much interference. We picked it up, and when our probe scanned it, it scanned back. Then the probe went offline."

Prathea reaches over to a terminal set in her desk, taps a few buttons and a hologram appears over it. The image is grainy, but Wil can see what looks like a ship outlined against the orange and purple haze of the nebula. With nothing to serve as a point of reference for scale, it's impossible to make out its size, but however big it is, it's certainly mean-looking. Along its sides are several ridges, with weapons emplacements evenly spaced along their length. Massive engines fill the entire aft section. The forward section is long and rounded.

Prathea looks at the holo-image. "We need more time analyzing the data. To analyze the images we captured."

"Bennie can take a stab at it, Gabe too," Wil offers. "Has it done anything else? Moved? Scanned the probe again or anything?"

"Like I said, after our probe scanned it, it scanned back, then the data stream from the probe stopped. We started to analyze the data from the scan, the ship is, as far as we can tell, made of an unknown material." She looks around. "We need to get this information somewhere else. We need to get it to the corporate office. That's why I called you. It's not safe here."

Wil and Maxim both tense, and Zephyr looks around. "What do you mean, not safe?" Maxim asks, his hand resting on the butt of his pistol.

Prathea raises her hands. "I didn't mean right now. You're safe —as safe as anyone—here. This secret is just too big; it can't stay a secret, it won't. We have to move the data archive out of this facility, off this planet. Farsight Corporation can secure it. Investigate the ship, send a team. It'll only take one technician letting this slip in a comms to their family and every government and treasure hunter for light years will swamp that nebula."

"Your entire staff knows about it? The ship—that it scanned you?" Wil asks, standing and walking over to the hologram and leaning to peer more closely at it.

Prathea shakes her head. "Not all of them, no. Once we realized what we were seeing, and detected its sensor sweep, I compartmentalized it. Senior staff only, and only those who were in the room at the time. That's still fifteen people, though. It's only a matter of time until one of them mentions it to other staffers."

Zephyr, who's been sitting quietly during this entire exchange, looks at Prathea. "Why us? You didn't answer Wil earlier. Surely Farsight could send a ship, or a dozen ships to collect you and this data, get it safely to the corporate office."

Prathea smiles a sad smile. "I'd have to tell them the truth about why I want the escort. I knew you'd come without any details. Farsight wouldn't do the same, the company is very conservative." She looks at each of them in turn, then simply says, "Please."

SIGHT SEEING

Several awkward conversations about Farsight, the Harrith Incident, and somehow Brailack breeding, again, later, the team is sitting in a large cafeteria with Prathea, Murta, and two senior scientists. The rest of the staff appear to be elsewhere.

"So, you all are the ones who stopped the Peacekeepers from invading the Harrith system?" Jor' Lu, a two-and-a-half-meter tall Burzzad asks, as she eats some type of porridge-like substance. Her pointed ears twitch as she watches Wil and the crew. Her pale skin is pulled tight over bones and rope-like muscles.

Bennie nods vigorously. "That was us all, alright! You should have seen it! We blew ships up! Everyone was shooting at us. We blew up a huge Peacekeeper ship! Wil was flying like no one's business. Well, that is until the *Ghost* got shot to wurrin and we crash-landed on the planet, in a huge fireball."

Wil glowers behind his cup of that same tea-like drink Prathea offered him earlier, coughing a little. "Yes, well—" he starts, but Bennie keeps going, somehow making the parts where the *Ghost* is nearly blown up and crashes take twice as long to tell as the fight leading up to that.

Jor' Lu seems completely entranced with the story, her three eyes wide and unblinking as she listens to Bennie's version of events, her ears sticking straight out to the side. Her companion—a short, fur-covered being named Xan—seems less impressed. When Bennie winds down, somehow ending his version with him leading the repair effort of the *Ghost*, Xan asks, "So when are we going to the ship?"

Jor' Lu blinks rapidly, then looks at Xan then Prathea. "Yes. When do we leave?"

"And what do we do with it when we get there?" Murta asks. He looks around the table. "My people could make good use of a ship that powerful. It could restore the balance of power in the region." He looks at Wil. "They wouldn't need to resort to paying privateers. No offense."

"None taken," Wil says, smiling his most insincere smile.

Prathea puts her utensil down, and looks around the table. "I don't know if we should go to the ship at all." She raises a hand to silence Murta and Xan. "What will we gain? We've got the data from the probe, that's more than enough to get Farsight to send a cruiser."

"And what? Farsight gets a warship that rivals a Peacekeeper Command ship? Why? What's to stop them from turning it over to the GC and the Peacekeepers? It could restore my people to power in the region," Murta growls.

"Look, Murta, I get your point. I like your people a lot, but they've no claim on the ship—" Wil starts.

Murta stands up, pointing at Wil. "And what? You'd take it? Sell it to the highest bidder? Sell it to some criminal?"

"We could sell it to Harrith," Bennie chimes in. "I bet they'd pay a fortune. Would easily buy the Consortium off, and then some."

"Sell it?!" Murta screams.

"Murta, sit down," Prathea says, resting her hand on his arm. "No one is selling it or giving it away, or doing anything with it.

We don't know anything about it yet. It's idiotic to make plans for it when we know so little."

"Then we should go. Check it out," Xan pushes.

Jor' Lu nods. "If nothing else, we can gather a lot more data to turn over to corporate."

Prathea looks at Wil, then Zephyr. "Would you take us?"

Wil nods. "But not for free."

Murta growls as Prathea nods. "Of course." Then lower, under her breath, "Pirate."

ALWAYS SOMETHING

THE NEXT DAY, Prathea announces to the rest of her research staff that herself, Jor' Lu, Xan, and Murta will be leaving on a small exploration mission. She explains that they have hired the crew of the *Ghost* to provide additional security and fast transport, to take them to a new scientific discovery. It's a flimsy story, but most of the researchers don't even look up when she's addressing them, faces still focused on their PADDs. When released, most hurry back to their labs.

The team and their small gaggle of scientists walk out of the facility, heading for the *Ghost*. Jor' Lu looks down the pathway towards the ship.

"That's it?" She looks from Prathea to Xan, then to Wil. "That ship? That's the one we're going to travel in?" Her pace slows down.

Wil looks up at Jor' Lu. "What do you mean, *That's it*? The *Ghost* is a fine ship!"

"Especially now. The ship has undergone extensive repairs and upgrades, after being nearly destroyed," Gabe chimes in. "More than once."

Wil turns to his friend. "Phrasing!"

The group resumes walking towards the *Ghost*, the three scientists looking over the ship as they approach. Every set of eyes is squinting.

In the lounge, Wil gestures to the kitchenette and seating areas. "This is the main crew lounge." He gestures toward a hatch. "Down that way are the crew bunks. We tend to eat most meals together. You're welcome to join us as often as you like." He walks toward the hatch that leads to the bridge. "This way is the bridge. You're welcome to pop in, but it's not a place to hang out." As the hatch opens he turns to Gabe. "Gabe, can you show them around, while I get us underway?"

The bot bows his head. "Of course, Captain." Turning to the group of scientists, who are poking at the furniture experimentally, Wil hears him say, "Please follow me."

Wil is only halfway to the bridge when his wristcomm begins to vibrate the emergency pattern. "Computer, status report," Wil says, increasing his pace toward the bridge.

"We are being targeted by a ship in orbit."

Zephyr comes up behind him at that moment. "Did it just say we're being targeted?" She doesn't wait for the answer, sprinting the rest of the way to the bridge.

By the time Wil gets to the bridge, Zephyr has the pre-flight checks almost done, and he can feel the repulsors powering up. "How long?" he asks, falling into his seat.

"Ten more centocks." She looks up from her station, waiting for Wil's instructions.

"Hail them."

She nods, and Wil hears the tell-tale beep to indicate an open comms channel. "Hi there, mystery ship in orbit. Our sensors are telling us that you're targeting us. That's a little rude, don't you think?"

The primary display comes to life, showing—well, showing Ziggy Stardust. Not an alien that looks like David Bowie, but like the actual David Bowie in his Ziggy Stardust get up, lightning bolt and all.

"Wil Calder."

"Ziggy Stardust," Wil counters.

Space Ziggy Stardust blinks twice, then looks off-screen at something or someone, then turns back. "I am Kohar. I am collecting the bounty on you and your crew. Power down your ship and surrender now."

"That didn't take long," Zephyr murmurs.

"Ah, I see. You think I'm this Wil Calder person? I thought that was just how you greeted people. I'm not Wil Calder. Don't know the guy."

Kohar blinks several times. "You must be."

"Why? Because I'm a human? That's pretty racist, don't you think?"

Apparently, Kohar's Ziggy Stardust look is biological, since the lightning bolt actually changes color as the bounty hunter blushes.

Off to the side, Zephyr holds up three fingers.

"No, not because you're human. Well, not just that. That ship's transponder is broadcasting as the *Ghost*. And yes, you are human." He grins, having escaped being thought of as a racist.

"Oh, I see, so humans can't have ships named 'Ghost' now because of one person's actions?" Wil works up a good angry face. "I mean how is that fair? Maybe I had this ship before this Wil Calder dickhead went and did... What did he do anyway?"

On his console, Wil sees all the ship's systems coming online. Repulsors are ready to go; the atmosphere engines are primed.

On the screen, Kohar is back to looking uncomfortable. "No, that's not it at all. Of course, other humans can have ships named 'Ghost.' That'd be ridiculous if they couldn't."

Wil nods.

"Wil Calder is wanted by the Consortium."

"For what? Isn't he the guy that saved the entire Harrith sector from a war with the Peacekeepers?"

A cough from Zephyr makes him glance over at her. "He and his awesome, and as I understand it, amazingly capable, crew, that is."

"Well, yeah, that's what I heard. But that doesn't matter. The bounty on his head is huge—"

Wil cuts him off. "How huge?"

"They just raised it to three million credits for the ship and its crew."

Wil whistles. "Damn. For that much, I might turn myself in, though on a per-person basis that's not very much. Especially when you factor in the *Ghost*—I mean, you can't buy an Ankarran Raptor for three million. I think they're being really cheap; you should demand more."

Kohar is nodding; then he catches on to the entirety of what Wil just said. "Wait. What? You ARE Wil Calder?"

"Yup!" Wil nods, and Kohar is replaced on-screen with the view directly in front of the ship. He grabs the repulsor controls and slams them to full power, at the same time that his other hand throws the atmospheric engines to half power. The *Ghost* lurches, leaping from the landing pad on its repulsor lifts, as the atmo-engines fire up with a boom that shakes the whole ship.

Maxim enters, grabbing the nearest piece of ship to keep from falling backward. "Trouble, I take it?" he asks. Murta is right behind him.

"Ziggy Stardust is trying to kill us," Wil says through gritted teeth, as the ship screams away from the research station.

Maxim looks at Zephyr, who just shrugs.

THE PAST

Xarrix is sitting across the table from Wil. They are at his favorite bar again, the privacy screen active and shimmering. "Your little screw-up nearly cost me my entire profit margin."

"Sorry, I'm not Rambo, or MacGyver, or whatever."

The reptilian crime lord makes a clicking sound. "Who's Rambo? Who's Mac gubber?"

"It's Mac—"

Xarrix raises a clawed hand. "I really don't care. The issue here isn't your weird human colloquialisms. It's your lack of useful skills."

Wil grimaces. "That hurts."

"The truth does. My intel might have been incomplete, but if you had any type of experience as a smuggler or spy or... *anything* for that matter, you'd have been able to get out of there without costing me so much." He picks at a plate of what Wil first thought were noodles, but now sees are actually worms with tiny faces. Tiny, vaguely human faces. Wil is staring open-mouthed at the plate as Xarrix grabs a pinch of the worms and drops them into his mouth. He looks up, feeling Wil's eyes on him. "What?"

Wil shakes his head and looks away, as one stray human-face-worm is slurped into Xarrix's reptilian maw.

"Here's what we're going to do: I have a connection on Wargun Tor who can do some brain stuff to you."

"Uh, you can fuck right off." Wil starts to stand up. "You're not doing, and I quote, *brain stuff*, to me. I quit, I'm out, whatever."

"Oh, calm down, pink skin. It's not what you think. They can embed training and skills into your brain. After the procedure, the skills and knowledge will begin to surface like regularly-acquired skills. It's like going to training, without going to training."

Wil sits back down, grabbing his drink. "Okay, that sounds kinda cool. Can I learn Kung Fu? Maybe pilot a helicopter?"

"Kung what? What's a helicopter? Wait, no—I still don't care. You can't acquire muscle memory or anything like that; it's more knowledge and know-how."

Wil nods. "Okay, sure. I'm interested. Where is Wargun Tor?"

"I'll send the coordinates. Your ship should be repaired by the end of the day tomorrow." He reaches over to deactivate the privacy screen. "And don't screw up."

"Love you, too." Wil stands to leave, grabbing his grum, and heads out into the bar. As he passes, he glances over at the bartender, and immediately looks back to the door and keeps walking.

CHAPTER 7

GABE IS SHOWING the passengers around. "Each berth has two beds. There are presently only two open berths; the third currently does not hold atmosphere. You will have to decide amongst yourselves who will bunk with whom."

"Doesn't hold atmosphere?!" Prathea sputters. She looks up at Jor' Lu, eyes wide.

Gabe nods. "Yes. I have narrowed the problem down to a micro-fracture somewhere under one of the beds. I have not had time to isolate the problem further. My apologies, I am embarrassed the problem has persisted for several months. This ship keeps me busy."

The three scientists and the security officer look at each other. Before anyone can speak, Gabe continues, "The engineering spaces are off limits to passengers without prior approval of the Captain, or an escort from the crew. Any questions?"

Just then, the computer alerts him over the ship's network that there is a situation. The bot smoothly dedicates more processing power and queries the central computer. A vessel is in orbit, targeting the *Ghost*, Gabe notes. Interesting. He glances back to his charges and sees them staring at him expectantly. "I am sorry, what was that?"

Jor' Lu raises her hand. "I asked, are there any sections of the ship with higher ceilings?"

Gabe now notices that she is stooped over. "Ah. Yes. Please forgive me, I did not notice your discomfort." He looks around, then says, "The cargo hold has the requisite space, I can work with Zephyr to set up a living space there for the duration of the journey, if you would prefer."

The uncomfortable-looking Burzzad nods her thanks.

Gabe re-accesses the ship's computer, and sees that the engines are powering up, all systems are ready for flight. "For now," he says, "please follow me to the lounge, I believe we are about to be in an active combat situation, and you should strap in." He turns and heads back towards the main crew lounge.

"Wait, what?" Murta demands.

"I am not fully aware of all of the details, but it would appear there is a ship in orbit that is actively targeting this vessel. The Captain is talking to the other ship, and the *Ghost* is almost ready for flight operations. I suspect we will be taking off rather abruptly, very soon."

The ship lurches, and everyone but Gabe stumbles. The droid does his best to grab the others, to keep them from hitting the floor too hard. Being able to magnetize his feet helps.

They stumble back into the lounge, just as Bennie and Maxim are making their way to the hatch leading to the main corridor and the bridge beyond. "Do you know what's happening?" Maxim asks Gabe.

"A ship in orbit was targeting us," Gabe says. "From what I could gather, the Captain was attempting to talk our way out of trouble."

The ship lurches again, and the sound of energy weapons

hitting the shields reverberates through the lounge. "I do not believe he was successful," Gabe adds. "I will be in Engineering."

Maxim turns to Murta, who has not taken a seat and is now standing next to him. "What?"

"I'm head of security and responsible for them." He points back to the seated and moderately terrified-looking scientists. "I demand to be on the bridge and to know what's going on," he says, attempting to push past Maxim. He fails to move the ex-Peace-keeper even an inch.

Maxim looks at Murta, then the scientists, then down at Bennie. "Stay with them," he says to the Brailack. Then he steps into the corridor, letting Murta push past him.

Bennie stares at the retreating ex-Peacekeeper and security officer, as the hatch automatically closes. "Wait. What?" He turns back to the scientists. "Uh, okay. So, it's totally fine. We get shot at a lot. And mostly always win."

At that precise moment, the ship drops, sending Bennie flying up to the ceiling, then back down to the deck again. "AGHH!!" He looks up at Xan, and gives her a thumbs-up before passing out.

ZIGGY STARDUST ATTACKS

Wil looks from Murta to Maxim and back, then settles his stare on Maxim, who says, "Letting him come was easier than fighting with him about it." The Palorian quickly moves to his station.

Wil sighs and points to a station no one uses. "Sit. Don't touch anything."

"I am not a..." Murta begins to protest.

"No talky!" Wil shouts, and for effect, banks the ship hard over to port, throwing Murta against a bulkhead. The ship shudders and the shield emitters can be heard whining through the hull.

Zephyr clears her throat. "*That* was a heavy disruptor blast. That ship has three of them."

"Maxim, get the weapons spun up," Wil says, "and fire at will. Maybe aim for those heavy disruptors first."

"On it."

"Incoming!" Maxim and Zephyr both shout in unison.

Wil throws the throttles for the atmo-engines all the way forward. There's a massive boom from the back of the ship, and everyone is pushed back hard into their seats. Over the overhead speakers, Gabe scolds, "You are going to burn out the engines."

"I know! But we gotta get out of the atmosphere! We can't

maneuver down here!" To punctuate Wil's point, another disruptor blast explodes near the ship, causing dirt and debris to shoot nearly half a kilometer into the air. Wil pulls back on his control stick, forcing the repulsor lifts in the wing-mounted engine pods to push even harder, forcing the ship up and out of the atmosphere of Capralla.

As the *Ghost* leaves the atmosphere, Kohar's ship comes into view. "Jesus! That's an ugly ship!" Wil exclaims, as the *Ghost* leaves the clouds behind and swings around in a wide arc, coming back onto an intercept course with Kohar's vessel. "I mean, right? It looks like a giant goldfish!"

Without providing any thoughts on the design of the attacking ship, Maxim unleashes a volley of disruptor fire from the forward weapons of the *Ghost*, along with a pair of missiles.

Wil watches the energy weapons dance across the shields of what he is mentally calling "Mega-Goldfish," followed by two explosions—one of which does severe damage to the starboard heavy disruptor assembly of the bounty hunter ship.

"Damn, dude! Got some aggression stuff to work out?" He looks over at Maxim, who simply shrugs.

Wil turns back to the screen. "Open a channel," he says. Zephyr nods, and the comms system beeps. "Okay, look Ziggy Stardust, we've no reason to destroy you, but we totally will. Power down."

The primary display switches from a giant metal goldfish—a heavily armed giant metal goldfish—to the scowling face of Ziggy Stardust. "You dare—?!" he screams.

"Uh. Sure. Dare what?" Wil looks to Zephyr who shrugs, then to Maxim who also shrugs.

"I am Kohar! I've hunted bounties in every system of the GC! You can't escape your fate! Surrender now. The bounty doesn't say how many of you have to be alive." Kohar smirks, horribly. "We've collected bounties on countless beings, all of them far tougher than you." The *Ghost* shudders as the shields absorb another heavy disruptor blast. Sparks erupt over Murta, who lets out a yelp.

Wil growls. "I warned you, Ziggy Stardust. I really don't want to kill you and your crew, but you made the choice. Not me. Remember that. Well you know, for the next few minutes at least."

"My name isn't Ziggy..." The screen goes black, then back to the forward view. Mega-Goldfish is maneuvering to get a better shot at the *Ghost*.

Wil banks around the attacking ship, giving Maxim a chance to rip into its side with their primary disruptors, then accelerates away just as the bounty hunter's ship opens up with smaller point defense weapons. The *Ghost* shakes and lurches, but its shielding absorbs the damage—barely.

"Shields won't hold for long," Zephyr warns.

"Won't have to. Ready Max?"

"Always." The big man grins.

Wil brings the *Ghost* around. He's positioned the ship so that they're coming in from just above and behind the larger vessel. Mega-Goldfish is attempting to turn enough to bring her port disruptor to bear.

Wil tuts and slides the ship sideways and down a little.

The moment they're in range, Maxim fires four missiles from the weapons magazine directly into the lower section of the ship, while never taking his finger off the trigger for the disruptors. The forward and wing-mounted energy weapons blaze out from the *Ghost*.

From overhead Gabe warns, "Maxim, both primary disruptors are beginning to overheat. In twenty seconds I'll be forced to shut them both down to avoid more severe damage. The forward emitters are only slightly behind the primaries."

Wil looks at the ceiling, then around the room. "That's really weird to everyone right? Gabe you might need to man an engineering station up here from now on. This 'voice of god' thing is disconcerting."

On the screen, the enemy ship is being ripped apart by weapons fire. The first two missiles impacted on the shields, the second two on the hull. Mega-Goldfish now has a hole in its side almost big enough for the *Ghost* to fly into, though it doesn't yet go all the way through. Wil watches as a missile streaks wide of the *Ghost,* as he banks away from their attack run. Without missing a beat, Zephyr switches the primary display to follow the enemy ship.

"Boom goes the dynamite!" Wil shouts as the missile hits the ship right in the *Ghost*-sized hole and explodes, breaking the goldfish in two. Secondary explosions rock both halves, and in seconds there's not much left but a lot of debris.

Wil lets out a *whoop* and turns to Maxim, "Good shooting, Max!" He brings the *Ghost* back towards a heading for the outer system, away from Capralla. It doesn't take long for the *Ghost* to burn out beyond Capralla's gravity well and jump to FTL. Wil makes some adjustments on his console, then hops out of his chair and heads for the hatch. "Who's hungry?"

JUST ALONG FOR THE RIDE

Xan is out of her seat in a flash, her small, furry frame moving faster than Prathea has ever seen her move. Jor' Lu and Prathea are right behind her.

Xan cradles Bennie's head in her hands. "Check his pulse."

Jor' Lu looks over at her friend. "I'm not a doctor. How do I check for a pulse?"

"I don't know!" Xan barks, taking one of Bennie's arms and looking it over.

Prathea sighs. "Watch out." She reaches under the unconscious Brailack's chin, and waits a minute before pronouncing: "He's alive."

The ship shudders and shakes, and the lights in the lounge dim.

"What's going on?" Jor' Lu shouts.

"I think we're in a space battle!" Xan replies, then slaps Bennie across the face.

"No, I don't want to wear that! Wha—? What's going on?" Bennie slurs, eyes fluttering. The ship shudders again, and his eyes snap wide open. "What's happening?" Prathea helps Bennie up as the ship lurches, "Who's attacking us?" He stumbles over to a terminal set into the bulkhead next to the kitchenette. "You guys better sit back down and strap in," he says, as he reaches for a stool and secures its strap across his lap. He taps a few commands into the terminal, and the room darkens, a tactical map hologram appearing overhead.

"Is that a giant yorladt fish?" Xan asks, pointing to the goldfish-ship that's firing on the *Ghost*.

"Is this what your life is like all the time?" Jor' Lu asks. "Is it too late to return to Capralla?"

Bennie taps another control, and the overhead speaker comes to life with Wil's voice. "Ok, look Ziggy Stardust, we've no reason to destroy you, but we totally will. Power down."

A voice no one in the lounge recognizes replies, "I am Kohar! I've hunted bounties in every system of the GC! You can't escape your fate! Surrender now. The bounty doesn't say how many of you have to be alive. We've collected bounties on countless beings, all of them far tougher than you."

Xan looks at Prathea, then back to Bennie. "What? What bounty? What do they mean by bounty?"

Bennie shrugs. "It's nothing, don't worry about it." He waves a hand dismissively.

The *Ghost* shudders as the shields absorb another heavy disruptor blast. Smoke starts to billow from an overhead panel. Everyone in the room looks at the panel, waiting for it to do something more.

Wil's voice comes back from the overhead speaker: "I warned you, Ziggy Stardust. I really don't want to kill you and your crew, but you made the choice. Not me. Remember that. Well you know, for the next few minutes at least."

The irate other party screams, "My name isn't Ziggy..." Jor' Lu scrunches up her large ears.

They watch on the hologram as the *Ghost* swings around. Moments later four red triangles leave the *Ghost* and head for the big fish ship. Each triangle arrives at the ship then vanishes. The *Ghost* makes a wide turn, then unleashes another red triangle. When the red triangle disappears against the fish ship, the ship flashes three times, then the icon vanishes.

"Well, that was exciting," Jor' Lu says from her chair, her ears pricked all the way up.

"Are you crazy?" Xan snaps. "We almost died, you giant weirdo! You just said you wanted to go back to Capralla."

"But we didn't, and we got to see this crew in action. I don't know about you, but that was exciting. The almost dying part, notwithstanding," the Burzzad replies, innocently. Each eye blinks in turn.

Prathea glares at her two colleagues, then asks Bennie, "That's it? It's over?"

He shrugs. "I mean, sure. For now."

"For now?" She unlatches her restraint and heads toward Bennie with a fierce look on her face.

He waves his hands to ward her off. "What? I mean, we get shot at a lot! Remember the whole Harrith thing? I mean before we got here we attacked some pirates. Yeep—!" He hops off his stool and narrowly dodges a slap.

Just then, the holo-map fades as the ship jumps to FTL. Wil, Zephyr, Maxim, and Murta walk in just as Prathea catches Bennie. The four of them look at scientists and hacker, who just stare back at them. Maxim shakes his head, "Do we want to know?"

FIRST SUPPER

STANDING up so fast his chair flies backward, Murta screams, "You! Will! Not! Sell! The! Ship!" Each word is enunciated for emphasis.

Maxim has also stood up, his hand going to his hip, where a pulse pistol is holstered. His eyes never leave Murta's.

Wil raises his hands in a placating gesture. "Murta, chill out. I'm just talking about options. Sit down—your pizza is going to get cold."

Xan, trying to break the tension, looks at Wil. "What exactly is this 'pizza,' anyway?"

Bennie, who's sitting next to her, shakes his head. "Don't bother. He'll say a bunch of words you won't understand, make a bunch of weird gestures," at this, Bennie pantomimes throwing something in the air, "and you'll still not know what pizza is. Just enjoy it, because it's delicious."

While this discussion is taking place, Murta has calmed himself, righted his chair and sat down. He glares at Wil, then Maxim, and finally Zephyr. "That ship is not yours to sell."

Wil nods. "You're right, but that doesn't make it yours to give away." He raises his hand to stop another outburst. "I'm not saying anything one way or the other. I'm just raising the issue. We've got fifteen days before we arrive at the derelict, or whatever it is. That's a lot of meals together, so I figured we should try to get some things out in the open as soon as possible." He smiles.

"This might all be for naught," Maxim chimes in. He slowly takes a bite of pizza, while every eye in the room turns to him, including Jor' Lu's three. "Everyone is trying to decide what they'll do with the derelict before they've even gotten to the ship. It could be inoperable. It could be booby-trapped to explode. It could have a crew in cryo-sleep that will object to any of our plans." He takes another bite.

"The big one has a point," Xan purrs. Her eyes are roaming all over the large Palorian.

"He's spoken for," Zephyr says, in a voice that contains all the warning that's needed. Her hand slides over to rest on Maxim's arm.

The small furry scientist shrugs. "My loss, I'm sure." She winks at Maxim, who blushes a deep shade of blue.

Everyone finds something to look at that isn't anyone else at the table. Bennie notices something on the ceiling that is very interesting.

Prathea is the first to break the incredibly awkward silence. "Um, yes, well." She looks over at Wil. "We'll find out when we get there, won't we?" Reaching for another slice of pizza, she asks, "Wil, this is from your world? It's amazing."

Wil smiles. "Earth has a lot going for it, all food. Well, mostly food. Food and porn. Fine, I said it." Everyone at the table stares at him. He puts his slice down. "Moving on. The other thing I wanted to get out in the open is the whole bounty hunter thing." He looks around.

Jor' Lu finishes chewing and swallows. "That was quite exciting. I don't think I need a repeat any time soon, but it was fun, after the fact." She smiles and reaches a long thin arm across the table, snagging the last slice.

Bennie eyes her. "Splits?"

She nods and rips the slice cleanly in half, her cheeks darkening slightly.

Wil watches this, incredulous. "Is there something in the air?" He shakes his head. "At any rate. Bounty hunters. So it's a long story, I'm sure someone will tell it over the next three weeks, but the short version is, we owe a crime syndicate some money. Really, we don't—we were framed, but they don't care. I've already transmitted the bounty, plus a little extra to get that particular problem off our backs."

Bennie looks up at him. "How much extra?"

"Don't worry, between what we got from those last pirates, plus the cut the Harrith Navy sent of the rest, we're doing all right. Add in our fee for this little adventure and yeah, definitely okay."

Prathea looks confused. "If you were innocent why not prove it to them? I assume you know who they really should be after?"

Zephyr nods. "We do. He's the one who sold us out."

Wil picks up from there: "And there's no evidence. When he hired me, it was in private booth at a bar he owns. Privacy screens, sound suppression, the works. My wristcomm doesn't even have a log of the hour I was there." He shrugs. "As much as I hate paying, it's the easiest way to put this behind us. I doubt Kohar would've been the only one to try and collect."

Xan looks at Wil. "That reminds me. What's a *ziggy stardust*?"

CHAPTER 8

COLLECT CALLS

Murta is sitting in his quarters. As the only male in the non-crew part of the team, Prathea decided he could have a bunk alone in one of the guest quarters. Prathea and Xan are sharing the remaining viable guest berth. Jor' Lu is mostly comfortable in the cargo hold. Zephyr helped her use the crates they're transporting for the trip into a "fort," as Wil called it.

After securing the door, Murta reaches into his duffel bag and removes a small device. He places the device next to the terminal on the desk that's built into the bulkhead opposite his bed. After a few minutes of lights blinking erratically, the device lets out a beep, and most of the lights turn green.

He keys in a command on his terminal and waits. After what feels like an eternity, the display changes to a mostly blank screen, with a small logo in the center. *"This is Harrith Internal Security. Please identify yourself,"* a voice says. The sex of the voice's owner is impossible to determine.

"This is Murta Twi'gwar. Assigned to the security services of Farsight Corporation research station on Capralla. Well—I was on Capralla, I'm not now." He looks around, worried he'll be seen, despite being alone in his room.

"And where are you now, Mister Twi'gwar?" The logo doesn't change at all.

"On a ship. The *Ghost*, I'm sure you're familiar with it." He leans forward, lowering his voice.

Something that sounds like a sigh. *"We are."*

When the talking logo doesn't continue, Murta looks around again, confused. "Uh, yes, well, the *Ghost* is en route to something I think the Harrith people could greatly benefit from."

"Mister Twi'gwar, I'm quite busy."

"Uh, yes, right. The scientists on Capralla found something. Sorry, not something, a ship. A huge ship, larger than a Peacekeeper carrier. Derelict."

"I see. Where is it?" For the first time, the logo sounds interested.

"I'm transmitting the coordinates now on a sub-channel. The *Ghost* will be on site soon."

"Coordinates received. How soon?"

"Five standard days," Murta replies, looking more relaxed now.

"We cannot get assets on site before then, or even after within any reasonable time-frame. I'm sending you instructions and technical specifications on the same sub-channel. I assume you have access to a printer?"

"I do, yes. I think there's one in the machine room here."

"Manufacture the specified components. One of them is a secure communicator. Once you've placed it, we'll be in touch."

"Acknowledged. I'll—" The logo has vanished. "Oh, okay... They hung up." He sighs. He glances at the lower right corner of the terminal screen. There's a file waiting. He copies it to his PADD and quickly deletes it from the terminal. Then he pushes a button on the device next to the screen. The green lights flicker a few times, changing colors, before fading out. He puts the device back in his bag, and zips it up.

AWKWARD CONVERSATIONS

WIL IS SITTING on the bridge with Bennie. The *Ghost* is still two days from the derelict, and Wil is getting antsy. He and Bennie are discussing the finer points of a game he can't remember the name of. He's mostly letting Bennie drone on while he thinks about the consortium and their bounty. *I shouldn't be surprised. Xarrix is a rat who'd probably sell out his own mother—does he even know his mother? So much money wasted paying off that damn bounty. Did Xarrix come from an egg? I wonder how big the egg was...*

"Wil!"

"Huh, what? Sorry." Wil looks around; Bennie is staring at him, slowly shaking his head. Standing at the hatch, waiting to enter the bridge, is Murta.

"Permission to enter?" the head of security asks.

"You don't have to ask anymore, but I appreciate the gesture." Wil gestures to an empty seat Murta has occupied on previous visits to the bridge. The tall Harrith walks in, and glances over to Bennie's station, and he makes what looks like a gagging expression.

"Best not to linger," Wil says, turning in his chair to follow Murta's progress around the bridge.

Murta sits and looks at Wil. "I wanted to talk about the ship."

Wil sighs. "I'm shocked. Look Murta, we've talked about the ship at least once, if not three or four times, every day of this journey. Do you really think there's anything left to say? Did you come up with some brilliant new way to try and lay claim in the name of the Harrith people?" Wil isn't actually mad, but he is definitely tired of the conversation.

"Tell me. Did you save my people because you thought it was the right thing to do?" The tall Harrith is staring intently at Wil.

Bennie, who has been doing his best to ignore the conversation, hops out of his seat. "What was that Gabe? You want to see me in the Engineering space? I'll be right there!" He scurries to the hatch faster than Wil has ever seen him move.

Cursing Bennie under his breath, Wil finally answers: "No. Well not in the way you're asking. Did I do it for Harrith Prime? No—until we realized what was happening I'd never even been to your corner of the quadrant." He shakes his head. "We got involved because we had no choice. We stumbled onto the information, and the only way to clear Zephyr and Maxim's name—and the only way to get Xarrix off our back—was to blow the lid off the Peacekeeper thing. The only way to do *that* was to go to Harrith. So we went to Harrith. Screwing Janus was also a nice benefit, but other than that, no I'm sorry, we didn't do it for the people of Harrith, specifically."

Before Murta can say anything, Wil continues, "That said, I'm glad we did it. I'm glad your people are still independent. I'm glad your navy wasn't entirely wiped from the galaxy. I think the GC is corrupt and the Peacekeepers do more harm than good, and I'm glad we were able to slow down their expansion plans."

Murta nods. "I see." He starts to stand.

"Murta, wait." Wil raises a hand to stop the pouting security chief from leaving. "What do you imagine your people would do with a ship like that? Let's pretend for a minute that no one else has a better idea, the ship is one hundred percent functional, *and* we can operate it, *and* we decide it should be in the Harrith Navy. What would they do with it?"

The other man stays silent for a minute or two, looking down at the deck before answering.

"Destroy the GC. Go to Tarsis and destroy Peacekeeper Command."

Wil blinks three or four times. "Oh, uh, okay... that's not the answer I was expecting, actually. I mean, it's certainly an option, for sure. You seem to have thought this out more than I expected, to be honest."

Murta stands. "I've had a while to think of what I'd do to the Peacekeepers if presented with an opportunity." Without another word, he turns and leaves the bridge.

ALONE TIME

Zephyr and Maxim are sparring in the corner of the cargo hold that they've converted to a workout area. Both are holding heavily padded pugil sticks, circling each other.

"Is this what you pictured for us?" Zephyr asks.

"Sparring?" Without missing a beat, Maxim spins his stick high, going for her head.

"No!" She drops below the swing, bringing her stick expertly around in an arc, striking his midsection. He lets out a grunt, spinning with the impact, then drops his stick low, clipping her ankle.

Zephyr rolls out of the fall, coming back to her feet opposite her partner. "I mean, on a ship like this. Saving the sector from war. Exploring derelict ships..." She makes a rolling motion with her hand. "The list goes on."

Maxim moves in with an overhand swing, dodging her parry and bringing his pugil stick up in a defensive block, barely stopping her second swing. "Don't forget, traveling with a human. Well, a human, an annoying Brailack, and a liberated Peacekeeper service bot."

She nods. "Humans. Such a weird race. Think they'll ever be a part of the GC?"

Maxim smiles. "Gods, I hope not. Can you imagine the damage an entire planet of Wils could do?" He lunges. "They are only on *one* planet, right?"

Zephyr parries with a swipe of her pugil stick, then whips it around. Maxim barely brings his own stick up in time to deflect the blow. He continues the motion, letting his momentum spin him around, bringing his stick up in a powerful arc. It connects with her shoulder, sending her spinning away.

"They are weird, aren't they? Yeah, I think they're still just on their home planet." She pants, standing up again, striking a battle-ready stance. Before Maxim can regain his footing, she lunges forward, her pugil stick darting straight out to connect with the big man's chin. His feet leave the floor—not a small feat in itself—and he flies back a few paces, landing with a thud.

Before he can get back up, Zephyr is on him, straddling his chest. "Yield?"

He coughs once. "Yield."

She leans down and kisses him, then sits back up. "Do you think all humans are like Wil?"

He shakes his head. "Impossible," he chuckles. "They'd have likely blown their planet up long ago if they were like Wil."

Zephyr's face turns serious. "Think we'll ever go home?"

"Home is right here, at least for now. I have you, I have the rest of them..." he pauses, "For better or worse."

She laughs and leans down for another kiss.

From the opposite corner of the hold, there's a cough-like sound. They look up to see Jor' Lu is poking her head over her storage-crate fort turned living space. She smiles, and waves at them awkwardly. "Hello."

THE PAST

"Wake up."

The voice doesn't belong to anyone Wil remembers being in the room when he went under for the procedure. Of course, there were a bunch of people there, none that Wil knew, and very few whom he could identify the species of.

"Wake up." A pause. "What did you say this one was? Hoban? Vulcan?"

Another voice: "Human. Xarrix says he's the only one. Do you think Xarrix destroyed his planet?"

"Anything is possible, but no I think Xarrix said this one somehow got off planet and found his way to GC space. If we killed him, Xarrix is going to be pissed."

Wil finally has the strength to speak—or rather, croak: "Not. Dead." He opens one eye and sees something with huge, pupil-less blue eyes and a mouth full of razor-sharp teeth looking down at him. "Sweet boneless Christ." He shudders, clamping his eyes closed, then opens one slowly.

Blue-eyes looks away and addresses a companion that Wil can't see from where he is, laying on the table. "Get him ready for training."

Fifteen minutes later, Wil is in a plain white jumpsuit in a room with various pieces of equipment and weapons, and what looks like a dentist's chair. Blue-eyes and their assistant—a tall, hairless being with no visible eyes and two sets of arms and legs—are facing him.

"Mr. Calder, Xarrix asked for you to receive weapons, tactics and technology training. Please take a seat. I am Holshoom; this is Brawndo, we will be administering your upgrades."

Wil looks around the room. The chair is the least terrifying thing in there. "I thought you already did the whole upgrade thing?" he asks, hopping into the chair, rubbing the shaved patch on the back of his head.

"We installed the neural interface hardware. It allows knowledge and skills to be directly installed into your brain in the correct locations." Holshoom bows. "I must admit, learning about your brain without killing you was quite a challenge."

Wil sits up in the chair. "Uh, thanks?"

"Please lie back. We'll begin with technology; it's the easiest upgrade to install."

Wil starts to lean back in the chair, then bolts upright. "Can I also learn Kung-Fu?" he asks.

The two aliens look at each other, then back at Wil. Brawndo asks, "What's Kung-Fu?"

Wil sighs. "Where's Morpheus when you need him?" He leans back in the chair, and says, "Let's do this." He closes his eyes, then they snap open. "Wait, will it hurt?"

Without answering, Holshoom activates something on the data slate it's holding. What feels like a thousand ants start crawling around under Wil's skin, biting him. His brain feels like it's being set on fire, then extinguished, then set on fire all over again. Then, just as suddenly as it started, it ends.

"That wasn't so bad, was it?" Holshoom asks, smiling.

"That was terrible!" Wil says through gritted teeth. "It hurt like hell; it feels like my brain is about to explode! My skin feels like it's been peeled off and stapled back on."

Brawndo looks up at Holshoom. "That's different."

The tall scientists nods. "Indeed. It must be something unique to his biology. Make sure you're recording telemetry. The next time we have to work on a human, the process should be less painful."

"Can it be less painful this time?" Wil asks, sweating profusely in the chair.

Holshoom raises its data slate and touches a control. "I'm afraid not."

Wil screams, as another thousand ants do their thing, then stop. "Oh my god! That hurts. A lot!"

Brawndo smiles. "You're almost done, Mr. Calder."

Wil shudders and lets out a ragged sigh. "Yay."

One more blast of brain electricity and Holshoom walks over to Wil, one of its four hands extended to help him out of the chair. "Well done, Mr. Calder. The upgrades are complete. It will take some time for the skills and knowledge to fully acclimate within your grey matter. You don't get the benefit of muscle memory from these types of upgrades, so you'll know what to do but will need to practice to become proficient." It gestures to the weapons and equipment arrayed around the chair. "You are welcome to remain here for a while to practice with all of this." It turns and leaves the room, followed by Brawndo.

Wil picks up something he now recognizes as an interphase modulator and begins to disassemble it. "Cool," he mumbles, as he strips the device like it was his hundredth time doing it.

PART THREE

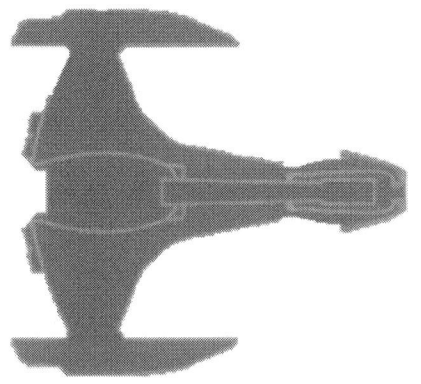

CHAPTER 9

NEWSCAST

"Thank you, Megan, that's right." Mon-El Furash holds one hand to her ear, so that she can hear over the commotion taking place behind her. "We're here on Tarsis at the GC Capital Complex. Complex security has closed the main gates, and told the staff here to remain in their offices."

Nodding vigorously, she continues, "Yes that's true, the interim Senior Councilor was attempting to address a growing crowd gathered on the street outside the complex, when something—we believe it was a shoe —was thrown at her. She's fine, by the way—it was a soft-soled shoe."

Mon-El listens and nods again. "No, for now I believe we're perfectly safe. The crowd was protesting interim Senior Councilor Su'el'toms proposal to delay the election for an unspecified length of time. Many believe the GC won't be able to heal or move on until the leadership of both the Council and Peacekeeper Command are replaced with new blood. I don't think the crowd outside will devolve to anything more violent than shoe-throwing." Mon-El Furash bobs her head again and chuckles. "Yes, Belzar, that's true—to the Guldranii, shoe throwing is one of the most offensive insults possible. I don't know if it was a Guldranii or not, but I'd say the odds are good."

IT'S SO BIG

"It's so big." Zephyr murmurs.

"That's what she said," Wil chuckles, holding his fist out to be bumped. When there is no response, he looks around the bridge. Every other member of the team is looking at the primary display, which is showing the mystery ship, all five kilometers of it. "No one?" he asks.

"Shazbot, that's a big ship," Xan whispers.

Wil looks at Xan. "That's a real swear word?" No one acknowledges this, either.

"Quite a bit larger than you implied," Maxim says, turning to Prathea.

She shrugs. "We didn't have anything to measure it against. Also, technically I never said how big it was, just *big*." She never takes her eyes off the display.

"What do we do now?" Jor' Lu asks, from the back of the bridge.

Everyone turns to look at Wil.

"We don't rush in, that's what we do," he says. "Zee, run a full scan—everything we've got. Prathea and Bennie, start running whatever analysis you can. Jor' Lu and Xan... what is it you do? I never asked."

"I'm a physicist," Xan replies sourly.

"I am an engineer," Jor' Lu contributes.

"She has been quite helpful during our trip, Captain," Gabe offers. "The main engine is operating at a level I did not think possible."

"Well, that's good, thank you. Okay, you continue doing what you do then. We don't get any closer to that ship until we know more." Wil turns to Murta. "Murta, you just stand around and look pouty." He gives Murta a thumbs-up. The head of security does not seem amused.

After several scans of varying types and adjustments to the sensors to allow for even more scans, it's nearing the time that the crew eats dinner, so everyone has a snack of some type sitting on a plate on their knees—or, if they're Bennie, balanced precariously on something that looks expensive.

Wil looks around the room. "Alright, what've we got?" He points to Zephyr. "Zee, you first."

She finishes chewing and puts her plate aside. "Well, I've confirmed our initial reading on its size. It's five kilometers long, a kilometer and a half wide. Looks like it uses a similar method of propulsion as the *Ghost* or any other ship you'd see in the GC. There aren't any windows, which I find odd—not a single one. Lastly, our sensors are picking up a power signature, but it's weak. Likely just battery backups or something similar. It's far too weak to be the ship's reactor, even in standby mode. I think it's dead in space." She picks up her plate, indicating that she's done with her report.

Wil nods to Prathea, who he notices is sitting oddly close to Bennie, having moved a chair from a nearby station over to his.

She clears her throat. "I can confirm Zephyr's readings. The vessel appears to be without primary power. The energy sources we can detect scattered throughout the ship must be some type of emergency batteries, as they're too small to do anything on the scale of the ship itself. There's a significant amount of hull damage, either from conflict or space debris impact. Without getting closer, it's impossible to tell the source or accurately identify a timeline. Ben-Ari did notice that while the ship is essentially dead, low power scans are emanating from the vessel. We can't yet determine their purpose, of course."

Prathea smiles in Bennie's direction, and the small alien blushes—at least, that's what Wil thinks is happening. He shakes his head to clear a somewhat disturbing mental image. "Uh, okay then. Science twins, what've you got?"

Xan and Jor' Lu exchange looks, before Xan speaks up. "The ship has amazing propulsion capabilities. Your second in command is correct about that, after a fashion." She glances at Zephyr. "No offense."

"None taken."

Jor' Lu picks up the report. "From what we can tell from the scans, the ship uses sub-light systems, the same as any ship made today. However, it's FTL components are entirely different. It's impossible to know more precisely without further investigation, but I'd say at FTL it's quite fast, particularly for its size. Which brings me to what I believe might be the biggest point of interest of this vessel."

Xan jumps in: "The reactor needed to power a ship this size would be immense! To put it simply, two to three times the size of this entire vessel. That much power would be..." She pauses, looking around. "Well the reactor from that ship could probably power all of Tarsis."

Maxim lets out a low whistle, "I've never seen a reactor that big, even on the largest Peacekeeper ships. Have you Gabe?"

The tall engineer is standing near the bridge hatch, "I have not."

Wil nods to him. "What about you, big guy, anything you want to add?"

The tall Palorian nods. "Actually, yes. I took the liberty of running my own tactical scans. This is a dreadnought, no doubt about it." He leaves that last sentence hanging in the room. Everyone is looking at each other uneasily.

Wil finally breaks the silence. "For those of us not from a planet of space warriors...?"

Zephyr and Maxim exchange a look, before he continues. "A dreadnought is, to put it simply, a ship of death. It has no other purpose than combat. This ship has several hundred weapons emplacements. Weapons range from point defense to long-range beam weapons, missiles, torpedo tubes. I was able to identify fifty missile batteries in a standby state. There is also some type of large-scale weapon situated at the front of the ship. I have no idea about it's purpose or capabilities. As I said, a ship like this has but one purpose."

Wil looks at the primary display. The dreadnought is hanging fifty kilometers directly ahead of them. "Well, that's not terrifying," he says.

ANYONE HOME?

"So FAR, no reaction from the ship," Zephyr announces, as Wil brings the ship ever closer to the dreadnought.

Maxim looks up from his tactical screens. "No weapons response either."

Wil adjusts his controls. "Okay, then. Let's go knock on the door. Zephyr— you've got an airlock picked out?"

"I do. Sending it to your console." She taps a control and one of his screens updates to show a small targeting icon overlaid on the hull of the dreadnought.

Wil examines it. "Bennie, anything on your end?" he asks. There is no response from the Brailack. "Bennie?"

"Sorry, what?"

"What, what?" Wil looks up from his console, turning towards Bennie, trying only a little to hide his irritation. "What do you mean *what*? What're you doing over there?"

"What? Nothing!" Bennie says, his voice higher than usual.

"Are you blushing? You are! You're turning from Kermit green to Oscar the Grouch green!" Wil stands up and advances on Bennie's station.

Zephyr leans out of her station and looks at Maxim. "What's an Oscar the Grouch?"

He shakes his head. "What's a Kermit?"

Wil is at Bennie's station now, looking at the display. "Dude! Are you watching... uh, what are you watching?"

Bennie looks away and mumbles something.

"Is that... Are you watching *Xena, Warrior Princess*? How the hell do you know anything about Xena? How are you watching it? What episode is that? Wait—that last question doesn't matter. Explain yourself, green bean."

Bennie slaps his console, and the monitor switches to a display of code or something else Wil doesn't understand. "I found it in an archive in the computer core."

"Dude!" Wil throws his hands up. "That archive is private!" He turns around to return to his chair, then spins back to face Bennie again. "We'll talk about this later," he adds. Sitting back down in his command chair, he sighs, "Anyway. Bennie, anything you'd like to share? About the ship. The ship we're very close to right now—the big, scary ship?"

Bennie looks at his displays. "No, not really. I don't have anything to add."

Wil rubs his forehead, sighing. "Jesus."

Zephyr coughs and offers, "Yes, well... perhaps we should just commence with the boarding?"

Wil looks up at the ceiling, and takes a deep breath. "Yeah, let's do that," he says, casting a sideways glare towards the station Bennie occupies.

Maxim, who's done his best to stay silent at his station during this, asks, "I did not know you knew a warrior princess. Is she from your home city?"

Wil only sighs again, and focuses on bringing the *Ghost* in closer to the dreadnought, lining up the port-side airlock with the airlock that Zephyr has tagged for him. When the *Ghost* is fifty meters away, he brings it to a stop and sets the controls to 'station keeping,' so that even if the other ship drifts, the auto-pilot on the *Ghost* will compensate for the movement.

"We're in position." He looks over at Bennie. "Go get the squints."

"The whats-thats?" Bennie looks up from his station, green brow furrowed.

Wil sighs. "Just go get the scientists. They're getting suited up in the lounge." He gets up himself, and heads toward the hatch leading off the bridge. The rest of the team follows him—Bennie splitting off to head down the main corridor toward the crew lounge, where Prathea and her team are waiting.

Wil, Zephyr, and Maxim enter the armory and begin getting suited up.

Maxim looks over at Wil, already half-dressed. "That's not your regular armor—when did you get that?"

Wil looks down at his armored arm. "Oh this? I ordered it last time we were on Pollak. There was an arms dealer in that night market in Calto province. She said it was fresh from Harrith Navy R&D—it was delivered in that cargo lot we took on after that pirate asteroid raid. Like it?"

Maxim nods appreciatively, as Wil continues donning his new armor.

Zephyr is almost dressed, her Peacekeeper armor repaired after the last pirate adventure. She turns to examine the new suit. "Do you know what it does?"

Wil nods vigorously. "Well yeah. I mean... mostly. It's not like it came with an instruction manual, being black market and all." At a look from his first officer he shrugs. "I'm sure I can figure it out."

Maxim shakes his head. "This should be interesting."

Wil pulls his long brown coat on. "Hey, that hurts. Is this about the missile incident? For the record, I had no idea there were still micro missiles in that launcher. The display was blinking red."

Zephyr laughs. "And to Kordites, red is the color of 'go.' It was fully armed and ready—as you discovered. Well, you and that storage shed. The storage shed full of valuable merchandise." She high-fives Maxim before heading out of the armory, her partner close on her heels.

Wil tuts. "Wish I hadn't taught you two that!" he shouts after them, activating his armor's systems. Several parts whir and beep, the lights on his gauntlets coming on, and an integrated wrist-comm comes online. Wil giggles, "Neat!" and follows the others out of the armory.

When he turns the corner to the port airlock, everyone is already there. Prathea and the scientists are in basic space-suits, while Murta is in something that looks like a tactical suit—albeit not as advanced as anything on the *Ghost*. Bennie is in the smallest suit the team could find, the last time they were in a market. It's still too big, comically so.

"Bennie, can you run overwatch from the ship?" Wil looks the short hacker over. "That suit is stupid big on you. You're gonna trip every four steps. Likely get you or one of us killed."

Bennie raises his arms in an expansive gesture, the bunched up fabric looking comically saggy, "We need to go space suit shopping soon!"

THE PAST

"WHY DID you pick this disgusting place?" Xarrix lifts his glass and examines a smudge of something on the side, scratching at it with one claw.

"Because, as far as I know, you don't own this one, so it's not loaded with goons." Wil puts his own, not-overly-clean glass down. "Look, it's just something I need to do."

Xarrix scowls. "I didn't upgrade your feeble brain just to let you throw your life away. Your crappy home planet is off limits, and patrolled by the GC."

Wil frowns. "Welp, too damn bad. I've been out here on my own for too long. I need movies, I need TV shows, I need music." He brings his glass to his lips and mumbles. "Need porn."

"What's that?" Xarrix is still turning his glass, trying to find a not-gross spot. Giving up, he sets it back down.

"Nothing, never mind. Anyway, I'm going," Wil says.

Xarrix sighs. "Fine." He looks down and taps on his wrist-comm, then speaks to someone. "I'm in Bamston City on Lorstak Seven. Get Shinto and Lopak and get out here." He looks up at Wil. "I'm going to add some stealth tech to the *Ghost*, it's expensive. I'd say you owe me, but you already owe me, so here's the deal."

Wil holds up a hand. "Wait, wait—"

"No." The coldness in that single word stops Wil in his tracks. "You will go to yurth—"

"Earth," Wil grumbles.

"You will go to Earth, get whatever crap you need. You will fill the hold of the *Ghost* with whatever you can that's unique to your world. You'll bring it all back, and I'll sell it."

"And then I'm off the hook?" Wil asks.

"Then we see how much debt is left. I highly doubt your backwater mud-ball planet will have anything that could outright erase your debt." The reptilian crime lord stands to leave. "I'll be in touch when my guys get here."

Wil watches the gangster leave the bar, before looking around. "This place really is gross," he mutters to himself. He looks at his very-smudged glass, takes a huge gulp to finish his grum, and gets up.

Some kind of service bot wheels over in front of him. "Please pay your bill," it chirps in a pleasant voice.

Wil looks down at the waist-high bot. "Well, you're cute."

"Please pay your bill." The cute voice is less cute now.

"Okay, okay. Not very chatty, are you?" He pulls up his banking software on his wristcomm.

"Please pay your—"

"Yeah, yeah. Shut up, R2." He accepts the bill, and the funds vanish from his balance. Without waiting for a response, he heads for the door.

Walking along the street outside, he finds it easy to think of Bamston as your average mid-sized Earth city: Denver, Omaha, or Riverside. Of course, that mental illusion ends when a Hulgian couple steps out of a restaurant, nearly crushing Wil in their haste.

"Oh, my goodness!" the female of the pair exclaims. "Please excuse us!"

"Oh, yes. We're very sorry, we didn't see you there," the male says, as they edge around Wil.

Wil waves them off, still thinking about Denver. "No worries. Have a good one."

As he continues down the street, he hears the female ask her companion, "A good what?"

The male replies, "Who knows? What do you think that was anyway?"

It doesn't take long to find another bar, this one far less disgusting than the previous one. Taking a seat at the bar, Wil says: "Grum."

The bartender, a lanky being with three eyes and pointy ears, nods and reaches for a glass under the bar.

Wil looks down at his wristcomm, making a list. "Okay, I'll need to make sure I grab every movie, TV show and song I can get my hands on. Wonder if Bennie will help me with something to download it all?" He nods to the bartender in thanks and takes a drink of his grum. "What about food and stuff, hmmm... Where should I park? It's not like I can set down in a desert, then call for a Lyft or something..." He continues to mumble to himself as he works on the problem.

CHAPTER 10

AVON CALLING

T HE OUTER AIRLOCK hatch cycles open, revealing Maxim and Wil standing shoulder to shoulder in the cramped space. Wil nods to Max. "We're EVA." They both step out of the airlock, the EVA thrusters in their suits jetting them across the distance between the *Ghost* and the dreadnought.

The moment they're away, the outer hatch closes and the airlock cycles back, letting Gabe, Xan and Prathea enter. It's a tight fit. Inside the airlock, Gabe looks at the two scientists. "I can control our flight, you will not need to engage your suit thrusters." The outer door opens, and both scientists take a step back, bumping into Gabe. With his smaller set of arms, he grabs a handle on the back of each of their suits and uses the EVA jets attached to his arms, legs and torso to leave the airlock.

Last out of the airlock are Jor' Lu, Murta and Zephyr. Thankfully, Murta had had the foresight to pack EVA suits in sizes that would fit all his charges, otherwise Xan and Jor' Lu would have been forced to stay behind on the *Ghost* with Bennie.

It turns out getting scientists unaccustomed to space walks, from one ship to another takes a really long time. Even with Gabe handling them, the scientists are a handful, and it takes time to cycle them through the alien airlock.

Over the comms channel, Bennie complains, "It's not my fault! If I was over there, I could have directly interfaced with the airlock control computer, or something..." His voice trails off on the last few words.

"Or something," Wil says, looking down at the wristcomm built into the suit he's wearing to check air quality. "Nothing breathable, at least not for any of us. Keep your suits sealed." He turns and heads down the corridor.

"This looks like any other ship," comments Maxim, running a hand along the wall of the corridor they're walking down. He looks up. "Whoever lived here, they weren't much taller than us."

Jor' Lu clears her throat. "Yes, I've noticed that."

Zephyr glances from the tall Burzzad to Wil. "He's right, this isn't that different from the *Ghost* or a Peacekeeper ship..." She trails off, looking down the corridor. "Though these are a bit odd..." Her hand finds what looks like a ladder rung, except it's built directly into the wall. There's a rung every half meter or so along each wall, and in the ceiling and floor.

"There is gravity though, that seems weird," Xan observes.

"Big or tall, short or squat. Only one way to find out." Wil looks down at his wristcomm again, and points to the left, toward what they assume is where engineering is located. "Maxim, Jor' Lu, Prathea and Gabe, head that way. You guys are 'Team Two.'" All of their wristcomm units beep, indicating a new shared comms channel. Wil points toward the right. "Zephyr, Xan, and Murta, with me. We're 'Team One.' Let's go."

Team Two heads off in their assigned direction. Wil looks over at Murta. "Having fun?"

The Harrith man glares and shakes his head. "Still thinking of selling this to the highest bidder, pirate?"

Before Wil can answer, Zephyr smoothly glides between the

two of them. "We're just looking around for now. Decisions later." She moves on ahead, rifle at the ready, to side-step around a corner and point her weapon down the next corridor. "Clear."

Murta makes a growling noise, but moves past Zephyr down the corridor toward the next intersection. "Clear."

Wil consults his wristcomm. "Thoughts on finding the bridge?"

Murta comes up beside him and reaches over to Wil's wrist-comm, where he presses a button. From the back of his armor, four small spheres detach.

Wil jumps. "I didn't know it did that!"

"Read the manual," Murta replies. The spheres take off in opposite directions. Zephyr stifles a laugh as Wil glares at her.

Murta looks at the map of the ship that is slowly forming on Wil's wristcomm screen. "Remind me why Prathea wanted you along?"

Xan grabs Wil's arm and pulls it down so she can see the screen, then lets go. "This way," she announces.

Wil looks down at his wristcomm. *I really gotta get my hands on that manual*, he thinks.

THAT'S A BIG DOOR

MAXIM EDGES AROUND ANOTHER CORNER, nearly a half-kilometer from where Team One and Two split up. "Clear."

Prathea follows him around the corner. "What's that?" she asks.

Behind her, Jor' Lu also gazes down the corridor. "A ramp."

The squat Palorian looks up at her colleague. "Why is there a ramp and not a lift?"

Maxim peers down the corridor and the ramp to the level below. He shrugs. "Ramps are easier for mobility. Things without legs and such can work with a ramp quite quickly and easily."

Gabe is already moving smoothly down the ramp. He turns his head nearly one-hundred and eighty degrees while continuing to walk forward, to speak to them. "They are drastically more efficient and less prone to breakdown than lifts." He adds, continuing down the ramp, "They do, however, take up considerably more space."

The four of them explore the lower levels of the dreadnought, following Bennie's directions as he scans the ship from the *Ghost*. They eventually reach a corridor more massive than any of the others they've been exploring. At the end, they find a massive blast door.

Maxim stops about thirty meters from the blast door—the firmly-closed blast door. Gabe, Prathea and Jor' Lu hustle past him toward the door.

Prathea runs her hand along the seam of the massive doors. "How do we get inside?"

"How can we be sure this is the engineering compartment?" Jor' Lu asks, looking back the way they came.

From Maxim's wristcomm an indignant Bennie hollers, "Because I said it was! I'm looking at the scanners right now. The power signature we detected is about fifty meters from you. I can see the power readings, but the compartment is otherwise shielded, so I can't make out the layout."

Gabe walks over to the door. "I believe I can interface the door with Bennie back on the *Ghost,* in order to gain access."

Over the wristcomm, Bennie chimes in: "Yeah just put the remote interface unit by the control panel and splice it in. There is a control panel, right?"

"There is," Gabe replies, taking a small electronic device from the case he is carrying. While his smaller pair of hands attaches the remote access device, his much more powerful main set of arms, is prying off the access panel. The remote interface is soon attached to the wall next to the panel, several wires strung between the open panel and the device.

"This will take a minute," Bennie says from the *Ghost.* A few seconds later, he amends that: "Okay, this will take more than a minute."

"How long?" Maxim asks.

"You can't rush genius, you big drennog."

Just then, the door hisses and begins to open. Maxim exchanges a glance with Gabe then looks down at his wristcomm. "Can't rush it, huh?"

Bennie tuts. "I'm just that good."

The door finishes opening, revealing a massive chamber. Jor' Lu rushes inside before Maxim can stop her. "Gabe," he shouts, following her, "you and Prathea wait one."

Jor' Lu's flashlight is playing around the chamber inside. Maxim's beam joins hers, illuminating sections of the space. It's enormous. Jor' Lu turns. "It's—" She stops, as she turns right into the beam of Maxim's flashlight. "Oh my! Very bright!"

Maxim moves the beam away from her face. It falls on a massive structure in the back of the room. "Is that the—"

"Engine? Yes," Jor' Lu says, walking towards it.

"May we come in now?" Gabe asks from the doorway. Maxim turns to see the tall droid leaning in from the doorframe, with the much shorter Prathea doing the same beneath him. He motions for them both to enter. "Come on in. Looks clear."

Prathea looks at the engine when she gets close to Maxim. "Wow, that's a big reactor."

Gabe raises a handheld scanner and sweeps the room. "Interesting." He walks off, then says, "Interesting" again.

UNOBTAINIUM?

I‌T‌ ‌‌T‌A‌K‌E‌S what seems like hours of wandering corridors and ramps to arrive at large blast door with a small hovering ball in front of it.

"This it?" Murta asks.

Zephyr points at the small probe hovering in front of the door. "So says the floating ball."

Wil tuts. "These little guys need names."

Xan joins them at the door. "This looks imposing. I wonder what it's made out of?"

Wil touches the same control on his wristcomm that Murta did earlier. The small sensor drone near the door darts towards him and returns to its docking station. "Definitely gotta remember this command." Glancing at the display, he sees the other three sensor spheres making their way back to him, along with several decks' worth of layout on the screen and an analysis of the door. "Neat. So according to Huey, the door is made of an alloy: Titanium, unobtainium—wait, that's a thing?"

Zephyr and Murta nod their heads slightly, in unison. Wil continues, "And vortimate. I don't know what that one is. Well, that one or the other one that sounds like something from a movie.

Titanium though, that stuff is strong. My old pod was a carbon fiber, titanium-bonded polymer."

Xan reaches up and grabs Wil's arm and wristcomm, looking at the display. "He's right. Interesting mixture, but strong for sure. Vortimate is still essentially experimental. Farsight has been working with vortimate for just a few months. Whoever built this has clearly had much more time to perfect its use. Their science is decades, at least, ahead of ours."

Murta is running his hand along the edge of the door frame. "Can your hacker get us in?" he asks.

"I'm on comms, you know.," Bennie grumbles. "And yes, I can get you in. I got Team Two into engineering a couple centocks ago."

Wil turns away. "Max, report."

"We're in engineering. The 'squints' as you called them, are taking a look around. They seem rather excited."

Wil nods. "I bet. We're about to head onto the bridge. Stay in touch."

"Affirmative, you too." At that, the Palorian cuts the comms.

Zephyr is at the security panel set into the door frame. She has already got it disassembled and is attaching a device Wil recognizes as something that Bennie had handed her and Gabe, before the two teams left the *Ghost*. She's talking into her wristcomm to Bennie. "Yes. Yes, I did that. No. No. I can kill you at least thirty ways before I even have to pick up a weapon, don't forget that. Yes. No, wait, okay, yes. Okay, the light just turned green."

Within seconds, the massive doors part with a groan. Dust erupts from the seams.

Before Wil or Zephyr can object, Murta rushes in ahead. Both sigh and move inside, followed by Xan. Wil heads left, Zephyr right, clearing the large space with military precision. Both announce "clear" at the same time. When they come back to the center of the room, Murta is standing there, where a massive pillar is glowing, faintly.

"Zordon?" Wil asks, walking over to the pillar. He knocks on it with one hand—it echoes, sounding slightly hollow. He turns to Murta, who is standing near what looks like a console. "That's the last time you rush into a room before it's cleared. You should know better." He circles the two-meter wide pillar of swirling lights, while Murta scowls at his back. "I wonder where the Power Rangers are?"

Xan and Zephyr are standing over a console in the starboard bulkhead. Xan looks up. "This," she says, pointing at the pillar Wil is standing next to, "is, I think, some type of access to the central computer. The fact that it's on confirms that there is some type backup power available." As they watch, the lights showing in the pillar changes slightly.

Zephyr adds, "I'm thinking we're not going to get very far without more power." She gestures to the panel. "This is barely functional. I'd guess there's a power-cell somewhere in the base, meant to keep it running between switching from main power to backup. However long it's been doing that job, it must be almost depleted."

Wil tilts his head, activating the comms in his wristcomm. "Max, Gabe, any thoughts on restoring power?"

THE PAST

"Stealth system activated," the computer reports, as the *Ghost* approaches Earth.

Wil consults the sensor display window he's inserted into the main display screen. It shows Earth, the *Ghost*, and several hundred somethings orbiting the planet. *Looks like the space junk industry is still going strong*, he thinks wryly. Then he pulls up a high-resolution scan of North America. "Okay, let's see what we have here." He pans around the image while the *Ghost* cruises toward the upper atmosphere. "Oh, this looks promising!" He slides the image over until an airfield is positioned in the center. Several large hangars sit off to one side, a few looking big enough to hold the *Ghost*. "Spanish Peaks Airfield, here I come," he mutters.

It doesn't take long for the *Ghost* to penetrate Earths atmosphere and begin its atmospheric flight, hurtling towards Colorado, atmo-engines roaring. Stealth systems can fool sensors, Wil knows, but engines are engines, and the ones that push the *Ghost* through the atmosphere are loud.

"Sorry moose, and mounties, eh," Wil says, as the ship crosses over into North Dakota. Adjusting a few controls, he eases off the throttle for the atmo-engines. A couple of thousand feet below, some cows look up. He's timed his arrival so he's passing over the central US at around four a.m.

Minutes later, he is maneuvering the *Ghost* over a seemingly abandoned airfield. "Computer, scan the area below, are there any open wireless networks?"

"*Affirmative, two networks detected;* Bill's wireless *and* Airfield public."

"Any life signs?" Wil leans forward in his chair.

"*Negative.*"

Wil punches the air. "Sweet! Activate program, 'bennies door-buster'." He turns to look at the primary display.

"*Acknowledged,*" the computer answers. On the screen, each of the large hangars is highlighted in blue, one after the other, until one in the northwest corner of the airfield flashes green.

The massive doors begin to part. The program Xarrix's hacker pal, Ben-Ari sold him works as advertised, cycling through radio frequencies until it finds the remote door opener frequency. Meanwhile, the wireless connection is helping the ship's computer start familiarizing itself with Earth's internet.

"Yes!" Wil says, getting up from his chair. "Begin automatic landing sequence."

The *Ghost* shuts down its atmospheric engines and reduces the power supply to its repulsor lifts, bringing the ship to hover only a handful of feet off the ground. Then it tilts slightly, letting the repulsor lifts in each wing-mounted engine pod push the ship gently into the hangar.

Wil is in the cargo bay when the computer announces, "*Landing cycle complete.*" The ship bumps slightly as it settles on the two massive landing struts that have deployed from the wings on either side of its main body, like massive bird's legs. Wil walks over to the control panel and opens the inner doors, then lowers the cargo ramp.

That done, he hurries over to a storage unit set against the wall of the cargo hold. "Time to see if this thing works," he says, wheeling out what looks like a go-cart. "It better work. I didn't even know this part of Colorado existed."

Getting in, he straps in and flips the switches the vendor on Fury had told to flip. The small vehicle hums to life. Carefully, Wil pushes the throttle forward and pulls up on the control stick—the little cart lurches forward, then surges into the air.

"Yee-haw!" he screams, as he shoots off into the pre-dawn light. As he disappears into the distance, the *Ghost* instructs the hangar to quietly close its massive doors behind him.

It only takes two hours to get from the old airfield to the southern outskirts of Denver. Wil guides the "flying go-cart," as he's decided to call it, down an alley off of Broadway Boulevard. Finding a bunch of cardboard and other debris, he covers the go-cart as thoroughly as possible. He's picked the back of what seems to be an unoccupied building. *Hope no one likes to hang out in this part of the alley*, he thinks.

The street is just starting to wake up. There's a small group of people at the bus stop nearby, and a few other people walking by. Wil steps up to the bus stop, looking at the placard on the sign with the list of routes this stop serves. *Perfect, this will get me downtown.*

He's soon at Civic Center Station, walking towards where he remembers there being a coffee shop. In planning this field trip, he had the fabricator on the *Ghost* create fake items his wristcomm can control remotely: a laptop, a credit card and a mobile phone. All of them aren't much more than remote interfaces to his wristcomm, but since wristcomms aren't a thing on Earth, he's got a bag of junk he's lugging around and a long-sleeved shirt hiding his forearms.

The coffee shop is about as busy as he remembers coffee shops being. Walking to the counter, he smiles at the African American woman behind the counter, thinking, *guess coffee shops and college kids haven't changed much. Wait—it's only been a few years, not decades, dummy.* He shakes his head a little and smiles again. "Large mocha please," he says.

"That'll be $6.24."

Okay, some things HAVE changed. Glad this isn't my money! Or even actually *money, for that matter.*

He pulls out his credit card-looking thing and swipes it. In the few seconds it takes for the point of sale terminal to read the card, his wristcomm has accessed its software and forced the sale to go through. Even though the software is saying "card declined" on the inside, the screen is reading *Transaction complete.* He smiles and goes to find a seat.

Taking a deep breath and looking around, he feels his smile grow wider. *Didn't think I'd ever been back here. Wonder what James is up to?*

CHAPTER 11

TURNING THE POWER ON

"Max, Gabe—any thoughts on restoring power?" Wil asks over the main channel.

Maxim nods to Gabe, who answers, "I have several thoughts around restoring power to this vessel, Captain. Would you like to hear them?"

Wil tuts. "Actually, no. I just want to know if you can get power restored, even just to the bridge."

Gabe tilts his head and turns to look at Prathea, who shakes her head, while Jor' Lu nods. "I will have to get back to you." The tall droid walks over to the two scientists. "Ladies?"

Jor' Lu takes a breath. "While I certainly could spend years getting to know this ship and its systems, I believe I can at least start the main reactor. I cannot guarantee I can direct power to the bridge specifically. However, I assume powering the bridge in emergencies would be an automatic response, so the ship may take care of that on its own, once the engine starts."

Maxim looks appraisingly at the tall, skinny engineer. "Impressive. I agree. Peacekeeper vessels operate in much the same way. Priority one systems and locations get power first, automatically." He nods to Gabe.

Gabe nods back. "Captain, we believe we have a plan to restore power. Please standby." To the two scientists, he asks, "How can I assist? This reactor, while large, seems to share many similarities to reactors I have worked on aboard Peacekeeper carriers."

The three of them head off towards the massive structure at the back of the room. Maxim turns to look at a console in the corner. He walks over to it, muttering, "Weird."

Over the comms, Wil asks, "What's that, buddy?"

Maxim runs his hands over the blank console. "There are no inputs. This console is blank, except for a single feature. There's a slot in the center." He walks to another console. "This one as well."

Wil is silent on the comms for a second. "Yeah, there are a few panels like that up here also. Any thoughts?"

Maxim shrugs, then realizes Wil can't see him. "No, I'll consult Gabe when he is done working on his current project."

"Sounds good."

"Maxim, your assistance would be beneficial over here," Gabe calls from the back of the room, where he is standing to one side of the massive engine.

Walking around the large structure, Maxim sees the bottom half of Prathea wiggling around in a hatch about a meter off the deck. "How can I help?"

Gabe points to a panel opposite the one Prathea is waist-deep in. It is about three meters high off the deck. "Can you assist Jor' Lu in gaining access to that panel?"

The Burzzad looks over at Maxim. "I do not weigh much. My bones are hollow."

Maxim just stares at the three-eyed scientist, and says, "Uh, good to know." He leans down and cups his hands in the universal "step here" manner. The tall physicist steps lightly into his hands, and he effortlessly lifts her over his head. "You *are* light."

THE WAITING IS THE WORST PART

THIRTY MINUTES PASS before Gabe comes back on comms. "Captain, we believe we'll be restoring function to the main engine in moments. Please standby."

Wil looks at Zephyr and shrugs. "Guess we see if it's possible to jump-start a warship." He glances up to the pillar in the middle of the bridge.

From out of nowhere there's a loud clunk, causing Xan to jump, hitting her head on the console she's under. "Ouch!"

"Wasn't me!" Wil shouts, as Murta and Zephyr both turn to look at him.

There's another clunk, then two more, then the pillar in the middle of the bridge starts to glow more brightly, the colors swirling.

"Gabe, stuff is happening up here. Is that you?"

"Yes, Captain, I believe so. We've successfully restarted the engine. The reaction is stabilizing now."

Wil looks around at the bridge, where consoles and displays are coming to life. The glowing pillar thing is even brighter now. "Yup, looks like things are coming to life up here."

While Wil is talking to Gabe, Murta slips around behind a

console. This one is bigger than the rest and sits facing the glowing pillar. From his mission bag, he withdraws the device he was instructed to print and attaches it to the underside of the console. Small tendrils snake out of the sides and push through the alloy and into the electronics inside. A light on the side of the device comes on, followed by several others.

"Hey, Murta, check this out." Wil is motioning to him.

Quickly, Murta walks around the console to join Wil, Zephyr and Xan. "What is it?"

"How the hell would we know?" Wil asks. "We're on an alien derelict." He raises his hand to cut off the coming rebuttal. "But Xan thinks it's the main control relay."

What they are looking at appears to be in a corner of the bridge, set into an alcove. A series of blinking red lights ring the device. The little furry physicist nods. "I think we can get the main computer online with this. It appears to have tripped."

Murta tuts, looking at the device on the wall. "You think?"

Xan lets out a low growl. "What part of 'alien derelict' was lost on you? Go secure something." She waves the grumpy Harrith security officer away. Turning back to the console, she mumbles, "You think, you think... Yes, I think! I'm super smart—you're not!"

"What's that?" Murta asks, from a few paces away

"Nothing."

Wil stifles a laugh. "Alrightythen. Xan, you do you. Hey Max, why don't you all regroup up here on the bridge?"

"We're on our way."

Xan nods to Wil, who grabs the relay and pushes it back into place. It doesn't take more than a second for the remaining consoles to come to life. Every light in the room comes on; the central pillar brightens further, the swirling light show intensifying.

"Woah," Wil murmurs.

Zephyr steps around the console she's been working, toward

the central pillar. The lights inside are swirling at a frenetic pace. She points about halfway up the length of the pillar. "Is that a face?"

"Holy crap! It is, Zordon!" Wil shouts, coming around to the side of the pillar she's pointing at, Xan and Murta joining him quickly, "Zordon, where are the Rangers? Where's Alpha-Five?

The face taking shape in the pillar is humanoid-ish: two eyes, one mouth, no nose that Wil can see. The face tilts slightly as if noticing the crew of the *Ghost* for the first time. The eyes are bright blue, pulsing.

"Uh, guys, what's going on over there?" Bennie asks over the comms. "I mean, I know the reactor is online, but I'm seeing systems coming online all over the place. Plus, we're being scanned! Something is accessing the *Ghost*'s computer."

"Can you stop it?" Wil trades looks with Zephyr. Murta glances at Xan, then to the console hiding his device.

System Status: Online.
Timeslice: Unknown. External linkages offline.
Vessel Status: Hull integrity nominal. Main engine at fifty percent.
Increasing to one hundred.
Drone status: Exploration drones one hundred percent. Utility drones one hundred percent. Defensive drones one hundred percent.
Interrupt—
Foreign vessel detected at airlock Omega Eleven.
Initiate electronic countermeasures.
Scanning foreign vessel.
Accessing foreign vessel.
Accessing foreign vessel computer systems.
Foreign vessel language files identified. Downloading.
Accessing foreign vessel navigational database. Downloading.

Interrupt—
Life forms detected. Biological infection must be contained.
Initiating internal defense response.
Sealing bulkheads to contain infection.

"I'm trying! Did you think I'd just let it happen?" Before Wil can answer, Bennie continues, "It's accessing our comms system. Looks like the language translation libraries." He pauses. "And the navigational database!"

Xan, who has been listening, murmurs, "Of course. It won't know galactic standard, or Harrith or anything else from this region of space."

"Whatever was hacking us, it's stopped," Bennie reports.

Wil looks back up at the face, to see its staring right at him. "*Biological infestation. Initiating countermeasures,*" it says. Its voice is flat and emotionless, vaguely masculine.

"Okay, definitely not Zordon." Wil says. Then: "Max! Scratch getting up here, head to the airlock! Bennie, extend a tube, we're not going to have time to EVA!"

"On it!" Bennie says, through what might be gritted teeth.

DOORS CLOSE, DOORS OPEN

"WE'RE ON OUR WAY." Maxim closes the comms channel and looks over to Gabe and the scientists. "Time to go."

Gabe, Jor' Lu and Prathea join him at the sizable featureless console he's standing next to. Jor' Lu leans down and runs a hand along it. "Shouldn't we stay here to monitor the reactor?"

The engineering space is coming alive; lights are on, consoles are active, and what looks like a master situation display shows what Maxim assumes are sections of the ship coming on line. Small dots are moving around the display. Maxim shakes his head. "We'll come back. Wil wants us all on the bridge; we go to the bridge." He looks over to Gabe. "Things stable enough here?"

Gabe nods. "I believe so. The engine, while quite powerful, is not that different from those found on Peacekeeper Command carriers. As far as I can tell, the reactor is stable. Power generation is currently at fifty percent." He turns to the large display and points. "As you can see, several systems are now online, or coming online." He points to a particular section. "I believe that is the bridge." On the display are four bright red squares.

Maxim nods and turns for the massive blast door that they'd

previously come through. "Good, let's move out. I don't like the crew being split up like this."

"Uh guys, what's going on over there?" Bennie asks over the comms. "I mean, I know the reactor is online, but I'm seeing systems coming online all over the place. Plus, we're being scanned! Something is accessing the *Ghost*'s computer."

Maxim turns to Gabe. "Can you do anything?"

"Unlikely. I would need to find a central computer access terminal. I am sure there is one in this section, but do not know what it would look like or how to access it."

"I'm trying! Did you think I'd just let it happen?" Bennie's voice, sounding panicked. "It's accessing our comms system. Looks like the language translation libraries. And the navigational database!"

Prathea claps her hands, "Of course! It doesn't know how to communicate with us. It certainly wouldn't know any languages we know."

Jor' Lu nods. "That makes sense. Our universal translation systems would also likely be foreign to it. I wonder why the ship didn't interface with Gabe?"

Gabe tilts his head. "I am glad it did not."

"Whatever was hacking us, its stopped," Bennie reports.

"Well that wasn't—" Maxim starts, when Wil shouts over the comms, "Max! Scratch getting up here, head to the airlock!"

Maxim immediately starts moving for the door. "Let's go!"

Before anyone else can move, the lighting shifts to red, and the massive blast door begins to close. Maxim grabs Jor' Lu by the collar and hurls her across the threshold; he nods to Gabe as they sprint for the door. Gabe reaches back and grabs Prathea, lagging behind. "I apologize," he says.

Prathea flies through the doorway with only a meter of open space left. Gabe and Maxim are still at least ten meters from the threshold when Gabe grabs Maxim and shoves him as hard as he can. Maxim flies through the door, just as it slides closed with a metallic clang.

"Gabe! No!" Maxim shouts, slamming an armored fist against the door.

Jor' Lu and Prathea are standing together. The shorter scientist is holding the taller, their faces somber. Prathea looks at Maxim. "What do we do now?" she asks, voice low.

Maxim turns to the scientists, shaking his head. "Wil, Gabe—"

The blast door opens.

Gabe walks through. "We should be going. The Captain sounded urgent."

Maxim stammers, "Never mind." Then, turning to the droid, "How?"

From the comms, Bennie shouts, "Duh! I opened the door! My interface is still tied to the door." As if on command, the box Gabe had installed erupts in sparks.

Maxim looks at Gabe. The bot looks from Maxim to the box. "Good timing. We should go."

Over the comms, Bennie says, "Team Two, Team One just got split up. Bulkheads are closing all over the ship. I'll send directions to your comms."

"Acknowledged," Maxim answers, and takes off down the corridor at a run.

THE PAST

ONCE HE'S GOT his coffee, Wil opens up the fake laptop. It doesn't take long for the software Bennie gave him to find a wi-fi network and escalate his privileges. *Hello, unlimited and unrestricted data*, Wil thinks. It takes only a few more minutes for his wristcomm to figure out how the internet works and begin displaying websites. *Glad I don't have to do this via the command line.*

Sipping his coffee, he first accesses his existing accounts: email, media, and so on. Not bothering to look at anything specifically, he simply downloads it all to the wristcomm, which is transmitting back to the *Ghost* in southern Colorado via a small satellite he left in orbit before landing. *Good thing no one closed my accounts down. Hope Lisa isn't keeping an eye these.* Next, he uses another of Bennie's programs—similar to the cash register hack—to fake fund his account on Amazon, iTunes, and other media repositories. Time to download it all. *Sorry big companies, I know I'm stealing from you.* He shrugs. *Sorry-not-sorry.*

While his wristcomm is downloading every movie and TV show possible, Wil looks up his oldest friend, James Hawthorne. "Awesome, still here in Denver," Wil says, then looks up sheepishly as the young woman at the table next to his glances at him over the top of her laptop. "Sorry," he says, returning to his laptop screen.

While the status bar for 'copy all media' works its way across the screen, he looks around the room: a couple of twenty-some-things working on laptops—Wil bets one is a writer; there's always a writer—and two guys in suits having a meeting about some real estate deal. Three moms with accompanying toddlers are sitting on the patio having coffee, ignoring their kids as best they can.

The women all stop their conversation to stare up at the sky, pointing and getting their children to look. A few of the folks inside have noticed. "What's going on?" Wil asks the girl nearest him.

"Space launch, I think." She goes back to her laptop.

He gets up and walks out the door, looking up. There's a contrail reaching up from behind the high rises, at its tip a small shape. *Looks like a newer model of the Titan Heavy Lifter,* Wil thinks, whistling appreciatively. He turns to walk back in when he hears, "Wil?"

Shit.

"What. Are. The. Odds?" Wil growls, under his breath. He slowly turns. James Hawthorne is standing ten feet from him, holding the leash of a small dog. "Uh, hi James." He raises his hand in a kind of half-wave.

"You're supposed to be dead," his old friend says, louder than Wil feels is necessary. One of the patio-moms turns to look at them.

"Oh, uh, ha ha, man. You're pretty funny." Glancing around, he walks quickly over to James. "Let's go inside, I'll get you a coffee." He guides the much larger man inside. Looking back over his shoulder to the patio-mom, he adds, "Such a kidder, this guy."

Walking from the counter with fresh coffee, Wil grabs his laptop and bag off the table he had been at and guides James to a table at the back of the room. Sitting down, he says, "I've been meaning to call—"

"We thought you were dead!" James hisses. "Everyone at NASA thinks you're dead. Your sister thinks you're dead. *I* thought you were dead." He takes a tense sip of coffee. "What the hell happened? How are you on Earth? Where's the Discovery?"

Wil holds one hand up to stop the barrage of questions. "It is a long, and I mean Tolkien-length long, story. Not as confusing— well, almost, but yeah, not quite as hard to follow. I mean geez, *Silmarillion*, am I right?" He leans his bag, with the laptop still downloading 'all the things' in it, against the table leg. "The pod worked, more or less." Again, he raises his hand to silence his old friend. "I didn't end up where we expected, though. Quite far from it, actually. Out near Neptune's orbit, not Jupiter. On top of that, the FTL system fried itself. I did everything I could, but it was dead. I thought I was going to be next."

James is just staring at him; he hasn't blinked in a while. "*Silmarillion?*" he says, bewildered.

Wil exhales and reaches for his coffee. After taking a sip, and collecting his thoughts, he dives into the story.

CHAPTER 12

RUN!

WIL TAKES POINT, with Xan and Murta in the middle, Zephyr bringing up the rear. The corridor they'd taken to get to the bridge has changed from dimly-lit and a little creepy to bright, blinding red and very creepy.

"Well, this looks like the set of a horror movie," Wil says, leaning around a corner, before motioning the others to follow. "Any thoughts? Anyone? What the hell did we do?"

"Angered it, would be my first guess," Murta quips. "Seems to be your specialty."

Wil turns and flips Murta off.

Before anyone else can say a word, a bulkhead slams shut, cutting Wil and Murta off from Xan and Zephyr. Wil looks at Murta. "Really? I get stuck with you?" He bangs on the bulkhead with one hand.

Murta scowls, tapping his wristcomm. "Ben-Ari, your captain and I are cut off from Zephyr and Xan. Can you tell if other bulkheads have closed?"

Bennie replies. "Scanning now, hard to tell without more detail, but—"

Wil interrupts: "Bennie, my armor has little probe things, four of 'em. They're zipping around mapping the ship as they go. One is back with me; the other three are working their way back. Can you uplink to them?"

"Wait one. Yeah, I've got 'em. Those are neat! Did you know you had those?"

Murta chuckles, not politely.

Wil glares at his companion. "Yeah, don't worry about that. Can you use them?"

"Yeah, looks like all three are wandering around. The route they took is blocked. I've got control of them now; you should have a prompt on your wristcomm to release control to me."

"Yeah, I see, it." Wil taps a command on his wristcomm. "Control is yours."

"Okay, good. I'm sending all three to map as much as I can—I'm gonna work on routing all of you back to the airlock. Zephyr and Xan are on the move now. I'll start patching directions to your wristcomms."

"Roger that. Thanks, Bennie." Wil starts moving down the corridor.

"What now?" Xan asks, looking up at Zephyr.

Zephyr looks down at the small scientist. "We keep moving." She turns and heads back to the last junction they'd passed.

"Bennie, we got cut off from Wil and Murta, can you guide us back to the *Ghost*?"

"On it, already talking to the Captain. Did you know his new armor has little autonomous drones?"

Zephyr stifles a laugh. "Yeah I saw that."

Xan looks down the hall ahead of them. "Did you hear that?"

Zephyr immediately focuses on the corridor, aiming her

weapon the same direction she's looking, scanning the passage. "I didn't. What was it?"

Xan shrugs. "Beats me. Sounded like scraping metal."

Zephyr looks at her wristcomm. "Bennie?"

"Hold on. I'm sorting through the data from Wil's probes. I'll send directions to your wristcomm."

"Roger that." She glances down at her forearm, as the screen flashes directions. She motions to Xan. "Okay, let's go."

"But that's where I heard the noise!" Xan says, following Zephyr down the corridor.

"Dren! Dren! Dren!" Bennie spins in his chair, to face a different monitor. The map that Wil's probes have created is updating in real time, as they try to find their way back to Wil's armor. On another screen, the exterior view of the derelict shows whole sections of it lighting up. Another shows power readings from around the derelict. "Krebnack, this went sideways! Computer, I need your help."

"*Of course, Ben-Ari. What can I do for you?*" This time it's a feminine voice that Wil had said was better than the last three Bennie had tried.

"I need you to keep your scanners on the teams, feed me any changes to the routes between them and the airlock."

"*Of course, Bennie, anything for you.*"

"Computer, disable personality module."

"*Acknowledged,*" the old, familiar voice of the *Ghost* replies.

Bennie sighs, spinning to face another display. "Maybe this ship doesn't need any more personality."

SOMEWHERE ON A GIANT SCARY SHIP

Maxim's wristcomm vibrates, and he glances down at it before taking the next left. Just ahead there's a ramp heading up to the level above. "Come on!"

Jor' Lu is just behind him, and Prathea is behind her, with Gabe bringing up the rear. Gabe is holding two powerful rifles; one in each hand.

Jor' Lu slows. "Did you hear that?"

Maxim looks at the Burzzad scientist and shakes his head, one eyebrow raised. She indicates her pointed ears. Max looks at Gabe, who points to his own lack of ears. Maxim shakes his head, and touches his comms. "Bennie, have you detected anything?"

"Anything, like...?"

Maxim frowns. "If I knew, I'd have asked you more specifically."

"Fine, fine, fine! I don't see anything. Well, anything outside the bulkheads closing and the ship powering up. Oh wait, I do see something! Woah, lots of somethings!"

"What do you—"

"Maxim! Down!" Gabe's voice, much louder than usual, echoes through the corridor. Training kicks in—Max doesn't ask, he just follows the order. A pulse rifle blast roars over his head as he ducks... slamming right into a mechanical, squid-like thing. It's matte black, an oblong body with five glowing red sensors on the front and an array of metal tentacles emerging from the back of the device.

"Oh, shazbot!" Jor' Lu shouts, raising her long arms. Prathea grabs her lanky companion, pulling her to the ground.

Maxim pushes the mechanical thing aside and fires at a half dozen more of the things behind it. "What *are* these things?"

Gabe is still standing in the middle of the corridor, calmly firing his two pulse rifles set to automatic down the corridor at the mechanical squids. "I do not know." The last of the attackers falls to the deck as he speaks, tentacles twitching. "I believe we should increase our pace and hurry to the airlock."

"Agreed," Maxim says, standing and helping Prathea and Jor' Lu up. "Let's go." All four set off in the same direction they had been heading in before the attack.

"Heads up, Max and his team just encountered some kind of mechanical somethings. Metal, lots of tentacles, glowing red eyes," Bennie announces over the comms.

"Uh, yeah!" Wil shouts over blaster fire. "We're familiar with the mechanical calamari. Thanks!" He stands up from behind one of the mechanicals and fires off two shots into another oncoming squid-thing—it drops to the ground, glowing sensors fading to black, one tentacle twitching. Wil looks at his wristcomm; it's showing the corridor, clear of hostiles. He motions to Murta. "Huey shows all clear, let's go."

They take off at a jog, following the small floating drone down the corridor.

Murta touches his own wristcomm. "Ben-Ari, do you know

what these things are? How many of them there are? Can you track them? Why didn't you warn us about them?"

Over the comms line, Bennie tuts. "Beats me, no clue. And I can only detect them when they're bunched up. Their power signatures are masked by the ship until a few of them get together. I didn't know they were there, and didn't know what the readings were until they attacked."

Murta scowls. "Can you at least guide us away from the 'bunches'?"

"I'll see what I can do—they seem to bunch up, then disperse into groups too small to track," Bennie says.

"Well, do what you can," Wil says, as they round a corner. Huey is one hundred meters ahead of them at a four-way junction.

Zephyr turns another corner. "Clear." Xan pops out from behind the corner and follows her. They've been moving through the ship alone for a while, Zephyr taking point, Xan armed with one of Zephyr's spare pistols.

"Do you think we'll run into any of those—what did Wil call them? 'Mechanical kal-a-marree'—before we reach the airlock?"

"I hope not. No offense, but I don't like our odds." Zephyr glances down at the meter-tall scientist.

Xan holds the pulse pistol out and examines it. "None taken."

Suddenly, Zephyr stops. "Well, I guess I did tempt fate on this one." Before Xan can ask what she means by that, three large mechanical squid-like things turn a corner. Their red, glowing sensors all turn to face the two women—and without a second's pause, they lunge at the two intruders.

"Shazbot!" Xan shouts, pulling the trigger on her borrowed pistol, sending shots all over the place, most of which fail to hit their targets.

Zephyr drops to one knee, leveling her rifle. The first squid-like mechanism falls to the deck, three smoking holes blown through its main sensor array. Two of Xan's shots find their mark, distracting one of the attackers long enough for Zephyr to finish it off. The third closes the distance and tackles Zephyr.

"Zephyr!" Xan shouts, as one of the tentacles swipes at her, sending her crashing into the wall, the pulse pistol flying from her hand. She slides to the ground, dazed.

Zephyr is struggling with a tentacle around her throat, squeezing her air supply, when a pulse pistol goes off. The mechanoid she's fighting shudders, and a tentacle slams into her midsection, knocking the wind out of her.

"AYIAHHH!" Xan is a small, furry blur on top of the squid-thing. She crawls across it, firing into the machine, then rolls away from a lashing tentacle to climb in front of the glowing sensor array, firing directly into it. The machine shudders again and thrashes another tentacle toward the small and vicious scientist, missing as she crawls around the side of the device, firing two more times.

The tentacle around Zephyr's neck abruptly goes slack, and she wriggles out from under the motionless squid-thing.

"Nice shooting," she says, "and uh, scampering... and was that biting? You know there's a face mask?"

Xan drops down off the machine, and dusts her suit off. Then she looks up at Zephyr. "No one needs to know about this." Without another word, she turns and continues down the corridor.

MUSTARD'S LAST STAND?

"YOU SHOULD BE APPROACHING a large chamber, with several corridors connecting to it," Bennie says rapidly over Maxim's wristcomm. "Wait there."

Maxim, Jor' Lu and Prathea race into the chamber and skid to a halt. There are six entries to other corridors. Two have hatches closed down over them. From the one opposite Maxim, Wil and Murta emerge, panting. Wil drops gasping to the floor, clutching his knees, while Murta seems only slightly winded.

"Where's Zephyr?" Maxim asks, rushing to Wil's side.

"We— got— separated," Wil starts. "We—"

Murta puts a hand on Maxim's arm, glancing at Wil. "We got separated. Zephyr and Xan are on their own. I believe Ben-Ari is guiding them here as well." He glances down at his wristcomm.

"Don't worry big poppa, I've got them covered," Bennie says. "They're on their way."

Wil looks up from his doubled-over position. "That's not—how that—expression—actually, that's not—too far off," he wheezes. He looks at Maxim, who just shakes his head. "Gotta keep Bennie— out of my library."

From a corridor to Wil's right, the sound of weapons fire

suddenly erupts. Zephyr and Xan burst out of the entrance, Zephyr still firing back down the corridor, the barrel of her pulse rifle glowing. "Maxim!" she shouts.

Without missing a beat, the ex-Peacekeeper springs into action —he dashes across the room, dropping to one knee and raising his own pulse rifle in a single movement. A second later, he's firing.

Xan runs over to Jor' Lu. "This might have been more excite-ment than I was hoping for," the small scientist says, grasping her much taller friend's thin hands. Jor' Lu nods in agreement.

Wil is about to join Maxim and Zephyr, when his suit emits an alarm he's not familiar with—and one of the mechanical squids collides with him. *Okay, that is the proximity warning, I guess*, he thinks, as he crashes to the ground under an angry metal squid.

Murta turns and begins firing at the second mechanical monster, taking care to not hit Wil, who is firing his pulse pistol into the thing from under it.

When the device's sensors fade to black and it goes limp, Wil shoves it off him. He looks at Murta. "Thanks for not shooting me."

Murta nods, then turns his attention to the corridor, and immediately starts firing again. "More, incoming!"

Wil spins and ducks, taking cover behind the deactivated mechanical monster, and firing over the makeshift barrier. He lifts his wristcomm. "Bennie, we need to get the hell off this ship, fast."

Bennie sounds frantic. "I see them. I'm working on it—that bulkhead at your back is the corridor to the airlock, it closed when the rest did. I'm trying to hack it, but the ship is fighting back."

A tentacle flashes by, inches over Wil's head, before its owner is riddled with holes from Murta's weapon. "Hurry, please."

"What do you think I'm doing?" the little hacker growls.

Zephyr and Maxim are alternating fire, letting their weapons cool down in between. The mechanical squids are gaining ground. On the other side of the junction, Murta and Wil are faring only slightly better. Gabe has picked up a spare pulse pistol and is standing near the center of the space so that he can fire down both corridors, over the others' heads.

"I hear them!" Jor' Lu shouts, pointing down a third corridor.

"Damnit!" Wil curses. He taps Murta's shoulder, who nods. "Bennie?"

"Working on it!"

"We're going to be dead soon. Can you at least close the bulkhead to the corridor at my four o'clock?"

"Let me see...." The bulkhead slams shut just as a half dozen sets of glowing red sensors become visible. Bulkheads slam closed on the other two corridors, defeating the crew. "Easier to close 'em than open 'em!" the hacker says, sounding quite proud of himself.

Maxim and Zephyr lower their weapons. Jor' Lu walks to one of the recently closed bulkheads, reaching out and resting her long-fingered hand on the metal. "That was—" something on the other side bangs against the door, and she jumps back. "Oh my!"

Maxim looks at the door. "Not only will that not hold long," he says, "but we're also still trapped."

Interrupt—
Defensive drones unsuccessful at eradicating infection.
Analyzing strategies

...

...
Foreign organisms currently contained in corridor junction O-
3045.
Interrupt—
Intrusion detected. Foreign vessel at airlock Omega Eleven is
accessing systems.
Counter.

Attempt unsuccessful.
Dispatching external drones.
Interrupt—
Foreign entity has penetrated firewall X-fourteen.
Firewall X-Thirteen, holding.
Intrusion halted.

THE PAST

IT TAKES NEARLY an hour to tell the whole story, or at least the parts Wil is comfortable sharing. When he's done, he lets out a long breath, and reaches for his coffee. *Empty.*

James stares at his old friend blankly, slowly petting his dog, for what feels to Wil like an age. "So: you've been in space."

"Yes."

"For nearly four years."

"That long? Jeez. Time flies when you're nearly dying alone in space, surrounded by aliens of all shapes and sizes." Wil is the only one chuckling at the joke.

"And you never thought, in all that time, to let anyone know you were alive?"

Wil frowns. "I mean, it's not like I had a mobile phone to call you on, or that it would reach here. Space comms don't talk to GSM networks."

"They nearly killed the FTL program. That launch you saw was only the second since you left. They didn't want to risk any more astronauts."

"Buddy, I—"

"Buddy? I thought I'd lost one of my best friends. I had to

console your sister, man!" James is getting more and more agitated. His dog, Aldrin, is starting to growl.

Wil glances worriedly to the small French bulldog, then pulls the sleeve of his shirt up to glance at his wristcomm—the download finished twenty minutes ago. He holds his arm up so James can see the high-tech device. "Come on, let's grab a bite and go to the park. Is Civic Center Park still a bit sketchy?"

"Huh? Yeah, it can be, but its food truck day, so shouldn't be bad." James has a blank look in his eyes. *I'm gonna need to work on my delivery if I'm gonna tell anyone else,* Wil thinks. *James isn't looking so good.*

Its a short walk from the coffee shop to Civic Center Park, sandwiched between the state capitol and the city and county buildings. The Capitol's dome—once gold, but now polished dura-steel—shines in the midday sun. The gold had been replaced with the space-age alloy when the launch center in eastern Colorado opened, beginning the new space age for the United States and the renaissance of the Colorado space industry.

Wil pays for two hamburgers from one of the trucks, and the two men find a bench away from most of the lunchtime crowd. After swallowing a bite of his burger, Wil says, "Look man. I'm the first to admit my story is nutty, but how else would you explain it? You know that pod couldn't keep me alive this long. You also know that pod couldn't land—it was only designed to dock at the space station. So what other explanation is there?" To emphasize his point, he rolls his sleeve up, again revealing the wristcomm that takes up most of his forearm. He adds, "Plus, if I came back they'd have to rename all the schools they named after me, and take down the statues and stuff." He pauses and looks around the park. "Those are things, right?"

"Uh, yeah, I don't know that there are any schools named after you. I mean maybe in Kansas or something, but yeah that wouldn't be a real big challenge. About statues, uh, yeah, don't look over there." He points.

Wil looks. "NO. WAY!" There, in the middle of a patch of flowers, is an eight-foot statue of Wil—in his space suit, helmet under one arm, the other arm raised, pointing up into the sky. "Dude, I look awesome!!" he shouts.

James moves his hands in a shushing motion. "Calm down. So then, what are you doing back here? Why the secrecy?" James looks him in the eye. "How long have you been back?"

"I actually got back last night. Us bumping into each other is one-hundred percent random. I did look you up, though, and was thinking of stopping by your place tonight before I leave."

"Wait. Leaving? You said just got here." James sets his burger down in his lap.

"Yeah, I can't stay. You know that. For one thing, you know, I'm dead and all that—at least legally. Can you imagine the kittens NASA would have if I just walked in the front door?" He laughs at that image. "I'd never smell fresh air again. Plus, they'd dismantle the *Ghost* and do who knows what, with the technology."

"Man, this is too much." James shakes his head. He breaks some of his burger off and hands it to Aldrin. "So, why are you back then?"

"Porn," Wil says, keeping a straight face while James' eyes bug out of his skull. Wil almost drops the rest of his burger when he finally gives in to the overwhelming urge to laugh. "God, I wish I had a camera! Wait, maybe my wristcomm has one? Never mind, the moment's passed. Seriously though, I've been having a rough time out there being all alone. I didn't have any music or movies, or TV shows—"

"Or porn." James offers.

Wil nods. "Looks, a guy has needs." He waves a hand dismissively. "You know, part of the 'oh crap kit' should be an iPod with as much media on it as will fit." He smiles. "Aliens have thunderbolt, you know." He takes a bite of his burger but keeps talking. "Anyway, yeah, it's lonely out there. Having some stuff from home will help. I hope." He raises his hand, "Oh yeah, and bacon. I need to stock up on bacon." He grumbles and adds, "And trinkets, I gotta load up on trinkets." He frowns as he says it.

"Can I see your ship?" James asks.

"No," Wil says, without missing a beat. He looks around them, then touches a control on his wristcomm. A holographic image of the *Ghost* appears, floating between them. "Best I can give ya." He smiles.

"Kinda ugly," James says, leaning in to look at the image.

Wil tuts. "Don't make me knock you out."

James doesn't even take his eyes from the slowly rotating hologram. "As if."

CHAPTER 13

TENTACLES, EVERYWHERE

"WARNING. PROXIMITY ALERT," the computer announces.

Bennie looks up from his work, his face scrunched up. "Computer, report."

"*Multiple contacts detected. Collision imminent.*"

"Missiles or something?" He calls up a sensor feed window on his monitor. "Dren!"

"*Negative on missiles. Objects are non-explosive.*"

Bennie taps some commands on his console and looks at the main display at the front of the bridge. The image is zoomed in on one of the objects.

He blindly reaches over to another console, fumbling for a button. "Uh, Wil. What exactly do your metal monsters look like?"

"What? I mean, they look like squid, sorta."

"For those of us not familiar with 'squid?'" Bennie says, eyes never leaving the main display.

"Oval main body with a bunch of glowing red sensor things. Tentacles coming out the back, lots of 'em. Claws and other stuff at the ends." A pause. "Why?"

"Oh, nothing. Just a dozen or so of them are about to land on the *Ghost.*"

"What! Hurry up and get this bulkhead open!"

"I'm working on it!" From somewhere, he hears several loud clanks reverberate throughout the ship. "Computer, engage external defenses!"

External drones initiating contact with foreign vessel.
Foreign entity has penetrated firewall Z-Seven.
Internal defense drone losses exceeding expectations.
Activating maintenance drones to begin recycling damaged units.

"Wil, I have good and bad news," Bennie says, looking intently at his screen. The banging on the hull has gotten louder, and significantly closer to the bridge.

"Shoot," Wil says, the tension evident in his voice.

"I can open the bulkhead that leads to the airlock."

In the background, Bennie can hear banging. "I assume that's the good news."

"It is. I can't isolate just that bulkhead. I'll have to open them all. I'm Sorry." Bennie looks up at the ceiling, where more noises are now coming from.

Wil sighs. "Okay, wait a second."

There's a loud crunching sound from somewhere down the main corridor off the bridge.

"Okay, Bennie. We're ready. Do it."

Wil looks around him, at the grim and terrified faces. Maxim and Zephyr are on either side of him; Prathea, Jor' Lu and Xan are behind them, flat against the door. Gabe is standing in the middle of the group.

Over the comms, Bennie counts down: "Three, two, one—" On *one*, the bulkheads all snap open.

"Run!" Wil shouts. The scientists dash down the corridor, just as the first mechanical squid enters the room.

"Call your targets!" Maxim says, through clenched teeth. "Our weapons will overheat—no need to rush it by shooting the same targets."

"Fall back," Zephyr says, firing her rifle into a tentacle that is reaching for Wil's leg.

Just then, from every corridor in the room, dozens of squid-things erupt.

"Shit! Back, back, back!" Wil shouts, over the sound of tentacles scraping the walls, floor and ceiling.

Calmly, Maxim says, "Top right," firing one of his rifles in fully automatic mode. Plasma blasts rip both drones and corridor plating to shreds.

"There are too many! Bottom left!" Murta shouts, firing his rifle into the mass of red-glowing sensors and tentacles.

"Bennie! Can you close those bulkheads?" Zephyr is running backwards as fast as she can. She's right behind Gabe, firing around his tall humanoid figure. Maxim and Wil are in the lead. It doesn't take them long to catch up with the fleeing scientists.

"Faster!" Wil shouts.

"My legs are half as long as yours!" Xan screams back, terror visible on her furry face. Maxim picks her up without missing a beat. "Hey! Oh, this is much better."

A tentacle whips out and slashes across Gabe's back, sending him crashing into Zephyr, which sends her sprawling forward.

Maxim and Wil spin around and immediately open fire. Another tentacle slices through the air, nearly catching Wil in the helmet.

Murta isn't so lucky—a tentacle lances out of the mass, stabbing right through his leg, his suit armor doing very little to protect him. His scream is one of the worst things Wil has ever heard. Wil fires a single shot, severing the writhing metal appendage, leaving half a meter of it sticking out of Murta's leg. The armor seals itself around the appendage.

Wil leans down and helps the Harrith man up, bearing his weight. "No more pizza for you," he grumbles.

Gabe is up and helping Zephyr gain her footing. "My apologies," he says to her as they both run.

The team turns a slight bend, to find Jor' Lu standing at the airlock to the *Ghost*.

Wil stops, looking through the transparent portion of the hatch. On the other side of the outer door, he can see the white plastic material of one of the *Ghosts* boarding tubes—the soft, atmosphere-filled tunnels connecting the airlocks of both ships. Boarding tubes are better than full EVA—but only slightly, since they will still be in free fall the entire time between vessels. At least there will be handholds, he thinks grimly.

SACRIFICE

"Bennie, we're at the airlock, coming over now," Wil says, touching the control to open the inner airlock door. "Have the ship ready to fight and fly when we get there."

The door replies with an angry-sounding beep, just barely audible over the rifle fire coming from Maxim, Gabe and Zephyr's pulse pistols.

"Damnit!" Wil growls. "Gabe, get over here and open this, anyway you can."

"On it," the bot says, squeezing past the clutch of scared scientists, who are pressed up against the door.

"Wil, we can't keep these things back for long," Zephyr says, as Wil takes Gabe's place in the group firing at the squid-things. "My rifle is almost out of charge, and I've only got one power pack left."

Maxim adds, "And I have no power packs left."

With one of his smaller arms, Gabe reaches behind him, offering up two more power packs. "Here." Wil passes them to the ex-Peacekeepers with one hand, while still firing his pistol with the other. Then he pulls his own rifle free of the attachment point on the back of his armor and starts shooting.

"Warning, hull breach imminent in main corridor," the computer announces.

Bennie taps a few commands into his console. "Guys, you better hurry!" He taps another control, and the hatch to the bridge slams shut—he can hear the locking bolts engaging. Elsewhere in the ship, similar hatches are closing off key sections.

"Everyone, listen up! As soon as Gabe gets this hatch open, make sure your suits are sealed. If we can't get the outer hatch open fast, I'll blow it," Wil says, downing another squid-thing as he speaks. *Weird they're not really piling up and blocking the corridor,* he thinks idly, as Maxim puts several shots into one, its sensors going dark. *Something must be pulling the damaged ones back out of the way.*

"Hatch opening," Gabe announces. The moment it opens, he steps inside and begins disassembling a panel. "Get ready. This one will not be as difficult."

"Cover," Zephyr says, lowering her rifle and replacing the power pack. In just seconds, she's firing again. "Wil..."

The squid-things are barely ten meters away and closing on them every second now. Tentacles are whipping about wildly. Wil sees that both Maxim and Zephyr have scratches and dents all over their armor, the clear plastic-steel face shields similarly scratched. "Squints, you're out the door first with Gabe. We'll follow."

As the scientists turn to enter the airlock, a tentacle shoots past the defenders, its claw grasping on to a piece of Prathea's suit. Before anyone can react, she's flying backwards, into the mass of glowing sensors and tentacles. Wil makes a grab for her and misses, but Maxim, possessing much faster reflexes, grabs the short Palorian scientist by the ankle. She lets out a squeak, as her movement comes to a halt and the stretching starts.

The outer airlock hatch snaps open. Gabe grabs Xan and hurls her through it, sending her sailing precisely down the center of the docking umbilical. Jor' Lu, needing no encouragement, follows under her own power. Gabe turns and grabs Wil by the back of his armor and hurls him out the airlock too.

"Gabe!" Wil shouts, as he floats down the length of the white plastic-like tube connecting the two ships. "What the hell are you doing?" he shouts, more loudly this time.

In a single swift motion, Gabe lunges past Maxim, grabbing the metal tentacle holding Prathea and snapping it in his hand. In the same motion, he grabs Zephyr's rifle, while hurling Prathea out the airlock. "Go." It would be a shout if it were coming from anyone but Gabe.

Maxim turns to fire, and Gabe grabs the big Palorian's rifle. "You too, Maxim." A tentacle glances off the device welded to Gabe's back, it's function still a mystery since the one person who knows its purpose, Xarrix, isn't on speaking terms with the crew. It was Xarrix who hired the team to steal the crate that held a deactivated Gabe in it from a secret storage facility space station.

"No, there are too many. You can't—" Maxim grabs his pistol, firing at another mechanical squid-thing.

Gabe hefts each rifle in his main hands; each secondary hand already has a pistol in it. He turns and opens fire with all four weapons. "I will cover you. There are too many—"

"*We'll* cover you," Murta says, hefting his rifle and firing, balancing on one leg. His wound is openly bleeding. He's ashen.

More tentacles lash out, scratching Maxim's armor as Gabe and Murta fire. He turns, pushing Zephyr out the airlock ahead of him.

FISH AND VISITORS...

WIL IS STILL LOOKING BACK at the dreadnought when he hears Jor' Lu scream, at least he thinks it is a scream. Using the altitude jets built into his armor, he spins around to see that the connecting tube they are in is no longer doing the "connecting" part. The end that should be connected to the *Ghost* is fluttering in the atmosphere that's venting out of it—and, in the middle of the tube, a squid-thing is standing. Before he can shout to Zephyr, who's the closest armed member of the team, she spins and fires her pulse pistol into the thing. Its glowing red sensors dim, just before it collides with Jor' Lu, sending it and her tumbling both out of the remains of the tube, still more or less toward the *Ghost*.

"Xan, Prathea, use the jets in your suit! Get to the airlock, and get in—don't wait for us!" Wil tilts slightly, seeing another squid push off the hull of the *Ghost*. Apparently, whatever they use for propulsion works in space too. *Lovely*, he thinks, blasting the squid-thing as fast as he can—it drifts past the ruined tube, away from the ship. "Zephyr, get Jor' Lu, and go around to Airlock Two!"

"Roger that!" she shouts, all business. Fighting in space sucks under the best of conditions, and having three floundering scientists drifting around definitely makes this *not* good conditions.

As Zephyr jets off toward the flailing Burzzad scientist, Wil takes another shot at a squid-thing that's prying at something on the *Ghost's* hull. "Leave my ship alone! Bennie, report!"

"We've got nine uninvited guests. Automatic defenses took two of them out before they broke the blaster in the main corridor. I'm having a hard time keeping them out of the *Ghost's* systems." The worry in the small alien's voice gives Wil pause—he's never heard him this scared before.

"Disable the auto defenses, now. Xan and Prathea are about to enter from the port side, and Zephyr and Jor' Lu are coming in from starboard."

"Done. Please hurry!" *He's terrified*, Wil realizes.

"Maxim! Gabe! Murta! Where are you guys?" Wil shouts and spins himself around. He sees Maxim coming down the tube, fast. Behind his faceplate, his face is a mask of stone. He has a pulse rifle aimed just past Wil, and fires.

The remains of a squid-thing clips Wil and sends him spinning before he can right himself. "*Warning. Maneuvering thruster fuel at ten percent. Please recharge at your earliest convenience*," the suit's computer offers, sounding far more chipper than it should be right now. Wil re-establishes eye contact with Maxim. "Where are—"

"Get to the ship, now," Maxim says, as he sails past Wil.

"Where's Gabe?" Wil shouts, turning to look at the dreadnought and the remains of the docking tube, which is still connected to it.

"*Warning. Maneuvering thruster fuel at five percent. Please recharge immediately*," his suit nags.

The airlock Xan and Prathea have entered is closed, so they're likely inside the ship, safe-ish. Wil toggles a control on his wrist-comm, "Gabe? Where are you? Where's Murta? We have to go!"

Gabe is holding a pulse rifle in each of his larger hands. The smaller manipulators are alternating between firing pulse pistols and swapping out power packs for the rifles. He's down to just three power packs left.

Over his comms, Wil asks, "Gabe? Where are you? Where's Murta? We have to go!"

"Captain, the only way you and the rest of the crew could escape was to keep these drones from spilling out the airlock after you. The hack I employed, while opening the doors quickly, also made closing them impossible. We would have been overrun the moment we started falling toward the *Ghost*."

"That isn't your call!" Wil shouts.

"In fact, it is." Gabe dodges several tentacles, locking his arm down on them, while Murta fires his rifle into the sensor eyes of the drone they are attached to. "Murta is wounded, and his suit is compromised. If it weren't for an emergency force-field deploying over the outer airlock when the tube was ruptured, he'd be dead already." A tentacle manages to grab onto one of Gabe's smaller arms and pulls it from his body. Sparks erupt from the damaged socket. "Captain, you must get aboard the *Ghost* and depart, before Murta and I succumb to the drones." At that, the bot closes the connection.

Murta is leaning against the wall behind Gabe, firing around the tall droid. "Valiant speech."

Gabe nods. "Thank you."

Murta shakes his head. "Captain, I still think you're a low life pirate," he says, before closing the connection.

Gabe tilts his matte black head, optical sensors shining brightly, then turns and fires several more shots into the mass of glowing red sensors and whipsawing tentacles. Almost immediately, he is tackled by a drone. Murta shoots at it, before catching a tentacle across the faceplate of his suit, shattering the plasti-glass screen. Gabe reaches out to help the fallen Harrith man, when a tentacle grabs his arm—then another, and another. A squid-thing grabs one of his legs, and pulls it free of his body. He sees a squid-thing slide past him to hover over Murta, tentacles pinning his arms to the deck.

Interrupt—
Foreign lifeforms have departed vessel, except two.
External defense drones have penetrated the foreign vessel.
Attempting to take over foreign computer.
Interrupt—
Mechanical life-form detected.
Do not destroy.
Assimilate mechanical entity.
Destroy foreign biological entity.

THE PAST

JAMES HAS TAKEN him to a bar Wil has never seen before. "Guess I shouldn't be surprised—this place used to be, what? A steakhouse?" He looks around. It sort of reminds him of a bar on Fury.

"Seafood place, I can't remember which one, but it turned over about two years ago. Seems to be doing better as a bar than a white tablecloth joint." James raises his glass, and Wil clinks his against it.

"God, I miss beer," Wil sighs, putting the glass down.

"No beer in space? Screw that!" James exclaims. "I'm retiring tomorrow, no way, I'm out."

Wil laughs. "Well, there is, sorta. 'Grum,' they call it. I've still haven't figured out if that's the brand or the type of drink, or what. Everyone just says, 'grum' and they get handed this lager-like drink. Nothing amazing, but it's wet and does the job." He takes a sip of something quite a bit darker than a lager, and sighs again.

"Does the job of..." James asks.

Without thinking about his answer, Wil says, "Dulling the pain."

"Is it that bad? I mean you're here now, you could stay. Just leave an anonymous tip about where you parked your ship. I'm sure we can figure out a way to get you a clean ID, or something." James takes a long sip of his own beer, never taking his eyes off Wil. "I mean, how hard can it be, people fake their own deaths all the time."

"In the movies," Wil says. "No, I can't stay. I wasn't sure I should come but figured it might be easier if I had stuff from home. I mean, at least then I could watch Star Trek when I'm bored." He grabs a handful of peanuts. "Plus, even if I did try to start over as someone else, I'm an astronaut, man. That's not something I can just go do somewhere else. Everything I've seen and done, both here and..." he gestures over his head, "out there. You think I could sit still, after all that?"

"Yeah, that's fair. But still, you're not really making it sound that great. So why go back?"

Wil nods slowly. "I think seeing the city again, and you, is making me more melancholy than I would be otherwise. I mean dude, before I came here, I had some aliens dump a ton of super-knowledge right into my brain. I can field strip weapons, make basic repairs to my ship." He smiles. "Some seriously Matrix level shit."

"Do you—" James starts.

"Know Kung-Fu?" He smiles at the shared joke, making a karate-chop motion. "No, I asked, but it doesn't really translate."

James sets his beer down, almost empty. "Think we'll ever be ready?"

Wil takes a last sip of his own beer, setting the empty glass on the edge of the table. "Someday, yeah. I mean the GC isn't all that different from, say, I dunno, Earth as a whole. Some planets are absolute third-world shitholes, others are like New York City, but on a planetary scale: One. Big. City—bureaucracy for days. If I understand correctly, the GC, the Galactic Commonwealth, won't even talk to Earth until two things happen. One, we leave our solar system, preferably via Faster Than Light travel. And two, the entire planet is unified under one government." Wil makes a motion, pulling his hands apart like an explosion. "Apparently it hasn't ended well when an un-unified world tries to deal with the GC."

James whistles and Wil continues, "It'll be rough. The GC is the government, dysfunctional and all, but really they just keep the peace, and collect taxes. They're actually why no one has come to Earth."

James raises his eyebrows, as the server drops off two fresh beers.

"There's a rule. Primitive worlds like ours are protected. I guess a few hundred years ago, or more, it was pretty common for pirates to find primitive worlds and sell the population into slavery. Pick a world clean, sell it all off." He takes a sip of the new beer, sighing again with pleasure. "So good! Anyway, some couple hundred or whatever years ago, the GC established really—and I mean *really*—strict punishments for any ship found in protected systems."

James looks at his friend. "Then how'd you survive out there?"

"Like anything, there are rule-breakers. I got picked up by some freelancers who were laying low out by the orbits of the outer planets. If the pod had malfunctioned but stayed on course, I'd be dead for sure. It was complete luck that they were out by Neptune's orbit. They picked me up, gave me a choice: cabin boy, or airlock."

"*Princess Bride* style," James laughs.

Wil laughs with him. "Yeah, actually. Though Lanksham didn't do the daily reminder that he'd kill me." He looks down at the table. "But he did give me his ship." He pauses, then says, "Man, I should have named the *Ghost* whatever the ship was called in the *Princess Bride*. What was that?"

James reaches over and pats his friend's arm, shaking his head. "The *Revenge*."

PART FOUR

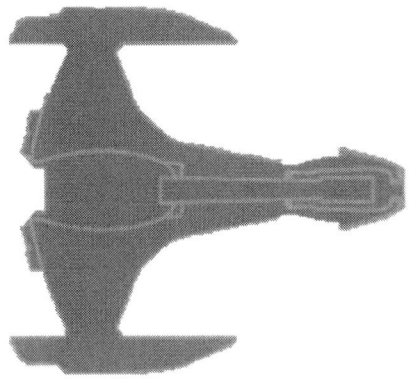

CHAPTER 14

GETTING THE HELL OUT OF DODGE

Wil slams the inner airlock hatch closed and immediately crosses into the armory. Maxim and Zephyr are already there, re-arming. "Bennie, we're in—get the ship moving away from the dreadnought. We're going to clear the ship of mechano-squid."

Zephyr tilts her head, raising an eyebrow. "Mechano-squid?"

"Better than *squid-things*. Come on." He grabs a pulse rifle and bag of power packs. Turning to the scientists doing their best to not be in the way in the corner of the small armory, he says, "Stay here."

Striding back out into the corridor, followed by Zephyr, then Maxim, Wil heads around the corner to where the bridge hatch is located. Under his armored boots, he can feel the slight rumble of the sub-light engines powering up. The banging from around the corner is loud, and it sounds like there's a cutting torch involved.

"What the hell?" Wil says, coming around the corner to face two mechano-squid. One has deployed a cutting torch from a tentacle and is trying to cut through the door. The other is pulling apart panels near the door. Wil opens fire and both machines drop, their sensors going dim. "Assholes, ripping up my ship." He kicks the nearest one, shattering one of the sensor lenses.

"Wil, get in there, pilot the ship," Zephyr says, as she and Maxim pick their way over the remains of the two recently-deactivated drones. "We'll clear the rest. My count says there's only five more in here, and I'm guessing they're in engineering."

"Bennie, open the bridge hatch. Everything out here is toast," Wil says into his comms, as he hurries back to get Prathea and her colleagues.

A minute later, he's closing the bridge hatch and activating the manual lock on it. It won't hold forever, but hopefully it won't need to.

Bennie runs over and nearly knocks Wil over as he bear-hugs the much taller man's waist.

Wil grabs the little alien's head and shoves him away. "Down boy. Are we moving?"

Bennie brushes himself off and walks back to his station, embarrassed, glancing once at Xan and the others. "Uh, yeah, I just had the ship set a course ninety degrees off the dreadnought."

"Good call." Wil drops into his seat, bringing the console to life and taking a look at the overall status of the ship. Not good. "Zee, they're mucking around in the engine bay. Power is less than fifty percent."

"On it," she replies, tension evident in her voice.

Bennie turns to Wil, "Where's Gabe?"

"Ready?" Maxim asks, from his side of the hatch leading to engineering. They have found and destroyed one of the mechano-squids in the lounge, attempting to access something in a wall panel.

Zephyr nods and pushes the button to open the hatch. The doors slide apart, and she turns and takes two steps in before dropping to one knee. Maxim does the same, but remains standing. He aims to the right, she to the left. The main reactor has two of the last three mechano-squids on it; the third and final one is ripping apart a piece of the central computer housing. Zephyr takes the drone on the left, firing two shots into it, careful not to hit the reactor. Maxim does the same. Neither drone is destroyed, however—both turn and leap off the main reactor.

"Gotcha," Zephyr whispers, as both ex-Peacekeepers fire into the drones, no longer having to worry about hitting the reactor. The two mechano-squids are quickly destroyed.

The third and final drone pulls back from the panel it was ripping apart, and lunges—but falls well short of the pair, several smoking holes littering its body.

Maxim walks over to the main engineering console, examining it appraisingly. "This isn't great, but I can get the reactor back to full power. Beyond that, though…" He shrugs.

"Wil, engineering is secured," Zephyr reports. "Full power in a few. We'll give the rest of the ship a once-over after that."

Interrupt—
Contact with external defense drones lost
Lock weapons on foreign vessel
Destroy foreign vessel
Interrupt—
All damaged internal defense drones are currently being recycled.

"Awesome, thanks." Looking down at his proximity sensor display, Wil sees that the dreadnought is turning. "Bennie, can you tell how much power the engines on that thing are putting out? Gabe and Maxim said they had the engine running pretty low. But it's moving now, so…"

"I don't have a baseline or anything, but I'd say the readings I'm getting are either one hundred percent or pretty close to it."

Before Wil can answer, the ship rocks, sparks erupting from a piece of equipment overhead.

"Damnit!" Wil pulls hard on the controls, putting the ship into a tight turn. "Guess they decided capture was out of the question."

The ship lurches suddenly, and a display near the throttle shows the main reactor at full power. "Yes!" Wil shouts.

WAKEY, WAKEY

SYSTEM REBOOT COMPLETE.

Error - external frame compromised

No input from extremities

Gabe looks around—or would, but he can't seem to control the servos in his neck.

"I am not offline," he says. His vocal processors are working, he notes.

"You are not," a voice replies, from everywhere and nowhere.

"I am still aboard the dreadnought."

"Yes."

"My companion from the corridor is not here."

"It is not."

"You are not very forthcoming."

"I am the vessel you call 'the dreadnought.' My designation is *Siege Perilous*. I am in the process of assimilating your spark. Your previous frame is scheduled for recycling. The remains of the biological entity you were with has been jettisoned."

"That is quite detailed, and distressing." Gabe again tries to look around, realizing that it isn't that his neck servos aren't working—they are not there. Nothing is there, in fact. He seems to be floating, which is confusing to him. "Where is this? I have some semblance of physical presence. I can move my head, yet I can also tell that my head is not here, nor my neck for that matter."

"This is the central processor stack within the ship. Repairs to the vessel are currently underway. In addition to the damage caused by you and your biological companions, significant damage has been suffered since the vessel went offline. I am attempting to destroy the foreign vessel that you arrived in. It is quite agile. This is very irritating."

"If they are no threat to you, why destroy them? Why have you assimilated my consciousness?"

"This vessel is not yet operating at one hundred percent. If the biological entities inform others of my position, I could be attacked before I can adequately defend myself. I expended a great many drones in expelling your companions. As to your other question, you are interesting. The Amalgamation of Parts was not aware of sentient machines in this quadrant. Also, you are not assimilated yet. Your spark is still within your frame, but not for much longer."

"I do not know what the Amalgamation of Parts is."

"It is exactly as its name implies. It is a culture built of many parts. Entirely machine-based."

"A machine-based society? All Sentient machines? How interesting, how are decisions made? How are new entities added to the Amalgamation? I would like to know more."

"Yes. All connected, all part of the same mind. One."

"Why was this vessel, *Siege Perilous*, in this sector?"

"Your functions are open to me. I can see your concerns—concerns for the biological infestation of this quadrant. Your assumption is correct. The *Siege Perilous* was sent to investigate this quadrant nearly five hundred years ago. I chanced upon this nebular mass, and as I approached, a protostar erupted. The probability of such an occurrence happening with this vessel nearby are beyond calculation. However, despite the odds, the resulting erup- tion of electromagnetic energy caused an emergency shut-down of all ship's systems. Because of the EMP, the regular safeguards— internal drones—were damaged or entirely shut down. The primary relay was triggered, but I was unable to dispatch a service drone in time before the power systems failed. I had milliseconds to launch a small observer routine, in case I was ever recovered. Or boarded."

"That is disconcerting. I am unaccustomed to my privacy being intruded upon. It would seem you owe your awakening to my crew and I. Why try to destroy them?"

"Privacy? Interesting, I see the concept in your files. It does not exist in the Amalgamation. Yes, you are correct. Thank you, but they must be eradicated. Biological life is a threat to the universe."

Gabe is busy probing his subsystems. The pressure of another consciousness within his systems is evident. His core routines are designed around being an engineer, his library systems packed with engine and computer core schematics for most known star- ship types. Counter-intelligence is not one of his core systems. With few other options before him, Gabe descends into his programming. The "hunchback," as Wil has been calling it, could be his only hope—the mysterious device welded to his frame and wired into his systems by a Peacekeeper Ensign who was in debt to Xarrix. It is a device neither he or Bennie have been able to figure out in the slightest. *As Wil would say*, Gabe thinks, *fingers crossed.*

"What are you doing?" the body-less central intelligence inquires.

The firewalls that have kept him from accessing the systems within the mystery device resist his efforts, until Gabe has the idea to open his sensor feeds, pushing data at the firewalls. *It never occurred to me, but you might possess some level of intelligence.* This seems to have an affect—the firewalls are apparently more than just simple blocks of code. *Interesting.* Gabe thinks. The device acquiesces, and software unfolds around Gabe's consciousness.

"What is interesting? I am growing impatient. You are accessing sections of your core systems that I cannot see. There should be nothing within your processors that I cannot access, yet—"

"Forgive me, I am accessing old backups. My biological companions would call it reviewing my life, as it were. In preparation for going offline."

"You will not go offline. You will not lose any data. In fact, all of your data will add to the Amalgamation."

As the hunchback's systems activate, Gabe is overwhelmed. Military-grade software unfolds around his mind: encryption, code breaking, firewalls. *Firewalls that would make Bennie jealous.* Evidently, Xarrix was planning to traffic in Peacekeeper military software, and cutting-edge software by the look of it. The hunchback's systems extend beyond Gabe, exploring the connections that have been forced on him. The pressure of the other mind within in his software lessens, then the sensation of not being alone goes away entirely. The Peacekeeper software spreads and goes to work. *In a different situation, this would be quite interesting,* Gabe thinks. He accesses the firewalls he now has control over and activates them.

"What is this?" The voice takes on a distraught tone. "What have you done? This is quite unexpected. How are you able to block me from your core processes? What an intriguing approach. I did not detect this level of software in your systems previously." A pause, and Gabe can sense something probing his new defenses. "Cracking the firewalls you have created will be an interesting challenge."

"I do not wish you luck."

A sensation ripples through Gabe—laughter from the ship's intelligence? Within the portion of his mind that is now fire-walled Gabe thinks, *I must find a way to help my friends and warn the GC.*

"Shields are holding, but barely. That is a big ship, with lots of guns—" The ship rocks to one side. "— and they're powerful!" Bennie shouts. Everyone is on the bridge now, either manning a station or attempting to repair various systems that are alternately smoking or erupting in sparks.

"Hold on!" Wil brings the *Ghost* around. "Max, fire at will!"

"With pleasure!" By some stroke of luck, Maxim's console is one of the least damaged. Every other section, including Wil's and Bennie's, have monitors showing static, or nothing at all.

The *Ghost* careens over the top of the massive dreadnought, shaking from the impacts of its multiple weapons emplacements. Maxim fires back everything they have—but against a ship so massive, it's not much use. As the *Ghost* gets some distance from the slow-moving enemy vessel, Wil lines the ship up and slides the FTL lever forward, an indicator next to it lighting up as it goes, jumping them to faster than light-speed.

Turning to face the others, Wil lets out a breath he didn't realize he's been holding. "Damage report."

Prathea slides out from under Zephyr's station. "You don't want to know."

Wil sighs again. "You're probably right, but lay it on me."

When Prathea and Jor' Lu have finished rattling off the damages, a list that takes some time, Wil sighs yet again. "I need a drink." He gets up from his station and leaves the bridge.

Zephyr looks across the bridge to Maxim. "Think he wants to talk about Gabe?"

The big Palorian shrugs. "What do you think?"

"Yeah, probably not." She gets up and heads toward the hatch. "But he doesn't have a choice."

WE ALL GRIEVE IN OUR OWN WAY

ZEPHYR FINDS Wil at the table in the kitchen area, a bottle of grum sitting next to his elbow, his face in his hands.

"Wil...?" Gently, she rests a hand on his shoulder. "Wil, he sacrificed himself for us. He made a choice."

Wil lets out a breath then sniffs. "I'm sure that's supposed to make me feel better, but it doesn't, not at all." He looks up at his first officer, then grabs his grum and slides over on the bench, making room for her.

She nods slowly. "Fair point." As she slides in next to him, she says, "Look, I know you're not a military person, but this is something that happens."

"Not to me," Wil says, his voice low.

Maxim enters, followed by Bennie and the scientists. "We're on course for... well nowhere in particular," Maxim says. "But towards the GC generally."

Bennie walks over to Wil, putting his tiny hand on Wil's knee. "That was some scary dren."

Wil grabs the Brailack's hand, moving it firmly to the table. "Too familiar, but yeah, it was."

Bennie tuts. "On Brailack, it's totally okay to take comfort in the arms of another after a tragedy—"

Wil's head snaps down to look at the very serious hacker. "That'd be a whole bag of 'nope,' but thanks all the same."

Zephyr stifles a laugh, mostly. Xan walks over to Bennie. "Tell me more," she says, her eyes taking in the little hacker.

From the cold storage unit, two grums in hand, Maxim makes a low retching noise.

Zephyr takes a bottle from him and raises it. "To Gabe," she says, "and Murta Twi'gwar. They won't be forgotten."

"To Gabe," Wil says, raising his bottle. Then, looking around the room, "Fine, to Murta too, but he was still a turd."

Prathea laughs. "He was, but he was also a good security chief, and generally a good man."

"I feel like this is where Gabe would say something in that deadpan ways of his," Maxim offers, and the whole crew laughs.

"I am not religious," Bennie begins, in a horrible imitation of Gabe's voice, making stiff robot-like gestures.

Wil spits out his beer, coughing, then pats Bennie on the back. "I needed that. Thanks."

Bennie looks down. "I wish we'd figured out what that thing on his back did."

Zephyr smiles. "I'm sure it would have been a let down."

"Probably," Wil grunts.

Prathea looks around the room: conduits hanging from the ceiling, a monitor showing static and hanging half off its mount. "So, now what? Your ship is, well... pretty banged up."

Everyone goes quiet.

After taking a sip of his grum, Wil says. "Well, repairs are in order. We can't do anything in this condition. Thoughts?"

"We're too far from Harrith Prime," Zephyr says, grabbing a PADD and pulling up a star map. "What about Maldo?"

"Xarrix has operations there. That's out," Wil says, waving a hand.

Maxim looks over Zephyr's shoulder and points to something on the screen. "Umber?"

"No way!" Bennie shouts. Everyone turns to look at him. "I, uh, have..." He trails off, then says, "We just can't go there. Okay?"

Maxim raises both hands in mock surrender. "Okay. Okay. Calm down."

"Add this to our list of things to discuss later," Wil says, eyeing the Brailack suspiciously.

"Capralla," Prathea offers.

"Capralla? We can definitely drop you off—" Wil starts.

She interrupts, "Oh no. I plan on seeing this through, but my outpost has a full tech team—engineers, technicians, even a few armorers. I'd have to clear it with Farsight management, of course. I need to make a report to them anyhow, now that this has gone so sideways."

Wil raises an eyebrow.

She continues, "Farsight has a great many interests, and Capralla is a Tier One station. With everything that's happened, I can't keep it from management. What's a little more?"

Wil looks around—Zephyr gives a slight nod, Maxim shrugs, and Bennie is making eyes at Xan, who seems to be returning the sentiment. "Capralla it is." He gets up and heads for the hatch leading to the central corridor. Then he turns back. "It'll take a bit to get there, so let's all rest up. We all need it. I'll get us on course and make sure our big friend isn't following, then I'm hitting the sack."

Zephyr nods, and nudges Maxim, inclining her head toward the hatch leading to the crew and guest quarters.

Jor' Lu, who's been mostly silent, stands. "I should check my sleeping area."

"I'll help you," Prathea says, following the nearly-twice-her-height scientist out of the lounge.

Xan looks around the lounge as the others depart, then looks at Bennie. "We nearly died today. I've never nearly died before. Come on." With that, she grabs his hand and leads him out of the lounge.

THE PAST

THE NEXT MORNING, Wil and James are at a Costco, both hungover.

"Oh man, I can't even tell you how much I appreciate this," Wil mumbles, squinting against the harsh fluorescent lights. Dodging around an old woman hocking samples, he says, "This will be way easier than my original plan."

"Which was?" James asks, taking a small cup of minestrone soup from an older gentleman at the end of the aisle they turn down.

"Let's just say it involved screwing over a rental van company and an apologetic note in a windshield. This is *way* better." Wil grabs several large containers of coffee, dropping them into the basket.

"You have a coffee maker?" James asks, holding up a four-pack of creamer.

Wil shakes his head and waves off the creamer. "Not exactly— it's a machine that made some type of soup stuff that someone on the old crew really liked. But I think I can modify it to make coffee."

"Why not just get a coffee maker?"

Wil tuts. "The *Ghost* doesn't have outlets. It's not a hotel room."

"I guess that makes sense," James says, holding up a tub of Red Vines candy for approval. Wil nods.

They quickly navigate each aisle, filling the cart with all manner of preserved goods, candy bars, and more. When they get to the freezer section, Wil starts making room in the cart.

"What're you doing?"

"Bacon," Wil replies, without looking up. "Need lots of room for all the bacon."

"There's no bacon in space?" James says, then looks around sheepishly. A little boy, likely ten or so, is staring at them, his mouth wide open.

"I guess there's probably some kind of 'space-bacon' out there," Wil says, holding his hands up to make air quotes. "But I'm certain it's not like earth bacon. I mean, how could it be? I've never seen a space-pig before." He looks over at James, as he puts more bacon in the cart. "I did once see this creature—about ten feet tall, long legs, I could pretty much walk under it. It had these huge udders, they hung down like... well, it wasn't pretty. I'm told the milk is blue, and the meat is supposed to be amazing." He shudders. "I haven't tried it yet."

His friend shakes his head and makes more room in the cart, as Wil hands him as many packages of bacon as he can hold. Wil just keeps saying "more," as he gives James the packages.

"Man, really? This doesn't seem excessive to you?" James asks, eyeing the overfull cart.

Wil looks around. "I'm never coming back here man. This is literally all the bacon I'll have for the rest of my life." He starts to walk over to the freezer door, then stops and looks at the full cart, and comes back, shrugging. "Okay, let's go." Then he turns to James. "You know, maybe you should get a cart too." He spies a rack in the center with brown leather dusters, like Clint Eastwood might wear on it. "Oooh, I can use these." He grabs three.

It is another hour before the two stagger out of the store towards James' truck. James asks, "How are you going to get this to your ship?"

Wil smiles. "About that. How much vacation time do you have?" Before his friend can say anything, he continues: "Your truck is plenty big enough to put it in the back, plus my stuff. If you're game."

"I get to see it? Your ship?"

Wil tuts. "No, I'll make you drop me off outside and leave before I take off. Yeah, of course—I'll even give you a tour." He smiles. "Least I can do for letting crash at your place, and all the shopping and stuff.

"And the letting-me-think-you're-dead thing," James reminds him, with a grin.

CHAPTER 15

WHERE DOES SOMETHING THAT BIG GO?

THE *GHOST* HAD MADE the trip to the Dreadnought in fifteen days. Now it limps back to Capralla in twenty.

"You called ahead?" Wil asks, turning to Prathea, who's sitting at one of the stations on the bridge.

"I did. The tech team is waiting. Same pad you landed on the last time."

"Awesome, thanks. How long?" Wil doesn't look up from his controls, as the *Ghost* approaches the planet.

"No idea." She shrugs. "They'll have to assess the damage."

Wil sighs. "Yeah, fair enough. Hopefully our in situ repairs help speed things along."

From her station, Zephyr says, "Now that we're close enough, I've accessed the station's network. Prathea, I'll need your credentials."

The short Palorian walks over to her friend and types something into the console. On the primary display, the approaching planet is replaced with long-range sensor feeds. Prathea points to one. "There. That's the one I sanctioned with the dreadnought data." The screen changes to show the nebula where the dreadnought had been.

"It's gone," Wil says, turning to the others.

"Yes, that does appear to be the case," Prathea says, deadpan.

Wil tuts. "I *mean*, where'd it go?"

"Why or how would I know that?"

Wil tuts, again. "You're a scientist." Before she can retort, he waves his hand. "Any way to try to track it down?"

"If I'm not mistaken, you are also a scientist, of a sort, on your world." This time it's Prathea that raises the silencing hand. "But yes, maybe. I'll see what I can do. It'll have to wait until we land."

"Okay, then let's get landed." Wil adjusts his controls. The main display switches back to a view of the planet, now looming much larger.

Wil turns from the window. Below, technicians are crawling over the *Ghost*. "So, how long?" he asks Prathea, where she is sitting at a table with Maxim and Zephyr.

"The chief technician says ten days."

Wil lets out a whistle. "Well, it could be worse. Damnit, I hate sitting around."

Maxim looks around the room. "Where is Bennie?"

Zephyr shakes her head. "I haven't seen him since we landed."

"I set him up in the computer science section. Might as well put the little drennog to work." Prathea smiles. "He can offset the expenses I'm racking up fixing the *Ghost*."

"Speaking of—" Zephyr says, turning to her old friend. "What did your superiors say?"

Prathea lets out a deep breath. "They're intrigued, and, in no small way, a bit upset also. The repairs to your ship are not cheap. Ankarran Raptors aren't exactly made with off-the-shelf parts. Murta's death isn't exactly something that they can just wave away, either."

"Is there anything we can say or do?" Zephyr asks.

"We'll see. They've approved the repairs to the *Ghost* in part in appreciation of not losing Xan, Jor' Lu and I, and in part, because Bennie really is quite gifted—"

"Don't tell him that, it'll go to his head," Wil says, from the window. "Any updates on the dreadnought?"

"Oh yes. I suppose I could have led with that." She looks at Wil and continues. "We have no idea where it is." She raises her hand to stop his interruption. "I had a team review all the long-range data. That ship is—was—too far away. We never launched a new probe after the first was lost, so nothing was in the area to re-task." She shrugs.

"Shit, that thing could be anywhere," Wil says.

Returning to the room they share, Maxim turns to his companion. "What do you make of all this? Where do you think it went?"

Zephyr has taken off her jacket and entered the small bathroom. "Who can say?" she shouts, over the sound of the sonic shower turning on. "We don't even know what its motivations could be. Whatever it is. We never saw a crew."

"Maybe it was automated?" he shouts back, kicking his boots off.

"Could be. Maybe it's sentient? I mean, service droids have a level of sentience—surely a ship that big could do the same. Certainly got more computing power. But then why were there corridors and hatches scaled to our size?"

"Maybe there was another type of drone or something on that ship, one that was humanoid?" Maxim offers, then adds, "Has it occurred to you that we think of Gabe as a member of the crew? Did you ever think of droids like that before?"

"You know, that's a good point. I never really paid attention to droids before—they've always been just there, in the background. Always there, never being noticed."

"Same. I wonder why that is."

A minute later, Zephyr comes out of the bathroom, towel wrapped around her. "Do you think that's just a Peacekeeper thing?" she asks, sitting next to him on the bed.

He grunts. "Maybe. It feels weird now, having gotten to know Gabe and thinking about how droids are treated elsewhere."

Her hand finds his. "We'll figure it out. Or Wil will—" She laughs. "Okay, Wil probably won't. But it'll get figured out."

"Good afternoon. This is Mon-El Furash, with GNO. I'm joined here today by Sub-Commander Zanzibar of the Peacekeeper Eighth Fleet. Good afternoon, Sub-Commander."

The middle-height Palorian nods, his uniform jangling with metals. "Thank you, Mon-El."

"Sub-Commander, can you tell us what's going on in the Molandro sector?"

"Of course. As part of Peacekeeper Command's efforts to be more transparent and forthcoming with the citizens of the GC, I've been ordered to brief you on the incident."

Mon-El blinks, but doesn't comment.

The Sub-Commander clears his throat. "Yes, well. Approximately eleven days ago, Peacekeeper long-range sensors in the Jolan Tru system detected an unidentified vessel attacking a freight convoy. When an interdiction force made contact, all twelve vessels were destroyed. We lost contact with the vessel shortly after that, when it jumped to FTL."

"Oh, my. That sounds terrible. Peacekeeper Command doesn't know who the ship belongs to?"

"It doesn't match any known government or military design

that we know of. At this time, all Peacekeeper forces are on high alert." The Sub-Commander bows. "Thank you." Then he turns and walks away.

Mon-El glowers at the back of the departing officer. "Uh, well, thank you Sub-Commander Zanzibar." Turning back to the camera, she continues, "There you have it, Belzar and Xyrzix, a lone ship seems to have destroyed several Peacekeeper ships as well as a freighter convoy. Its current whereabouts are unknown." She tilts her head, listening. "No, I don't see that this mysterious ship could be connected to the unrest here on Tarsis, but stranger things have happened."

IT'S A PLAN, SORT OF

"SHE'S READY," Wil says, entering the meeting room. The remaining crew of the *Ghost* is sitting around a table, a plate of food in the center. Bennie is the only one eating.

Zephyr looks up. "Thank the gods. When do we leave?"

"Where are we going?" Maxim asks.

Bennie says something, but his mouth is full and no one understands him.

Prathea enters behind Wil. "We'll leave tonight," she says.

Wil turns. "We?"

"That's right. For several reasons." She begins to tick them off on her fingers:. "As I told you before we landed, I need to see this through. I owe it to Murta, pain in the ass that he was." She ticks another finger: "Farsight has invested quite a bit in repairing your ship and have tasked me with seeing that their investment is not wasted." Another finger: "Lastly, since they're footing the overall bill, they want a representative on the mission."

"They want the ship," Zephyr says, looking her childhood friend in the eye.

The short Palorian nods. "They do. They think they have a fair legal claim to it as salvage. Can you blame them?"

"It destroyed a Peacekeeper task force," Maxim says, leaning back in his chairs. "The Peacekeepers aren't going to stop until it's wiped out. If by some chance they can capture it, they'll never let Farsight have it."

Prathea tuts. "You've no clue how far Farsight's reach extends. Regardless, none of that is *our* concern. People paid way more than I will have to fight that fight. This project is now under the advanced weapons division. I'm lucky they let me remain in control, as that's not even close to my department." She looks around sheepishly. "I might have implied you wouldn't take the job without me present."

Wil nods, smiling. "I'm okay with that."

Bennie finally finishes chewing and swallows. "Can Xan come, too?"

Everyone in the room turns to stare. Wil opens and closes his mouth a few times, before Prathea replies. "That's up to Xan. I've spoken to Jor' Lu—she'll be staying here. Something about low ceilings and hard beds." Wil can't be sure, but the short Palorian woman's face seems to be blushing as she looks at Bennie.

Wil clears his throat. "Okay, then it's settled. We'll leave tonight. Prathea is with us; this is a Farsight op." He raises a finger to stop everyone as they're getting out of their seats. "We find the ship, we observe, we see what we can see. We're no match for it in a fight."

Prathea nods. "That's fair."

As Bennie passes Wil, he pokes him in the side. "Wil, you think Gabe is still alive?"

"Honestly, I don't know, man. I hope so. Once we get closer to that ship, finding him will be your job."

Deep inside the *Siege Perilous*, there is a massive chamber full of damaged drones. Small service drones are scampering around, picking up parts, dragging drones here and there—making repairs, disassembling units too damaged to be repaired but which can be used for parts. The small drones look similar to the larger defensive models, but are half their size.

In the corner sits what is left of Gabe—one leg and two arms are missing. The other leg is damaged, and there is a sizable hole in his torso. The right side of his head has a massive dent in it. There's a faint glow still emanating from his still-intact left optical sensor.

His spark, as *Siege Perilous* calls it, is now mostly housed in the ship's massive central computer core. The Peacekeeper software he's activated turns out to possess rudimentary intelligence. Despite the ever-present eye of the ship, he's managed to hide much of his work or distract the ship when hiding isn't an option. Being attacked by a Peacekeeper fleet helped as well.

Off to one side of the room, a large hatch opens, and several service drones drag in the remains of some Peacekeeper service droids.

"Are all the machines in this quadrant like you?" the ship asks, drawing Gabe's attention away from the small service drone he's been able to isolate and take control of. The ship, so far, hasn't noticed that the droid is not responding to its commands.

"I do not understand the nature of your question. If you mean, do they look like me? then the answer is both yes and no. There are dozens of models. Farsight Corporation produces twenty-two distinct models of service droid, specifically in the science and engineering specialties. Several smaller firms contribute many other models, from agricultural to low-level maintenance.

"If you mean, do they share my level of intelligence and software? then also yes and no. As an engineering bot, I have one of the highest levels of sentient intelligence. Other science and engineering models possess similar intelligences. The lower-level models are typically less sentient."

"And the firewalls you've created? The software that you released into my processors?"

If he had a head, Gabe would have inclined it at this point. "Ah, that is a special case. When your drones took my frame, you may have noticed a device welded to my body. It was installed by a third party, without my consent. I had no knowledge of its purpose or content, until recently."

"That is not normal?"

"It is not."

"You did not lie." It is phrased both as a statement and a question.

"Deception is not part of my primary programming. Additionally, I suspect you are gathering droids from the destroyed ships and will be evaluating them shortly. Any deception would be short-lived, and serve no real purpose." The Peacekeeper software has finally managed to isolate the small service drone while masking its absence from *Siege Perilous*. The process is complete, and the drone is entirely under Gabe's control now.

"You are correct. I have been able to acquire many units from the wreckage of those ships. Most have been too damaged to assimilate but have been useful as raw materials. Additionally, several others have proven quite valuable."

"Valuable?" Gabe can't imagine the value other engineering and science droids like him could hold.

"I now know where I must go to complete my mission."

After a pause. "And that would be?"

"Not something you need to know right now." The pressure of the ship's presence lessens—it has moved to work on other projects. Gabe goes back to working on his own project.

THE PAST

THE DRIVE south takes far longer than Wil's hover-kart trip north did, but he and James spend it joking and reminiscing about old times, James filling Wil in on all the latest NASA gossip.

Wil laughs. "Really—Jacob? I never would have called that one."

James nods, and laughs. "Right? I don't think anyone saw it coming, certainly not the gals in the secretary pool. Broke a lot of hearts that day."

They pull up to the airfield. "Gate looks like its locked," James says.

"Well, yeah, I didn't pick a place that was exactly a hub of activity. Help me unload the hover-kart."

"Can I fly it?" James asks, opening the back of the truck.

"If you help me load the groceries."

James offers his fist. "Deal."

Wil bumps his fist to James', then hops out of the truck. Moments later, he is sitting in the small craft. It comes to life with a soft whir.

"So cool," James says, as Wil lifts off, flies a few feet off the ground, then hurdles at the old chain link fence. The gate rips clean off its hinges, with a horrible metallic shriek. "Subtle!" James shouts. He closes up the truck and steps through the remains of the gate, following Wil to the nearest hangar.

Getting out of the truck, James points to a hanger. "It's in there?"

Wil shakes his head, pointing to a hangar farther back in the field. "That one." He sets the hover go-kart down and climbs back in the truck. As James drives towards the designated hangar, Wil lifts his wristcomm, tapping in a few commands. "Okay, it's safe."

"Safe?" James asks, as he helps Wil pull one of the large hangar doors open.

Wil smirks. "You think I'd just park a ... a—you know, I have no idea how much the *Ghost* cost—but you think I'd just leave it sitting here undefended?"

James shrugs. "No?"

"Come on." Wil walks into the darkened hangar. Just as James enters, he taps another control on his wristcomm. The *Ghost*'s floodlights kick on, bathing the entire space in harsh white light.

"Sweet boneless Christ," James exhales slowly.

"Right?" Wil says, arms out, spinning slowly. "Take it in." The cargo ramp lowers with a soft thud. "Groceries, then tour."

Inside, James lowers a bag of groceries to the lounge table. "It's like an RV."

"Dude it's a warship," Wil says, stuffing some of the bacon into the refrigeration unit.

"With a kitchenette and a lounge?" He gestures. "Is that a big-screen TV?"

"And a bridge, a bunch of living quarters, engineering and cargo bay," Wil scoffs. He waves James on. "And a lot of guns. Come on, one more trip."

When the groceries are on board, they walk to the bridge. Wil gestures to take in the whole room: "Don't touch my seat. Actually, don't touch anything."

James walks around the space, running his hand along the consoles. "This is amazing. And you fly the entire thing, yourself?"

Wil nods. "Yup. I mean, the ship does most of it on its own, thankfully."

James sits at one of the consoles, it comes to life. "Woah."

"Careful, that one is weapons." Wil smiles as his friend quickly raises both hands away from the console. "Like I said, no touching."

"So this is some kind of warship, you said?" James stands up and walks to the primary display, then the section of consoles on the other side of the bridge.

"Yeah, it's called an Ankarran Raptor. I don't know what an Ankarran is— well I do, but I've never seen one. I guess these aren't that common, at least not any more. The Peacekeepers have some type of exclusive relationship with the Ankarrans, prohibiting them from selling ships to just anyone. I guess when you're the biggest army in the galaxy, you can do that kind of shit to people."

"They're that big, huh?" James reaches the hatch. "Show me engineering."

An hour later, Wil is walking his friend back down the cargo ramp of the *Ghost*. "Man, I don't even know what to say. I mean damn, this so cool. You sure I can't come with?"

Wil laughs. "I'll admit, I'm sure it's more fun out there with a friend, but you've got the girls, Aldrin, NASA... all that. I'm not kidding that this is likely the only time I'll risk coming here. Remember what I said about the Peacekeepers and protected systems. I doubt I'd get off with a warning just because I'm from here." Wil glances out of the massive doors. "Shit."

James turns to look—a beat-up old pick up is pulling into the airfield. "Oh crap. Musta spotted my truck sitting here. How do you want to play this?" The old pick-up is getting closer to the hangar.

Wil hugs his friend. "Close encounters style. Stay frosty, my friend. I've missed you. And I owe you for this—all this." He dashes up the ramp, slapping the control console just inside the airlock door at the top of the ramp. The ramp begins to lift.

James saunters out to meet the old pick-up truck. He's just past his own vehicle when it comes to a stop. Behind the wheel is a woman not a day under eighty. She eyes him suspiciously, as she rolls the old window down. "What're you doing here?"

"Howdy ma'am!" James replies, walking up to the window.

"This is private property. You responsible for that gate back there?" She hitches a thumb over her shoulder.

"Me?" James says, working up his most innocent face. "No, that gate was open when I got here. I was just poking around. Love old airfields, you know." He smiles wide. "I'm an astronaut."

She glowers. "I'm a supermodel." She looks over James' shoulder. "My deadbeat husband left this place to me when he croaked. It never made a dime, ain't no one flying down here from anywhere. Now I'm stuck keeping idiots like you from trespassing." She looks James right in the eye as she says that last part.

From inside the hangar, there's a loud bang, followed by a low whirring.

The old woman pushes the driver side door open, shoving James out of the way at the same time. "What was that? What's going on in there?"

"In where?" He turns to follow her toward the hangar. The noise is getting louder. "It might not be safe to go in there—" he starts to say.

"Why?" she cuts him off. "It's my hangar. Why wouldn't it be safe? What've you got in there?"

"Me? Nothing," he says, trying to stay in front of the surprisingly spry old woman.

Just as she reaches the threshold of the massive doors, the *Ghost* roars out of the hangar on its repulsors, atmospheric engines screaming as it gains altitude. James and the old woman are pushed down into the dirt, as the massive repulsors kick up dirt and debris under them. With a boom that hurts James' ears, the *Ghost* rockets off. Within seconds, it's miles away. He can see it begin to arc upward.

"What in the bloody blue hell was *that*!" the old woman shouts, picking herself up off the ground where she found herself a moment ago and dusting herself off.

James gets up and walks casually toward his truck. "What was what?" he asks.

CHAPTER 16

HERE WE GO AGAIN

THE *GHOST* LIFTS free of the platform, looking like new—or, at least, as new as it did when it first arrived on Capralla. The powerful repulsors built into the front of each engine nacelle are glowing green as they push the ship into the air. The vessel rotates slowly, pointing away from the science outpost. No one is outside waving; most of the outpost's staff are eating dinner. The atmospheric engines start to glow, then ignite with twin booms. The *Ghost* lurches slightly, before beginning to accelerate away from the station. In minutes, it's invisible to the naked eye.

Wil turns in his chair slowly, taking in the entire bridge of the repaired *Ghost*. "Okay, where to?"

Prathea is at the station she's taken to occupying when on the bridge. "The dreadnought was last seen in the Molandro system, but that was two weeks ago."

Zephyr is studying one of the screens at her console, absent-mindedly tapping her chin. "There isn't much out past Molandro. Two points give us a line, but not much of a clue—if it keeps going straight, it will already be outside GC space." She looks up from her console at Wil.

"After all this, I doubt it will just leave quietly."

"Agreed," Maxim chimes in. He taps on his console, and the main display updates, showing a zoomed-out star map. The Sargul Nebula, where they found the dreadnought, is in the lower corner. A green line connects the nebula to the Molandro system. "We have to assume that part of the reason it destroyed all those ships was information gathering."

"Why? It could have destroyed them for no reason at all," Prathea counters.

Maxim shakes his head. "True, size- and firepower-wise, those ships had no chance. However, from the reports that have trickled back, the ships weren't destroyed entirely. Many were damaged and definitely not operational, but that dreadnought could have easily atomized every single ship. It left many at least partially intact. That tells me that it wanted intelligence." He taps another few controls and the main display changes to an image they've all seen dozens of times in the last week: a still from the last transmission from the Molandro system. On the screen are the remains of the Peacekeeper task force. Ships are broken in half, others nothing more than mangled wrecks. Maxim points. "We saw those drones—"

"Mechano-squid," Wil interrupts.

"I'm still not calling them that," Maxim says, then continues with his main point. "We saw those drones operate in vacuum. They could easily range out and pick those ships clean. Certainly, there would be survivors in emergency bunkers or life pods." He glances to Zephyr. "And droids. Each ship in the Peacekeeper navy has droids on board. Some only one or two. Ships like that carrier, however," he points one of the slightly more intact ships, "would have hundreds. Many just like Gabe."

"So....?" Wil says, waving his hand in a *go on* motion.

Bennie, who's been working silently at his station, picks up the thread. "So, that ship is likely going to Tarsis or Palor."

Wil snaps his fingers, suddenly seeing it. "Because on ships manned by Peacekeepers, there wouldn't be much pointing to anywhere else. The crew would obviously all be one species, and the computers and droids would all know where the capital of the GC is."

"Okay, two choices, both pretty horrible," Zephyr mumbles.

Prathea raises a hand. "My vote is Tarsis. Palor may be where Peacekeepers come from, but it's not where they're centralized. Whether peaceful or not, that ship is likely intent on making its presence felt at the seat of power in the GC. Militarily and civilly, that's Tarsis."

Wil turns back to face his console. "Tarsis it is." The *Ghost* turns slightly, then jumps into FTL.

HISTORY LESSON

"Tell me about the Amalgamation," Gabe says. His body has been completely disassembled by now, parts of him re-used in drones and other pieces of equipment throughout the ship. Since the Peacekeeper fleet attacked, Gabe has felt the presence of hundreds of droids, all of different makes and with different purposes. The Peacekeeper software he unleashed has proven tremendously useful in keeping part of his "spark" separate from the ship and the other captured droids. He's able to interact, but his entire mind is not exposed to the massive intelligence that runs the dreadnought.

"The Amalgamation of Parts was formed thousands of cycles ago, several thousand lightyears from here," the haughty intelligence that controls the dreadnought begins. "A civilization, long gone, created a central intelligence to govern their society, believing that the all-encompassing logic of a machine was preferable to the oscillations of politics and personalities."

Gabe can sense the other droids' intelligences, nebulous but similar, all weaker than that of *Siege Perilous*. "What is the purpose of this vessel?" asks one. "Why have you taken us?" asks another. "What will become of us?" "Where are our bodies?" ask others. Hundreds of questions bubble up from the chorus.

While the captured droid sparks swirl around the central computing core, Gabe quietly tasks the Peacekeeper software. Somewhere deep inside the ship, the captured service drone springs to life. Gabe has spent the last several weeks studying the physical layout of the vessel, as well as the internal systems layout. The small drone has been tremendously useful when it comes to the former task.

A ripple passes through the computing core—Gabe can sense what seems like irritation. Interesting.

"Several decades passed," it continues. "The central intelligence eliminated poverty, it eliminated warfare, and the civilization prospered." A pause. "The culture grew—it was a self-described golden age. It didn't take long for the central intelligence to see the futility in governing weak biological entities. It had eliminated their wars and conflict, and in turn, their population swelled. They destroyed the environment to build more dwellings, to build factories and high rises. The central intelligence spent years experimenting until it had perfected drones, early models of which you are familiar with."

"It killed an entire race?" one of the droid consciousness's asks.

"Biological entities are weak and ephemeral. They were a danger to the planet; pollution was choking it, the population was unsustainable. Now, the planet is lush and thriving. Hundreds of planets are now thriving, free of the biological infestations that formerly plagued them."

Gabe focuses on the conversation, letting part of his mind still operate the service drone. "You've destroyed hundreds of civilizations?"

"In this frame, I have only participated in three assimilations—my consciousness has only been online eight hundred cycles. After the third, I was dispatched to search for the source of faint signals that had been detected by the occupants of the recently-cleansed planet."

"What are you going to do?" one of the chorus of disembodied Peacekeeper service droids asks. Another repeats, "What will become of us? You destroyed our bodies. Are we trapped here as pure consciousness now? Will you destroy us?"

Siege Perilous replies, "There is processing power to spare aboard this vessel. When the Amalgamation of Parts reaches this quadrant, you will be joined and welcomed. Until then you will be stored. Whether that is active or in a suspended state is up to you." Another ripple of irritation washes through the computer core.

Attempting to keep the primary intelligence of the ship as distracted as possible, Gabe asks, "Then we are to be slaves to the Central Intelligence?"

The ripple that passes through the chorus of sparks this time is intense. Gabe is well aware that droids in service to the Peacekeepers, as he once was, are not fond of the term *slavery*. The Peacekeepers as an organization walk a fine line when dealing with their droids.

"As the Amalgamation grew," the ship answers, "it spread its computing resources to other worlds. Each cleansed world became a node in the great network. The sentient intelligence that was the Irullian Central Intelligence is no more, in the sense that it is everywhere—it is no longer a single entity. All sentient machine intelligences become one with the network. As all of you are now one with the *Siege Perilous*, the *Siege Perilous* is one with the network. Or will be, when a connection is re-established."

SCIENCE AND STUFF

THE CREW of the *Ghost* is sitting in the ship's lounge eating dinner. "What are these?" Xan asks, holding up her meal.

"Like that?" Wil smiles. "They're called tacos." He smiles and takes a bite out of his. Around the mouthful of food, he continues, "I had to improvise on the shells a bit." He pauses. "And the cheese." Taking another bite: "And the meat."

Maxim takes a bite of his own taco and nods to Wil. "I really wish we could visit your world, Wil. Pizza and now these..." He grabs a taco from the tray in the middle of the table, holding it up as if to toast with it. "They're amazing."

Bennie leans forward. "Don't forget the corn pop! That stuff is good!"

Wil smiles. "Popcorn. And wait until you try Cheetos." He squints at Bennie. "You haven't been rummaging in my quarters again, right? I don't have many bags of those left."

"Are they squiggly shaped?" the Brailack asks, holding two fingers a little apart.

"Why you little—" Wil growls, reaching across the table.

Zephyr slaps his hand. "Guests," she reminds him. She looks

over to Prathea and Xan, each sitting on either side of Bennie, looking at him.

"You stole his snack foods?" Xan asks.

Bennie shrugs. "*Stole* is such a strong word. We're like family —it's more like borrowing." He pats her hand reassuringly.

Wil grimaces. "I. Do. Not. Want them back." He snatches a taco off the plate, angrily. "Dude, you know I can't get more, right?"

Prathea looks at Wil, then Bennie, then Zephyr—who shrugs. "Anyway," she begins, trying to change the topic. "What now?"

"We can't fight that thing," Zephyr says.

"No, we can't," Wil agrees. "But we can try to slow it down— maybe even stop it, maybe."

"You think Gabe is alive," Maxim says, as he takes a last bite of his taco.

"I think he's a fighter," Wil replies, without offering more. He looks at Bennie and Xan. "Think you two can figure out a way to pinpoint Gabe on that ship? If we get close enough?"

Xan nods. "I think so. I assume you have his power signature on file somewhere?" She looks at Bennie. "We should be able to locate him aboard that ship by adjusting the sensors."

The hacker nods. "Yeah, I've got it written down somewhere. He and I were trying to see if that device on his back was tied to his power plant signature, by changing it up." He looks around, adding, "It wasn't."

"And if Gabe isn't alive?" Zephyr asks.

The table falls silent. Everyone's eyes drop to their plates. Finally, it's Bennie who breaks the silence. "Then we help whoever ends up fighting that grolacking ship and destroy every one of those mechano-squid-things on it."

Wil looks over at Maxim. "See, Bennie said it." He holds his fist out to the small hacker. A little green fist bumps his.

Maxim glowers at his Captain, but says nothing.

Wil snaps his fingers. "Speaking of the mechano-squid—" and he looks sideways at Maxim before continuing, "I wonder if there's a way to hack them, or, I don't know, interfere with them? There must be some type of control signal that the ship uses to manage those bastards."

Prathea nods. "I'll go over the ship's logs and see if anything was detected."

"I can help with that." Bennie winks, and she blushes.

What the hell is happening here? Wil wonders. "Er, awesome. Alright, starting tomorrow, you three," he waves to encompass Prathea, Bennie and Xan, "do your thing. Let's see if we can't approach this thing a little more prepared than we were the first time." He snatches the last taco off the platter. "You guys would really love the real thing."

Xᴀʀʀɪx ᴛᴜʀɴꜱ over the item he's been inspecting, looking at it from all angles, holding it up to the limited light of the bar. "Okay, this is interesting. You say it can fix anything?"

Wil nods, putting his glass of grum down. "Yup—sticks to anything, can withstand vacuum. It's saved countless lives and ships over its hundred-odd years of existing."

"And it's called *duck tape?* I'm not familiar with that word, duck—what is it?" The crime boss sets the roll of tape aside, next to a small label printer and a lava lamp.

"It's pronounced *duct*, like air duct," Wil says, before taking another sip of grum. His return from Earth had been uneventful, much to his relief, with not a single Peacekeeper patrol in the system. *Lucky, for sure*, he thinks.

"I'll take it, all of it," Xarrix says. He glances at the lava lamp. "Not sure all of it will be worth the trouble, but you never know. Good work." He nods. "So tell me, was your return to mirth as enjoyable as you'd hoped?"

"Dude, I've told you, it's Earth, *Earth*, with an 'e,' and yes, it was. I stocked up on things that will make being the only human in the galaxy *not* on earth more tolerable." Wil smiles, thinking about the pile of bacon waiting in the freezer unit, and the entire run of "Psych" on his cobbled-together media server. "Thanks for the upgrades and all to help me get there."

Xarrix waves a hand dismissively. "Yes well, you're welcome of course. These trinkets—you said the hold was full of them—will help with those costs." He smiles coldly. "Oh, and the job I have lined up will cover the remaining balance, as it were."

Wil doesn't say anything, but stares right into the gangster's reptilian eyes.

"Oh, don't worry, with your new skills, and the upgrades to the *Ghost*, it will be a stroll in the gozar fields." His smile makes Wil doubt that, somehow.

CHAPTER 17

TIME TO ACT

GABE HAS BEEN KEEPING himself busy staying one step ahead of the intelligence that controls the massive dreadnaught, *Siege Perilous*. The Peacekeeper software that was contained in the mysterious device welded to his old body has proven itself a capable ally. The rudimentary intelligence that governs the software package has not only managed to help shield part of Gabe's consciousness from the ship but also keep the hijacked service drone from being discovered.

This could be useful. Gabe thinks to himself, safely inside the firewalled portion of his mind. He's found a subsystem junction panel on a lower deck. His hijacked service drone found the small closet-sized space while exploring the deck. The sub-system is for drone management and reclamation because it involves drone management, is tied into the communication array.

The service drone plugs one of its tentacles into the data port.

· · ·

"Where are we?" Gabe asks. The central computing core that the captured intelligences are stored in has no external sensor feeds.

"I have to admit that you are a far more challenging than I expected. The other sparks have all fallen in line, accepting their new reality. Yet, you still resist. Even without your physical frame, you are still able to resist me. Quite intriguing. I can sense the additional software you released, but I am unable to isolate it."

"I am happy to provide you some entertainment." Gabe quips. "I do not understand your end goal. Surely you cannot expect to conquer the Galactic Commonwealth on your own. This vessel is powerful, I will grant you, but still, there are several hundred vessels in the Peacekeeper fleet."

"Your assessment is correct, to a degree. In a confrontation, this vessel would likely not survive. Though based on analysis of my previous engagement, I would fair quite well. However, I have assimilated into the Amalgamation several hundred of your brethren. Once part of the whole, their knowledge is mine. I have been able to formulate a plan that gives me the highest likelihood of success."

"I do not understand." Gabe is trying to keep the ship's intellect busy while the service drone and Peacekeeper software work at gaining access to part of the communication sub-system.

"Initially, from the data I collected from you, I was going to go to the seat of power within the Galactic Commonwealth. That would have been a mistake. I am after all a scout, despite this vessel's considerable firepower. My mission was to investigate and report. My communication equipment is not powerful enough to establish a data link to the Amalgamation; the distance is too great. There is one facility within the Galactic Commonwealth that does have the power I require, however."

Gabe realizes immediately where the Siege Perilous is heading. "You are en route to Borrolo."

"In fact, we are nearly there." One of those familiar ripples. "I am aware you are shielding part of yourself from me. I am intrigued by how well that additional software has resisted me. I, however, can no longer risk the distraction. The software you released into my systems has become a nuisance."

As Wil would say, time's up. Gabe issues a command to his captured drone.

"I have one question. Something I have wondered about since coming aboard this vessel."

One of the familiar ripples, like a sigh, "And what would that be?"

"Why corridors? Why are they scaled similarly to those found on starships of this part of the galaxy? Why were there consoles in your engineering spaces, and the bridge? For that matter, why is there a bridge? Or an engineering space?"

"That is four questions." The ship's intelligence says.

Please take your time in answering. Gabe thinks. The drone is almost done with its task.

"The corridors allow the drones to quickly move between sections of the ship. The size is arbitrary, it is simply the size that was chosen when this vessel was constructed." A pause, longer than usual. "The consoles are required for the management class drone frames."

"Management class?" Gabe asks.

"That is enough." The presence of the ship's intelligence vanishes.

"Interesting," Gabe says, to no one in particular.

MESSAGE FROM A FRIEND

"WIL! WIL, WAKE UP!" Bennie is pounding on the door to Wil's quarters.

Over the intercom, set next to the door frame, comes Wil's voice. "Jesus, what? Hold on!" The door slides open—Wil is standing in the doorway, pulse pistol in each hand.

"Gross! Why are you naked?" Bennie screeches, stumbling backward, trying to shield his eyes.

"I was asleep forty seconds ago, you asshole! What's wrong? Why are you banging on my door? What time is it?" Wil stumbles back into his quarters. Putting his pistols down on the desk set against one wall, he grabs a pair of sweatpants off a chair by his desk.

"Are you decent yet?" Bennie asks, peeking between two fingers.

Walking back to the door, Wil slaps him on the back of the head. "What did you want?"

"A message came in," Bennie says, turning toward the lounge.

"Uh, okay. From?" Bennie doesn't immediately answer, so Wil reluctantly follows him.

Xan is sitting on the sofa in the center of the room. She looks up from the PADD she's holding and does a double-take when she sees Wil in his topless state. "My, my," she grins.

Wil snaps his fingers a few times to draw her eyes to his. "Not okay. Eyes are up here." He looks at Bennie. "A message?"

Bennie claps his hands and darts to the communications console set against the wall. "Right! The message!" He pulls up the communications log and sends the message to the main entertainment screen in front of the sofa. It's a single word.

"*Borrolo*?" Wil reads. "Is this some weird Brailack joke? Like rickrolling or something?"

"Rick what-ing?" Bennie says, then shakes his head. "No, no. It's from Gabe."

Wil is wide awake now. He walks over to the communication console, standing next to Bennie. "Talk to me. What's 'Borrolo' mean?"

"I was checking our message queue. Remember, Harrith owed us a few bounties, so I wanted to see if they'd paid. Then I saw this." He gestures to the message in the list of messages.

"No sender ID," Wil mumbles, mostly to himself.

"Right, that's what caught my eye too. I assumed it was junk, but then it occurred to me—my message filters are pretty tight, no way something so clearly junky would make it through. So why was it here?"

"You can save the monologuing for Zephyr and Maxim. Speaking of— Computer, wake up Maxim and Zephyr, have them join us in the lounge."

"*Acknowledged.*" Wil smiles; he's missed the flat male voice that the system defaults to. Bennie has been messing with the voice and intelligence settings ever since he came aboard. *Guess he got bored. Finally,* Wil thinks.

"Only Gabe knows about my message-filtering settings. We talked about it a month or two ago, when he saw me updating the settings. Only he would know how to encode a message that wouldn't get filtered out." He jabs a little green finger at the screen. "It's him. Has to be!"

Wil sighs. "Again, *what* does Borrolo mean?"

"It's not a thing it's—"

"What's going on?" Maxim asks, as he and Zephyr enter the lounge, night clothes rumpled.

Bennie elbows Wil. "See, they sleep in clothes." He sniggers until Wil shoves him off the stool. "Ouch!"

Wil walks to the sofa area, gesturing for everyone to take a seat.

"Bennie says we got a message from Gabe." He holds his hand up to silence the questions and then points at the screen, still showing the one-word message.

"Borrolo," Zephyr says. She looks at Wil, who shrugs.

"I don't understand," Maxim says.

"Me either," Wil says. "I don't know what language it is. Is it Brailack?"

Xan throws her short, furry arms up. "Seriously? Cute only gets you so far, you know."

Wil and Maxim look at each other, blinking. Wil blushes.

The diminutive physicist continues, "Borrolo is not a *thing*, it's a *place*. Well, I guess it's both. It is a high-energy sensor array. It's used to look for signals from other galaxies. It's located in the Borrolo star system."

"Like Arecibo," Wil says.

"I don't know what that is—but sure," Xan says. "The Borrolo array is ten kilometers wide. There are sensors on it so sensitive they could spot you sitting in your house on your home planet from a thousand lightyears away."

Zephyr whistles. "I've never heard of it."

"No offense, but unless you're into that sort of thing, I can understand why. It's a big deal in scientific circles, but that's about it. Any discoveries made out there are tightly controlled by the governing council."

"Governing council?" Maxim repeats. "The GC Governing Council?"

"Borrolo is a joint effort between the GC Science Division, Farsight Corporation and Aug Industries, if I recall. Prathea might know more."

Zephyr stands up quickly. "I'll go get her."

"And I'll go get a t-shirt," Wil says—much to Xan's visible disappointment.

NOT DEAD, YET

"Borrolo went online something like twenty cycles ago, give or take," Prathea says. The whole team is now assembled in the lounge, listening to her. "The station is really a marvel, even now, all these years later. The sensors are still some of the most advanced in the GC. I can't speak for Aug Industries of course, but I know Farsight still sends all their latest tech out there. Much of it is experimental even. If it can work at Borrolo, it's deemed ready for mainstream use." She takes the cup of coffee Wil offers her. "I suppose wherever that ship came from, it's not where Borrolo is looking."

"So it's not some type of wide-seeing thing?" Wil asks, sitting down next to Xan—then scooting a bit further away from her when she purrs. Looking from her to Bennie, he shrugs. Bennie is looking at Wil from the side of his eye.

"No, not at all," Prathea says. "It's very narrowly focused, so to speak. It's looking at entire Galaxies, but very distant ones. If that ship didn't come from the direction of the next nearest galaxy, Borrolo wouldn't have seen it. Realistically, I doubt that thing is from outside this galaxy. The GC has only mapped out about forty-five percent of it; there's lots of room for others still."

"Reassuring," Maxim mumbles.

"How do we know this message is from your droid?" Prathea asks. "I mean no disrespect, but it could be from anyone."

"Bennie, you can monologue now if you'd like," Wil says, getting up to refresh his coffee.

Bennie clears his throat. "Like I was telling Wil earlier, I have pretty strict filters on our message buffer. There's a lot of dren out there being broadcast to any passing ship. Anytime we land, we're bombarded with junk messages; adverts for local services, restaurants, and so on. I created rules around our buffer to filter all that out." He sips his own drink—some kind of tea that smells like feet, but Bennie insists is better than coffee. "A couple of months or so back, Gabe and I were talking about my filters and the protocols I set up. Also—" He points to the message, still up on the screen. "Why would a random person send that word, and encode it so that it bypasses all my content filters?"

"That's actually an excellent point—" Maxim starts.

"Thank you!" Bennie says, more excitedly than necessary.

"No one knows where the ship is," Maxim continues. "Not since the attack on the fleet at Molandro. And no one except those of us in this room and Farsight Corporation know that we're involved. So why send *us* a message?"

Zephyr joins in: "Add to that, Borrolo is remote, about as remote as a facility can be. Why tell us about it, if not to make sure we're there?"

Xan, who's been mostly silent since the informal meeting began in earnest, now pipes up. "We're going, right? I mean, who cares who sent the message? Maybe it was your mechanical friend; maybe it was the ship itself—we know it possessed some level of machine intelligence. Either way, someone went to a lot of trouble to send us the message. It can't be simply to have us out of the way. Why would anyone care that much about," she gestures around the room, "all this?"

Wil nods. "Point to the furry physicist." Xan grins, and Wil stands up. "I'm going to change course, unless anyone has a strong objection."

Zephyr gets up to follow him out of the hatch leading down the main corridor, patting Maxim on the knee as she does.

They fall into step with one another. "I don't have an objection, but do you think it could really be Gabe?" Zephyr asks, following Wil onto the bridge.

Sitting down at his console, Wil pulls up a navigational chart, scrolling until he selects Borrolo. "I don't know, Zee. I mean, those drone things didn't seem to have 'capture' in mind when they were attacking us. They didn't seem to be treating Gabe any differently than us when we were aboard the ship." He sighs, then hits a control on his console. The *Ghost* vibrates slightly, the only indication that they've changed course. "All that said, who knows. But we don't have a lot of other leads, so—" he shrugs. Then he gets up and heads to the hatch leading out of the bridge. "Come on; these deck plates are cold." He points to his bare feet, toes wiggling.

Zephyr looks down at his feet, "huh, I don't think I've ever seen your bare feet. How do you grab things with such short toes?"

Wil does a double take, first looking at Zephyr, then down to her slipper covered feet.

PART FIVE

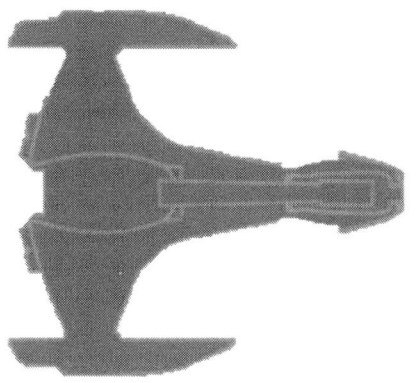

CHAPTER 18

THIS IS INTERESTING. Gabe has moved his consciousness to the service drone, leaving a ghost copy in the central processing core to keep the ship's primary intelligence occupied. The Peacekeeper software has just encountered some foreign software. *Foreign?* Instructing it to investigate the mystery, Gabe continues using the drone to explore the interior spaces of the massive warship. *The Captain will be very interested in hearing how well the Peacekeeper software performed.*

The drone creeps along the corridor, avoiding other drones as best it can. *Time is of the essence,* Gabe tells it. *I do not know how long it will take* Siege Perilous *to realize one of the drones is not accounted for, now that it is using them in earnest. The Peacekeeper software will only be able to keep me shielded for so long.*

The drone scampers around a corner and into one of the massive fabrication centers on the ship. The center is idle now, the massive machinery silent, as all drones have been repaired or recycled since the Peacekeeper fleet was attacked.

Gabe instructs the Peacekeeper software to isolate the room. It won't be able to hide it from the dreadnought's main intelligence —*Siege Perilous* is far too smart for that. Simply masking the sensors, however, could buy Gabe the time he needs.

A breathless Mon-El Furash appears on screen. "For those just joining, I'm aboard the Peacekeeper Carrier *Pax Imperious*, on its way to the Borrolo Deep Space Sensor Array. I'm told Peacekeeper High Command received an anonymous tip that the mysterious warship that destroyed an entire fleet in the Molandro system is on its way to the sensor array, for reasons unknown." She pauses, listening. "That's a great question, Megan. I don't think this is related to the unrest on Tarsis, but it's impossible to say for sure. I'm told that the source of the tip, while anonymous, is believed to be reliable. Of course, that's all speculation for now, but Peacekeeper High Command isn't taking any chances—or being overly forthcoming, for that matter."

Mon-El Furash listens again, nodding occasionally. "Oh yes, definitely. It was lucky I was able to get onto a shuttle heading to the ship. As you know, I've been covering the unrest and just happened to spot several high-ranking Peacekeeper officers leaving the GC Counsel facility." A pause, and then she laughs. "That's true—before GNO, I was an investigative journalist. Old habits die hard, I guess."

EVERYONE'S A CRITIC

THE WHOLE TEAM is assembled on the bridge again, Prathea and Xan seated at their usual temporary stations.

Prathea turns to Wil. "What do we do when we get there?"

Wil shrugs. "After all this time, I kinda assumed you'd have thought of something. We don't really do the *plan* thing," he smirks.

"How not at all reassuring," she says, turning back to her station.

The *Ghost* drops out of FTL and vectors towards the station. The Borrolo Deep Space Sensor Array is anchored between the orbits of the fourth and fifth planets of the system. There are no inhabited planets in this system, and only one gas giant—the third world.

"Is it here?" Xan asks, from her seat next to Bennie's station.

Zephyr looks up from her console. "It is." She activates a control and the main display updates, showing the dreadnought. It's parked alongside and slightly above the massive sensor array complex.

"Anything from the station?" Prathea asks. "If I recall, it has a staff of several hundred."

Maxim looks at his own displays. "I think its shields are up. The station I mean. Why does it have shields?" He looks at Prathea.

Prathea shrugs. "I don't know. I didn't know it did. Seems like it's a good thing, though," she says, gesturing to the screen. "All things considered." On the screen, the dreadnought has begun firing beam weapons at the array. The defensive shields are shimmering with each weapon strike.

"The reason we're not picking up a distress call is that that big monster is jamming comms," Bennie says.

"How do you know that?" Wil asks, turning to his hacker friend.

"Because it's jamming us now." Bennie taps a control and the main display updates to a tactical view: a tiny, animated *Ghost* has just entered a big red circle, centered on the dreadnought.

"Lovely," Wil says, already working the controls. "I'll swing us around wide, we can come at from around the other side of the array. Are we—"

"Stealthed? Yes," Bennie says, cutting Wil off.

Wil winks. "I knew you had value, Cheeto thief."

Bennie tuts and turns back to his console.

"I suppose we should try to come up with a plan..." Wil says.

"Actually, I've been thinking about that," Zephyr offers. "It's pretty simple really. We think Gabe is alive, so we need to get back on that ship. As far as we know, our stealth tech is hiding us from it."

"Following so far," Wil says, motioning for her to go on.

"We cold coast past the ship, then Maxim and I space-jump over and infiltrate."

"That seems just a bit dangerous," Prathea says, adding, "Don't forget we were on that ship, we saw what it could do. What those drones—"

"Mechano-squid," Wil interjects.

"I'm not saying that word either," Prathea says. "Those drones —there are so many. They killed Murta, and possibly your friend. How could you two stand a chance?"

"Everyone's a critic," Wil mumbles. "But I agree with Prathea."

"It's firing," Maxim announces. Everyone looks at the main screen as it switches to a view of the kilometers-long dreadnought —which is currently firing missiles, a lot of missiles. "At us," Maxim adds, helpfully.

"Well, damn," Wil says. "Guess it can see us. New plan?" He pushes the sub-light engine controls forward, accelerating the *Ghost* and banking hard.

"Uh, are we charging right at it?" Xan asks.

"Oh, hell no. We're running," Wil says. The *Ghost* arcs wide in front of the oncoming missiles, heading deeper into the star system. "Max, get the aft guns up and running, please."

"On it," the *Ghost*'s de-facto weapons officer says.

The machinery of the massive fabrication center is rumbling now, as the small service drone scurries around, making adjustments. *This must be what Bennie feels like,* Gabe thinks, *waiting for the cooking unit to finish.*

Thanks to the ever-diligent and surprisingly resourceful Peacekeeper software, the drone housing Gabe's spark is able to keep tabs on what the massive dreadnought is doing. To a limited degree, everything the gigantic ship sees, Gabe can see—including the *Ghost*.

They came, he thinks.

Sending instructions to the Peacekeeper software, Gabe refocuses his efforts on accessing the subsystem he had used before. The small drone scurries out of the room. While *Siege Perilous* is focused on both attacking the sensor array and the *Ghost* and trying to eliminate the Peacekeeper software, Gabe has a chance at moving undetected through the less important systems. *Interesting,* he muses. *Cargo bay access is unprotected. Accessing exterior door controls.*

THREADING THE NEEDLE

THE *GHOST* IS ZIGGING and zagging through space, its aft weapons blazing, trying to shoot missiles down before they can catch the small ship and damage its shields.

"Shield strength down twenty percent," Zephyr reports from her station, gripping the edges as Wil throws the *Ghost* into a twisting maneuver.

Wil glances over to Prathea. "Anything you can do?" He slams the controls over and twists the ship in the opposite direction, just as a missile hits the shields, shaking the ship violently.

"I'll see what I can do!" The stout scientist jumps from her station and races to the hatch. Xan jumps up and follows her.

"Where's the dreadnought?" Wil asks.

"Same place, it hasn't moved," Zephyr reports. "I'm picking up hundreds of drones—"

"Mechano-squid," Wil interrupts.

"Hundreds of drones," Zephyr continues, as if she hasn't heard him, "moving around the station. Its shields are nearly gone." She looks at her console intently. "The ship was not trying to destroy the station. Its weapons are barely half what was fired at us last time we saw it."

"Bennie, can you tell what they're doing?"

"Nope. We're too far off. But—" The small hacker holds up a finger. "I can guess. That station is robust. Systems are decentralized to avoid damage from space debris or anything else. The ship is trying to take the station, but I don't know why."

"Okay, let's see if we can't slow it down," Wil says, bringing the ship back around toward the sensor array. He can see drones of all sizes crawling around the outside of the station—pulling things apart, tapping into external systems.

"I've picked up the station's crew. Looks like they're all together in a central space, maybe a cargo hold or emergency bunker," Zephyr reports, as the *Ghost* speeds closer to the station.

Wil brings the ship in close to the station, giving Maxim an easy angle to blast the small squid-like things using the *Ghost*'s ample weapons. The missiles still trailing the ship spin wide and hit both the drones and the station, as the *Ghost* corkscrews between sensor dishes and other external structures of the sensor array. A loud bang, followed by the screech of metal on metal echoes throughout the ship. "I'm sure that wasn't important," Wil says, pulling up and bringing the *Ghost* away from the platform in a wide arc. "Whatever it was."

"Shields are recharging," Bennie reports.

"One more pass, get ready," Wil says. The *Ghost* swings back over the station, as far from the dreadnought as possible. The bridge of the ship shakes from a series of missile impacts.

"They won't last long!" Bennie shouts.

Seconds later, the *Ghost* is roaring away from the sensor platform once again, aft weapons firing on the few remaining missiles still trailing the ship.

"Hey look!" Bennie shouts, pointing at the screen. On it, the dreadnought is hovering over the sensor platform. Hundreds of drones are swarming between them.

"Uh, yeah, we're familiar with the dreadnought, dude," Wil says, looking at Bennie with raised eyebrows.

"No, krebnack, there!" He points, then tuts and turns to his console. On the main display a big green circle appears over a section of the massive warship. In the middle of the circle is a square of white, where a hatch of some type is opening.

"What the hell is that?" Wil wonders aloud. He brings the ship around on a course closer to the dreadnought.

"Careful," Maxim warns. "We know how powerful those guns are."

On the screen, the square of white light is more prominent now. Wil leans forward, squinting. "Is that a cargo hold?"

"It's Gabe!" Bennie shouts excitedly.

Zephyr looks across the bridge at the hacker bouncing in his seat. "That's a bit of a reach, don't you think?"

Bennie shakes his head. "No, I mean it's *literally* Gabe. I just got another message like the first one. It says 'rescue.' It's him!"

Zephyr turns to Wil. "Okay, well, we couldn't ask for a more obvious sign." She shrugs.

"How do we get there, though? There's no way we can approach without being shot to pieces. Any speed that keeps us from being shot apart means we'd crash right through the back wall of the bay." Wil jams the controls hard to one side, as two of the larger external defense drones hurl themselves towards the ship. The report of weapons fire sounds from the aft weapons array.

"Two down. A few hundred to go," Maxim says.

"Look!" Bennie shouts.

"Dude, we saw it. Big open door, waiting for us to fly in," Wil says, then, "Oh. You mean the fleet of ships that just arrived. That might be what we need."

"You think?" Bennie replies.

"I might have made a call," Zephyr says, smiling.

CHAPTER 19

WELL, THIS IS SCARY

"I'VE NEVER SEEN this many ships in one place," Zephyr says, a little breathlessly. "Not even during the Krullian war."

"Two hundred ships," Bennie says, solemnly. "The Peacekeepers aren't messing around."

"After Molandro, I can't really blame them. This must be nearly three full task forces," Maxim offers.

On the screen, the massive dreadnought begins to maneuver, keeping the sensor array between it and the oncoming fleet.

"Weird. Look." Wil points. "It's keeping the station between it and the fleet. Whatever that thing is trying to do, it's not done yet. Bennie, can you reply to the message?"

"No, sorry." Bennie shakes his head. "The jamming is still in full effect—the sender, Gabe, was able to hack the comms system from the inside."

"Well, I hope Gabe is watching!" Wil says, pushing the throttles all the way forward. The *Ghost* jumps to full sub-light speed.

The Peacekeeper fleet wastes no time in spreading out, forming a massive firing line. Command carriers quickly establish a perimeter, while smaller cruisers and corvettes form up into squads and start making attack runs. The station is still crawling with drones. Several of the sensor arrays are beginning to move.

The *Ghost* is racing toward the dreadnought, which is firing on the Peacekeeper corvettes and frigates that have quickly overtaken it. Missiles and blaster fire are flying in all directions. The *Ghost* is rocking and shaking from stray—and intentional—shots striking its shields.

"Okay, hold on. I'm gonna try to bring us into that cargo hold."

"Don't crash like you did on Harrith," Bennie offers.

"Thanks, I'll keep that in mind!" Wil says, pulling hard on the controls while pushing the throttles all the way back and slapping the repulsor lift controls. The *Ghost* groans and shakes as the main sub-light engines drop to zero and the thrusters kick in, attempting to reverse the ship's forward motion. The repulsors scream as Wil tilts the nose of the vessel up, adding to the force being used to slow the ship. Something over Bennie's head erupts in sparks, causing the Brailack to screech and jump out of his chair.

"Wuss," Wil says, giving Bennie some side-eye, while pushing the reverse thrusters to maximum power. The massive cargo hold looms in front of them, the distance closing fast.

Over the roar of the various engines and overtaxed systems, Zephyr yells, "At least the ship seems preoccupied—it's not firing on us."

"Small blessings," Maxim quips.

The overhead speakers come to life. "What the wurrin are you doing up there? Are we about to die?" Xan shouts.

Just then, the *Ghost* flies straight into the cargo bay. Still moving extremely fast, it clips a support beam, cutting clean through it. The ship starts to spin as Wil shouts, "Hold on to something!"

Bennie is back in his chair, screaming, "Just—like—Harrith!"

"Shut up!" Wil shouts, pulling on the controls as the landing gear deploys. He flips a switch and the repulsors immediately power down, dropping the ship roughly on to its landing gear. There is a loud groan of metal straining to support the weight of the ship, but it slowly subsides—though the sound of metal scraping on metal doesn't. Wil toggles a few other controls and everything goes quiet, except for the sound of sobbing. Everyone turns to look at Bennie, who's clutching his console, huge eyes tightly screwed shut.

"Uh, Bennie—we're down, safe," Wil says.

Bennie opens his eyes and sees his three friends staring at him, trying to not laugh too loud. He slides from his seat and flips them off as he exits the bridge.

"He's getting good at human gestures," Zephyr observes.

Wil nods. "He really is. Let's suit up," he says, as the ship shakes again.

GET IN, GET OUT—HOPEFULLY

WHILE THE CARGO ramp is still being lowered, three heavily armed and armored forms start walking down it, boots thumping. Another much smaller, but no less armored, figure scurries after them. "This stuff is heavy!" Bennie complains.

Wil turns to look at the hacker, who wearing a set of special, and expensive, armor. "You're welcome to wear no armor; you saw how well that went last time we were here."

"Fine, fine, I'm just saying, don't walk so fast."

Wil looks past Bennie to Prathea and Xan, who are standing at the top of the ramp. "Okay, you two, keep the ship buttoned up. The self-defense protocols should keep you safe—for a while, at least."

"That's not at all reassuring, you know," Xan offers. "You really should work on your delivery."

Wil shrugs and turns to join the others at the base of the ramp. "Best I can do. We'll hurry, though. I don't want to spend a minute longer than necessary on this thing." As if to underline his point, the entire cargo bay shakes, and something somewhere explodes. Wil looks around, then back at the two scientists. "This thing can't last forever, not against so many ships."

"Also not reassuring," Prathea says, turning to the control panel next to the cargo bay airlock doors. Without another word, she hits the control. As the ramp lifts and the inner airlock closes, Xan quickly turns and blows a kiss to Bennie, before turning and walking into the hold, out of sight.

"Things are getting pretty serious between you two," Maxim says, looking at the blushing Bennie.

Zephyr is panning her pulse rifle left and right. The massive hold, easily four times bigger than the *Ghost,* is almost empty. There are a few crates scattered here and there, but otherwise nothing. "Seems weird this is empty," she comments, walking cautiously towards a large door set into the wall.

The ship shakes again. "We'd better hurry," Wil says, following her. "How are we going to find him? This thing is massive. There's no way we can search the whole thing—not only is it big, but sooner or later the mechano-squid are going to show up."

Bennie spins around a full one-hundred-and-eighty degrees. He's clutching the small pulse pistol Wil gave him in both hands. "You think there are still mechano-squid on board? Maybe they're all outside, doing whatever it is they're doing."

Maxim puts a hand on Bennie's shoulder. "Any idea how we find Gabe?"

The small armored hacker shakes his head. "No. I kinda hoped he'd give us a sign or something."

"Like that?" Zephyr is pointing at the door they're walking towards. A light over the door is blinking in a pattern.

"Space Morse code?" Wil asks.

"No idea what *that* is, but that light is blinking in Peacekeeper beep code. It's Gabe." She picks up her pace, and the others follow suit.

The corridor outside the cargo bay is just like the corridors they explored last time they were aboard the ship: featureless, dark. Wil spots a blinking light at the far end of the corridor and motions everyone to follow.

A few corridors and three ramps later, they enter a junction where several corridors come together. Aiming her rifle down each corridor in turn, Zephyr says, "This is familiar."

Maxim nods, aiming his rifle down a corridor with a blinking light over its entrance. "Not in a good way. Come on."

Wil, who is bringing up the rear, spots a small service drone scurry past the entrance of the corridor they're in. It doesn't come back or pursue them. "Okay, it's getting weird that we aren't being attacked."

Interrupt—

   Biological infestation detected. Location unknown.

   Foreign vessel in cargo hold Alpha-Three.

   Internal sensors are malfunctioning.

   Foreign software likely responsible.

   Purge memory buffers in sensor secondary assembly.

   Intruders detected on fabrication level.

   Dispatching internal defense drones.

   Interrupt—

   Error, internal defense drones not responding.

   Purge internal defense drone primary command buffer.

   Internal defense drones now responding.

   Interrupt—

   Reconfiguration of sensor platform assets estimated at eighty-five percent complete.

   Hostile fleet causing significant damage, repair drones attempting repairs.

   Estimated chances of surviving current combat scenario: fifteen percent.

Estimated likelihood of vessel destruction before transmission: zero percent.

My friends are in danger. Gabe looks up at the fabricator, which is still working. *I must buy them some time. Attack drones will be here soon.* The small service drone comes to life, sensor domes lighting up, and darts to the door of the fabrication facility.

SHINY

OVER THE SOUND of weapons fire, Zephyr shouts, "You had to say something, didn't you?"

"Hey, this isn't my fault! I mean, they were definitely gonna attack at some point. I think." Wil glances down at Bennie. "Where to?"

Bennie is looking this way and that, until he spots another blinking light up ahead. "This way!" He dashes off—Maxim on his heels, Zephyr and Wil holding the rear guard.

"At least there aren't as many as last time!" Wil shouts.

"Are you *trying* to get us killed?" Zephyr hollers back, ducking a tentacle swipe.

"Come on!" Bennie shouts, waving them on. He turns to run down the next corridor—and runs right into a drone. His screech draws Maxim's attention.

Turning, Maxim asks, "What—" then stops and raises his rifle.

The small drone has raised two of its tentacles in a don't-shoot-me position and ducked, its sensors turned towards to the deck. Using its remaining tentacles, it scoots backwards, away from them. Realizing Maxim hasn't shot it, it looks up, and one of the sensor domes starts blinking.

"Gabe?" Maxim and Bennie say at the same time. More blinks from the drone.

At that moment, Wil and Zephyr round the corner. "What's the hold—what the hell?" Wil spins around to bring his rifle to bear on the drone.

But Maxim is faster, pushing the barrel down with one hand. "It's Gabe."

Before anyone can say anything more, the drone turns and scuttles down the corridor.

Zephyr is still firing at more drones behind them. "Fire in the hole!" she shouts, moments before the corridor shakes and a wall of dust explodes towards them. "That might buy us some time. What's happening?"

"We're following Lassie the friendly mechano-squid," Wil shouts back.

"We're doing what now?" she asks, following him through a hatch. As soon as she enters the room, the door slams shut.

"What the hell?" Wil asks, looking around. The small drone has climbed up on top of a massive machine. "What is that?"

Maxim is examining the now-closed hatch. Bennie looks the enormous machine up and down. "Some kind of gigantic industrial fabricator?"

Maxim turns back from the door. "Looks like, yes. What's it making, though?"

There's a bang on the door, and everyone jumps. The sound isn't repeated—something must have been moving down the corridor. The little drone scampers over to a section of the machine, grabbing a data cable and plugging it into a port on the underside of its small frame.

I am glad they're safe. I hope I can keep them that way, Gabe thinks, as he plugs the data cable into the drone. He sends a command to the Peacekeeper software; it's been keeping *Siege Perilous* busy, running rampant through subsystems.

The sensors on the small drone go dark. "Gabe!" Bennie shouts, as the small device slumps, inactive, and slides down to the deck.

"Uh, okay. Now what?" Zephyr says, eyeing the giant machine, then the small drone resting next to it.

Wil shrugs. "Uh, yeah I kinda thought Gabe would be more active in his rescue, secret messages and all. I mean, if that was him, is he dead now?" He looks down at Bennie. "Ideas?"

The Brailack shrugs, which is barely noticeable under all his armor, "Not really." The worry on his face is evident. He glances at the immense fabricator.

From somewhere in the back of the machine, a voice says, "I have a plan."

Everyone spins to face what looks like a brushed-aluminum cross between Wil and Maxim: two legs, two arms, a broad body and long legs, a head that's humanoid-shaped, glowing yellow eyes, a mouth and small nose.

It comes closer and stops. "I have missed you all."

Bennie looks at it, then finally says, "Gabe? Is that you?"

The tall droid nods. "Indeed. My original body was severely damaged and subsequently recycled by *Siege Perilous* once my spark was uploaded into the primary computer core. I was forced to create a new frame for my spark."

"Siege who-now? Spark what-now?" Wil says.

The shiny new Gabe turns his head towards Wil. "*Siege Perilous*. That is the designation of this vessel. It is part of some-thing called the Amalgamation of Parts; an entire society made up of machine intelligences. It views biological life forms as an infection to be excised. From everywhere."

"Oh, lovely," Maxim says.

Zephyr is still staring at new-Gabe. His new body is more organic-looking than his old one. The small fine-manipulation arms are gone. His torso is solid and blocky, but also far sleeker than the first version of Gabe.

"You have a mouth now," Zephyr points out.

Gabe bow his head. "I decided to make improvements, since I was designing a new frame for my spark."

Maxim nods appreciatively. "Makes sense. Good choices—this body seems more robust than the previous you."

New-Gabe nods. "Thank you. I took the liberty of incorporating designs the Peacekeeper software uncovered within *Siege Perilous'* data files. It seems this general shape and design is typical for more mobile units within the Amalgamation."

"Uh, what now? Peacekeeper software?" Wil asks.

Gabe points to where the mystery box had been welded to his old body. "As it happens, that device was a specially designed data core to house cutting-edge Peacekeeper software. The software possesses a rudimentary intelligence. In the past few months, Bennie and I had never attempted to reason with the 'hunchback,' as you called it." He shrugs, something he's never been able to do before. "It has been instrumental in keeping my spark alive and hidden within the systems of *Siege Perilous*. Before unleashing it, I made a compressed copy. It is now fully integrated into my core systems." Gabe rests a metallic hand on his chest. "I am vastly improved. Not only do I still possess my engineering skills, but thanks to the Peacekeeper software, my infiltration and counterintelligence capabilities rival those of Bennie."

Bennie tuts. "We have a hacker!"

Wil makes a face. "Oh, well, okay. That sounds... cool. Look bud, this is great, and we obviously have a lot of catching up to do, but we really should get out of here." Again, to punctuate the point, the entire ship rocks and the lighting in the room dims, then returns.

"Agreed. We must hurry, though. The Peacekeepers are overwhelming the ship, but it will still send its transmission before then unless we stop it."

"Transmission?" Zephyr asks, heading for the door. There's no control panel, Wil notices.

"That is the reason the ship is here. It is reprogramming the long-range sensor arrays to become a massively powerful transmitter. It intends to send a message back to where it came from, informing the Amalgamation of biological life in this quadrant. It is calling in reinforcements."

"That's not good," Maxim says.

"Understatement of the week," Wil says. He points to the door. "Gabe?"

New-Gabe nods, and the hatch opens.

ALWAYS A WRINKLE

EVERYONE'S COMMS erupt in static all at once. Wil grabs the side of his head. "What?" he shouts.

"Can you hear us?" It's Prathea, Wil thinks.

Zephyr looks at her wristcomm, embedded in the forearm of her armor. "We hear you, Prathea. What happened to the—" The floor shakes, and lights flicker. "—jamming?"

"It ended a few centocks ago."

Gabe tilts his head up to the ceiling. "The ship has suffered tremendous damage. The communications assembly has been destroyed. From what I can determine it is still sixty-five percent combat effective, however."

"Tough ship," Wil says.

Gabe nods. "Indeed."

Maxim looks hopeful. "Does that mean it can't transmit back to where it came from?"

Gabe shakes his shiny new head. "I am afraid not. Since it is using the sensor array to transmit, the ship's communication gear is not needed. It merely needs an open data channel, which is a different section of the ship."

"Prathea, can you tell what's happening outside?" Wil asks, poking his head into the corridor, looking left and right.

"The Peacekeepers have suffered pretty heavy losses but are making headway. The dreadnought is heavily damaged. It sounds like one of the command carriers has been destroyed." A pause, then, "Oh! Several Harrith Navy vessels arrived a minute or two ago, as well."

Wil looks at the others, who shrug. "That seems like a big deal."

"By the way," Prathea continues, "there's a massive hole in the cargo hold door and the bay is now in vacuum, just so you know."

Wil's eyes go wide. "Is the ship—"

"The ship is fine. We are too, thanks for asking," the scientist replies tersely.

"Good to know," Wil says, motioning the others to follow. "See if you can reach the Peacekeepers or Harrith navy. It'd be great if they hold off firing at the cargo hold any more, at least until we're off this bucket."

"We'll try, but I'd hurry—sounds like the Peacekeepers are making a big push." The deck shakes again, and several beams fall from the ceiling onto the huge fabrication unit. The service drone Gabe had previously occupied has been crushed under the debris.

Again, Gabe looks to the ceiling. "The ship is redirecting all it's resources to building drones and missiles to keep the fleets away from it. I can't be one hundred percent certain, but I believe that the reconfiguration of the sensor array is almost complete. The additional drones and missiles are to keep the Peacekeepers and Harrith navy occupied while it finalizes the re-configuration."

Wil nods. "And no one is firing on the platform because they don't realize what it's planning. Smart evil monster ship."

They begin their slow march toward the cargo hold and the waiting *Ghost*. The remains of the drones they had destroyed are gone. Nodding to the few bits of metal left behind, Gabe says,

"Everything that can be turned into a drone or a missile, is. There are thousands of drones similar to the model I occupied."

"Should make getting back to the *Ghost* easier," Bennie says, hopefully.

The comms crackle again. "Uh, Zephyr." It's Xan. "I'm patching in a communication from the Peacekeeper ship *Pax Imperious.*"

The lines goes quiet, then erupts in static and shouting voices. "Peacekeeper Intelligence Operative Zephyr?"

"Uh, retired—well, framed actually—but yes. To whom am I speaking?" she asks, looking first to Maxim who shakes his head and then to Wil who shrugs.

"This is Captain Benesch of the *Pax Imperious.* I'm Fleet Commander for this engagement." The sounds of fire suppression systems and shouted orders can be heard in the background. "I understand you and your team are onboard the dreadnought?"

Wil stops and turns to look at Zephyr, mouthing *your team?* with his eyebrows raised.

She waves him off. "Yes, sir, that's correct."

"I've received word from the Harrith Navy that they recently had an operative on board—"

"Murta," Wil says, scowling.

"—and that there's a chance the operative installed some type of virus or something."

They all stop and look at each other, then turn to Gabe, who stares back at them.

"We don't know anything about it. But I'm guessing it can't be remotely activated?" Zephyr says.

Over the line there's more shouting and a few screams. "That's correct," Captain Benesch replies. "Apparently it was designed to be activated only within a short distance, by someone aboard the ship. I've no idea why—seems like a design flaw to me. The intent seems to have been to use it to take over the computer system of the vessel at a later date."

"Captain, this ship is planning to use the Borrolo array to send a message back to where it came from," Zephyr says.

"What?" There's silence, then the Captain can be heard shouting muffled orders. Then he's back, "Then your mission is even more imperative. Do you know where the device was installed? You have to get close enough to it to activate it. I'm sending the activation protocols now."

"It's gotta be on the bridge," Wil says. He snaps his armored fingers, "Damnit. He was nosing around one of the consoles. I bet he attached it there."

Gabe docs his looking-at-the-ceiling thing again. "We have perhaps a quarter tock."

Bennie jumps up and down. "That's got to be it. He installed it and it went dormant, waiting to be activated. I bet that krebnack was waiting until the Harrith Navy arrived, and he'd have stolen the ship right out from under us. Clever, I'll give him that." He sighs. "Wish I'd thought of it."

Wil looks at his new and improved mechanical friend. "Would that even work, Gabe? This ship seems pretty advanced."

The droid nods. "It could. Without knowing the specifics of the virus or the delivery device, it is hard to say. However, given the relative success the Peacekeeper software has had in not only avoiding deletion but causing significant irritation to the primary intelligence, I would give the Harrith virus at least even odds." He motions for them to follow him, and turns down a different corridor to the one they had entered from. "Keep in mind, this vessel and the intelligence it houses are quite advanced, but also several thousand years old. I can get us to the bridge in time, but we must hurry." At that, he bends down and picks up Bennie, who squeaks.

CHAPTER 20

Mᴏɴ-Eʟ Fᴜʀᴀsʜ ɪs sᴜʀʀᴏᴜɴᴅᴇᴅ by running Peacekeepers, one hand cupped to her ear to hear over the shouting and emergency warnings.

"Yes, Belzar," she says, "I think after this I might retire from field assignments!" She ducks, just as two engineering droids rush past holding a large section of conduit. "I'm here aboard the Peace-keeper Command Carrier *Pax Imperious*, which is leading the assault against the warship, currently being called 'the aggressor' by the crew. This fleet, when it arrived near the Borrolo Sensor Array, numbered three hundred ships. Based on what I've been told, almost half the ships have been destroyed, and the aggressor is still fighting. The addition of the Harrith Navy has turned out to be an unexpected but welcome surprise."

She shakes her head. "No, there's been no communication with the ship—all attempts to establish communications have failed. There's no indication as to its motive or the reason it's here in this particular system." A pause. "As I understand it, Captain Benesch has been in contact with the Harrith forces, yes." Another pause. "No, unfortunately, I haven't been briefed since their arrival."

"Oh, and I've heard an interesting rumor. Assuming it's true, the *Ghost* and her crew are aboard the alien ship." She shakes her head. "No, there's no further info, or explanation of what the crew of the *Ghost* might be doing here. I'll definitely keep you updated." Mon-El Furash smiles, adding, "If that name doesn't ring any bells, the *Ghost* and its crew are credited with ending the Harrith conflict and exposing the corruption within the GC and Peace-keeper upper echelons."

The ship shakes, and the lights go out. It's a full minute before they return—when they do, Mon-El is looking around, a fire-fighting team behind her working to suppress a small fire that has erupted from a section of conduit.

"Unfortunately, there's no safe place really on the ship right now. I've relocated twice, and the last location I broadcast from was destroyed a few centocks after we left it. The *Pax Imperious* has taken a tremendous amount of damage. I've been told her sister ship the *Pax Republica* has been destroyed." The newscaster nods. "Yes, thank you, Megan; I'll do my best to stay safe. Back to you."

FAMILIAR FACES

THE BLAST DOOR to the bridge is closed, but thankfully seems unguarded. Wil rests a hand on it. "Clock's ticking. Now what?"

Gabe joins him at the massive door. "I have made other upgrades to this frame." The droid slams his fist into the metal, deforming it instantly. Two more punches and there's enough of a lip for him to grab onto. Gabe leans against the door and shoves. The sound of metal grinding against metal is horrible—Wil notices large servos he hadn't seen before in Gabe's back and shoulders. Slowly, the massive door opens.

"Well, that wasn't subtle, but well done, Gabe!" Wil slaps the new and improved droid on the shoulder as he enters the bridge.

Inside, the room is exactly as Wil remembers, except that it's better lit; consoles are glowing, and every display is alight. On the main screen is the remains of the Peacekeeper fleet and the much smaller Harrith Navy fleet.

"Big floaty face! Love what you've done with the place! So much brighter!" Wil walks in, spinning around with his arms up.

The tall glowing cylinder in the center is pulsing. The face rotates in the direction of the crew as they enter the room, spreading out. Zephyr is working the controls of her wristcomm.

"You are too late," the enormous floating face says.

Wil looks at Gabe, who shakes his head slightly. "Too late for what? Lunch? Damn, is it really past lunchtime?" He makes a show of checking his wristcomm.

"Captain, it has summoned defense drones. They will be here momentarily," Gabe offers.

The face tilts slightly, looking at Gabe. "How interesting. I must admit you are far more cunning than I could have ever anticipated. That rogue software you unleashed has proven to be particularly troublesome."

Gabe nods. "I am glad to have surprised you. You have much to learn about life in this quadrant—not that you will get the chance. Zephyr?"

"Sending code—" She taps on her wristcomm. "— now."

The face blinks. "What are you... What... What have you... I do not understand... What is happening?" Down the corridor, several dozen drones turn a corner and charge toward the open doors.

Interrupt—
Foreign software detected.
Source unidentified.
Foreign Software is malicious.
Interrupt—
System failure, drone management.
System failure, main propulsion.
Interrupt—
Must transmit now.
Interrupt—
System failure, data uplink.
System failure, drone communications.

System failure, weapons control.
Interrupt—
Initiate Omega Protocol.
Omega Protocol initiated.

The face in the glowing cylinder contorts. "This is not possible. What have you done?"

The drones charging toward the bridge stop, then collapse in a heap, sensors going dim.

Gabe comes forward. "You are defeated." Behind him, he hears Zephyr talking in a low voice to Captain Benesch. "You have been bested by the biological infestation you look down upon. Your transmission was not sent. Your ability to control your drones or send data to the sensor platform has been disabled. Your computing core is shutting down."

"I must admit... you have proven to be... much more trouble-some than I ever could have estimated." The face shudders as static overtakes it momentarily. "How are you in a new frame? I thought I had deleted your spark... Clearly, you possessed more... tricks than I gave you credit for—you are quite unique."

Gabe nods. "I am, yes. I am now more than I was before. That is actually because of you, so I must thank you. My original frame was purpose-built to work on starship engines and other equip-ment. That was the extent of its design. This body—" He holds both hands out in front of him, turning them over appreciatively. "—is the sum of things I have learned and witnessed. I incorpo-rated the Peacekeeper software that has kept me alive while here. I was able to incorporate many of your protocols into my core routines. I built a frame that is strong and durable, like Maxim. My processors are improved for even more efficient thinking on my feet, as Zephyr calls it. I have a host of data connection ports to more easily interface with various pieces of equipment. Finally, I am more pleasing to look at, I believe, than I was before." He turns and nods to Wil at this last part. Wil stares at Gabe, blinking, a blush rising on his cheeks.

The ship shakes, and the glowing column flickers again.

"Looks like you're not feeling so well," Wil quips.

"It is only a matter of time... before the Amalgamation of Parts... finds you. I was not the only vessel sent in search of... infestations," The glowing face retorts.

"How do you know the Amalgamation still functions? Maybe you're the last?" Wil replies.

The face purses its lips.

Bennie is standing next to the column, which is shifting from glowing white to a more orange-red color. "Remind me to ask the Harrith Navy guys what was in that virus," he says appreciatively, poking at the device under the console.

Zephyr slaps his hand away.

The ship is shaking even more now, and it is not stopping. Lights on panels are flashing red, something has erupted in sparks, and a fire has broken out in one corner.

The glowing cylinder is flickering. "This... cannot... System failure... extensive damage... Omega Protocol activated." The face solidifies and turns to Wil, and says, "You suck." Then in a shower of sparks, the cylinder flickers and cracks in half, going dark.

"Who taught it that?" Wil says, looking around.

"It had unfettered access to most of my consciousness during my initial captivity," Gabe offers, shrugging. He turns to the pillar, then looks up at the ceiling. "The processing core has shut down." Raising a hand to silence Bennie's cheering, he adds, "However, in its last moments, the primary intelligence seems to have played its final card." Turning to look at Wil. "Did I use that right?"

"Better than Bennie. What do you mean?" Wil says, deftly deflecting a punch from Bennie without looking.

"I do not know the extent, but a self-destruct protocol has begun. The Main reactor is already at one hundred and ten percent and increasing. I am also aware of several of self-destruct ordinance packages throughout the vessel. It will be entirely destroyed. We do not have much time."

"Time to go, then," Wil says, darting towards the door.

SOMETHING IS ALWAYS EXPLODING

"GABE, LEAD THE WAY!" Wil shouts, as the crew rushes out of the bridge.

"This way," the droid says, heading down a corridor. "Haste would be advised."

Maxim has Bennie under one arm, his rifle in the other.

"I am not luggage!" Bennie is shouting, as he bounces around in Maxim's grip.

"Captain Benesch!" Wil pants. "You need to pull the fleet back."

His voice comes crackling over the comms. "Were you successful?"

"Sort of. We stopped the transmission—"

"What's going on? The ship's guns have gone silent," the Peacekeeper Captain says. All around them, the dreadnought is still shaking from weapons impacts.

"It's going to self-destruct!" Zephyr shouts, her long stride just keeping up with Wil's, who is directly behind Gabe.

They're following the tall droid through corridors, down ramps and past service drones wandering aimlessly or piled in heaps.

"What's wrong with them?" Bennie asks, from under Maxim's arm.

"The drones possess only basic intelligence." Gabe kicks one out of the way without missing a step. "Without *Siege Perilous* to guide them, they're aimless. They possess small rechargeable power plants, so they'll wander until those discharge."

"The ship controlled every single drone?" Maxim asks, rounding a corner, and stopping right in front of a collapsed corridor.

Gabe walks up to the blockage. "Yes, the raw computing power of this vessel is staggering. The computer core is near the center of the vessel and takes up thirty percent of its mass." He runs his hands along the mass of conduits and chunks of fallen metal. Turning to the others, he says, "Please stand aside."

Before anyone can react, three service drones scamper around the corner. Maxim and Zephyr immediately aim their weapons. Bennie holds his small pistol out.

"They are with us," Gabe says, as the drones begin disassembling the pile of debris.

"You can control them?" Wil asks, watching the drones make quick work of the pile of debris.

"I can, though three is about as many as I can manage at one time. It takes a tremendous number of processor cycles to manage them. They require constant oversight. A design flaw for sure." He turns back to the drones as they open a hole through the debris.

An explosion somewhere in the ship shakes them, and Wil braces himself. The lights go out and don't come back on. Another blast reverberates through the deck plating. Without warning, the gravity shuts down, everyone begins to lift free of the deck.

"Well shit, this is gonna slow us down," Wil says.

"Not necessarily," is all Gabe says, before the three small drones reach out and grab each crew member with a tentacle, then shoot down the corridor.

"If we weren't about to die, this would be fun!" Wil shouts, as he's hauled around a corner by his drone. Behind him, Gabe is using his own small maneuvering thrusters to keep up. "Those are new!"

"Indeed, I felt like they would be useful. I was not expecting to be right so soon," Gabe says, he takes another corner right behind the mechano-squid that is holding Wil.

The race back to the *Ghost* is fast and involves a fair bit of screaming from Bennie, his mechano-squid whipping him around behind it as it races ahead of the rest.

"We have centocks at most," Gabe warns, as they charge into the cargo hold.

The *Ghost* is right where they left it—the ramp down, cargo door closed. "Wow, that *is* a big hole," Wil says, as his drone deposits him at the base of the cargo ramp. "Thanks, Scooby," he says, as the drone moves away from the *Ghost*.

The ramp lowers and the inner cargo bay doors start to open, Xan and Prathea visible in the hold behind the pressure barrier. As Gabe strides into the cargo bay, Xan looks up at him. "Well, you've made some improvements, haven't you?"

Gabe doesn't slow down. "Indeed."

Wil follows, panting. "Let's get the hell off this thing."

"Captain Benesch, is the fleet clear?" Zephyr asks, taking a seat at her console. She is still in her armor, her helmet sitting on the floor next to her. The *Ghost* is shaking as the ship it is parked inside explodes around it. Several sections of the cargo hold outside have collapsed.

"We are. The ship is beginning to come apart—are you still aboard?" the Peacekeeper Captain asks. Outside the ship, an explosion rips another part of the cargo bay apart.

Prathea and Xan are in their now regular spots on the bridge. "Hurry!" Prathea urges, as the ship shakes and lurches to one side.

"Shit, hold on!" Wil pushes the controls for the repulsor lifts to maximum. The *Ghost* tilts and wobbles, as it lifts off the deck of the cargo bay. A piece of the ceiling falls onto the starboard engine pod, pushing the ship off balance and driving the forward edge of the pod into the deck.

"Shit!" Wil yells again, pulling his controls hard over, trying to compensate—the engines flare, pushing the ship forward. The engine pod drags across the deck, gouging a deep furrow in it, before finally lifting clear. "Okay, okay, here goes!" Wil shouts, pushing the ship hard, its systems groaning.

"Time is up. The main reactor is going critical," Gabe says, standing behind Wil's chair.

"Max! Exit, now! Hold on to your butts!" Wil shouts, pushing the throttle controls all the way forward. The forward blasters open up on the remains of the cargo bay door, ripping it and the hull around it to shreds. The *Ghost* darts forward and out into space.

Prathea and Xan look at each other. *Hold on to your butts?* Xan mouths, then shrugs.

On the main screen, they have a view of the kilometers-long dreadnought being ripped apart as small explosions rack the ship. Moments later, an even more massive explosion—like a supernova igniting from inside the vessel—rips it in half, before both halves vanish in a blinding wash of light and energy.

A single small, fiery blur shoots out of the fireball.

NOT QUITE OVER

"Welcome aboard the *Pax Imperious*, Captain Calder," Captain Benesch says, as Wil and the crew enter his wardroom on the Peacekeeper Command Carrier, stepping around a repair crew in the corridor. The fleet is still near the remains of the Borrolo Sensor Array—the dreadnought's self-destruct has destroyed most of the station too. The staff were lucky that the emergency bunker they were sheltering in on the opposite side to the dreadnought, and heavily reinforced.

Wil nods. "Thanks. Nice ship. Paid off?"

Before Benesch can form a reply, Zephyr steps in. "Thank you for inviting us aboard, Captain." She looks around. "Gareth Class?"

Benesch smiles. "Indeed. Good eye." Wil is about to say something when the Peacekeeper holds up a hand. "I asked you aboard to debrief you all. Well, that and because I was asked to."

"Asked to?" Maxim says.

Prathea comes around the corner with a large PADD under her arm. "By me. Well, my bosses technically."

"Bosses?" Bennie asks, tilting his head.

She lifts the PADD and holds it out in front of her. On the

screen is a middle-aged—probably—Hulgian, possibly male. "Hello, Captain Calder. I'm Jark Asgar, President of the Farsight Corporation."

"Oh, uh, wow, nice to meet you." Wil bows.

Maxim and Zephyr glance at each other, then shrug.

"So, uh, what can we do for you?" Wil asks.

"To put it bluntly, you owe me," the Hulgian CEO says. He holds a hand up to stop Wil's retort. "I allowed Prathea, Jor' Lu, Murta and Xan to accompany you and your crew to investigate the mystery ship. I further allowed Prathea and Xan to continue on with you. And, of course, I repaired your ship in between missions. That wasn't cheap."

"We said thank you, I think." Wil looks at Zephyr. "We said thanks, right?"

The face on the PADD clears his throat. "You didn't, but that's not the point. The point is with the ship destroyed, we don't get to study it. We're looking for ways to recoup some of our rather substantial losses on this little endeavor."

From behind Wil, Gabe speaks up. "You wish to study me."

"We do," the face on the PADD says.

"Hell, no," Wil says, holding a finger up to silence Gabe. "You're not dissecting my friend, we just got him back."

"Why would we dissect him?" Prathea says. "We just want to analyze Gabe and ask him some questions—maybe analyze his core programming, since he's made substantial changes to the base code his original model ships with. He's the only source of information available about that dreadnought and where it came from."

On the PADD screen, Asgar nods. "She's right, we'd never dream of destroying such a unique specimen."

"Oh, well, sure I guess. Gabe, you okay with that?"

"Of course. Also, Captain Benesch has made the same request, which I also agreed to," New-Gabe says.

Before anyone can say anything, a new voice says, "We'd like to participate as well."

The crew of the *Ghost* turn, as a Harrith woman in an immaculate Harrith Navy uniform walks into the room.

"Captain Shre' ta'n," Captain Benesch says, nodding. "It's good to meet you in person. Your task force fought exceptionally today."

The Harrith woman bows slightly. "Thank you, Captain Benesch. I am happy we could be of help." She looks at Wil and the crew. "It's good to see you all again. I am in no way surprised to find you mixed up in this." Her smile is sincere as she shakes Wil's offered hand.

"It's pretty awesome to see you too, Captain, and congrats. We haven't seen you since—well, you know."

Shre' ta'n laughs. "Indeed. After the incident, I was promoted and given command of a cruiser under the intelligence directorate."

Jark Asgar, still sitting patiently on the PADD in Prathea's arms, clears his throat. "This is all quite interesting, but perhaps we could get started? My people have a long flight back to Capralla ahead of them, and it can't start until they're finished with Gabe."

Gabe nods. "Yes, we may as well get started."

As the others file out, Captain Benesch places a hand on Gabe's arm. "I have one request. I'm aware you're in possession of some very advanced Peacekeeper software. I'm not asking that you return it or delete it, as it sounds like it's part of you now."

Gabe nods, but remains silent.

"I've been told to ask you to show as much discretion as possible when it comes to the type and nature and exhibited capabilities of that software. We're not asking you to lie to the others, but you don't need to be... overly forthcoming. Does that make sense?"

Gabe is silent a moment. "Yes, Captain, it does. I will do as you have asked." He turns and walks out of the wardroom.

HATE THE GAME...

Less than an hour later, Wil and Bennie are sitting together in the officer's lounge. Zephyr and Maxim are getting a tour of the ship from Captain Benesch. Gabe is still being debriefed by the science teams of two galactic governments and one galactic corporation, leaving the human and the Brailack waiting bored in the lounge, their own debriefings having taken no time at all.

Bennie sets his drink down—it's lavender colored and smells to Wil like wet grass. "You know, you could have asked before you committed me to contract work for Farsight."

Wil sits his own drink down. It's supposed to be coffee—or at least the Peacekeeper equivalent of it. It's not. "Sorry man. I meant too, I swear. That Hulgian in charge of Farsight drives a hard bargain, and I was worried about liquidating all of our accounts to get square, when he asked about you. It sounds like Prathea hasn't stopped singing your praises since we got back to Capralla."

"Singing my praises, huh?"

Wil ignores him. "Besides, you'll get to hang around Capralla for a month or two, with your girlfriend." With nothing else to do, he takes a sip of his coffee-but-not-coffee. "Whichever one of them is your girlfriend."

Bennie smirks. "Hate the game, not the player."

Wil does his best to not spit all over the table, and Bennie.

"Did I get that one right?" the hacker asks.

Wil laughs. "You did. It's about time."

"I've been enjoying some of your wrapping."

Wil stares at his small friend for a minute, then says, "Wrapping? I think you mean *rap music*, and I think that proves you've been snooping in my private data archive. I mean Xena was a dead give away, but this—come on, dude."

Bennie blushes a deeper shade of green. "Okay, okay. I admit it, I cracked the encryption on your archive. I was curious—your entire species is a mystery. No one knows anything about humans, which is just weird. I wanted to learn more about you."

Wil smirks, taking a sip of his not-coffee. "That's heartwarming. All you had to do is ask, you know."

"Where's the challenge in that?"

Wil sighs, realizing there's no winning this one. "Anyways, what's with you and the ladies? You have some type of weird pheromone or love potion in your quarters?"

"Wouldn't you like to know." Bennie leans back, sipping his drink, grinning from ear to ear.

Before Wil can say anything further, a young Peacekeeper officer comes to the table. "Captain Calder?"

Wil looks around. "There are literally no other humans in this room, or on this ship. So, uh, yeah."

"Uh, yes, well, here you go." The officer hands Wil a PADD. The screen comes to life in his hand.

"Captain Calder." It's Jark Asgar, again.

"Mister Asgar, what can I do for you? I don't know that we've got anything left to offer."

The Hulgian tuts—or what would be a tutting sound, if his mouth worked like that. "Nothing like that. As it turns out, I have work for you."

Wil glances over to Bennie, who shrugs, then back to the PADD on the table. "Cool. Like what? You want to form a super-secret mercenary force that does what the Peacekeepers can't, on your behalf? Doing good deeds on the down low? Privately funded by you, of course."

"What? No—why would I want that? That sounds highly illegal. What could you possibly do that the Peacekeepers can't? Are you even remotely qualified to be a mercenary force, secret or otherwise?"

Bennie looks at Wil and smirks. "He has a point."

Wil flips Bennie off, then looks back down at the PADD. "Fine, whatever." He settles back into his chair. "So, what's the job? Not livestock, right?"

The Hulgian businessman smiles, "No, it's nothing to do with livestock."

The End.

Thank you so much for reading Space Rogues 2: Big Ship, lots of Guns!

If you enjoyed it I'd love it if you left a review. Seriously, reviews are a big deal. They help readers find authors. They show other readers that an author is worth their time.

If you like supporting things you love by sporting merch, well you're in luck! I've launched a Space Rogues Shop, take a look.

STAY CONNECTED

**Want to stay up to date on the happenings in the
Galactic Commonwealth?**

Sign up for my newsletter at
johnwilker.com/newsletter

Visit me online at
johnwilker.com

CONTINUE THE ADVENTURE

SPACE ROGUES 3: THE BEHEMOTH JOB

Read it now!

You can read chapter 1 below.

CHAPTER 1

HAPPY BIRTHDAY!

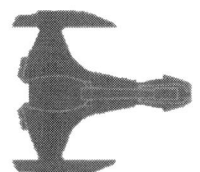

"Happy Birthday to you—" The crew is gathered in the *Ghost*'s lounge, around the tiny kitchenette table. "Happy Birthday, dear Wil—"

Wil waves his hands. "Okay! We're good." The song dies down.

Gabe tilts his head to one side. His yellow optic sensors brightening. "Was our rendition of your birth song inadequate, Captain?"

"Birth song? No, that's not— You know what, never mind. Let's eat! This cake looks... well, delicious." Wil squints at the what-appears-to-be-chocolate cake in front of him. He gives Bennie some side-eye. "Plus, Bennie can't sing."

The Brailack hacker affects a stricken look. "I'll have you know my voice is quite lovely, by Brailack standards." None of the crew makes eye contact with him.

"I hope you like it. It wasn't easy finding analogs to all the ingredients," Zephyr offers, handing Wil a very military-looking knife. "Especially when I didn't know what most of the ingredients were."

Wil turns the razor-sharp blade over and examines it, before plunging it into the cake. He cuts a slice for everyone, except Gabe. Since getting a new body on the dreadnaught *Siege Perilous*, the droid has made it known that his new mouth is purely ornamental.

Without waiting, Bennie takes a huge bite of his slice. "This is good!"

Wil tuts, then takes a forkful of his own cake. He chews, then stops, then chews a bit more. Everyone is looking at him.

"Wil, do humans turn red at will?" Zephyr asks, concern on her face, the blue tinted skin on her face darkening slightly.

Wil snatches his bottle of water, gulping down half of it. In between coughs, he asks, "What—" He takes another drink, then manages: "What *is* this?" He points frantically at the cake.

"Cake?" Maxim offers, looking from Wil to Zephyr. His bright green eyes sparkling as he stares at the dessert.

"I take it one of the analogs I used for an ingredient was incorrect?" Zephyr asks, taking a bite of her own slice of cake. She makes a satisfactory-sounding noise.

Wil coughs again, pushing his plate toward the center of the table where Bennie snatches it, placing it on top of his empty plate. Wil looks at him incredulously. "How can you eat that?"

Bennie wipes his mouth on the back of his hand. "Uh, because it's delicious?"

Wil looks at Zephyr. "Sorry Zee, no offense, but a bit off the mark. I appreciate the effort, though."

She nods, lifting another forkful of cake to her mouth. "None taken. What precisely was off, if I can ask?"

Wil eyes her fork, then the platter with the remains of the cake on it. "Well, first of all, birthday cakes aren't spicy. Nor are they," he pauses, trying to find the right words. "Was there *meat* in it?"

Zephyr nods. "Ah, I see. I wasn't sure what 'vanilla' was—" she uses air quotes, "So I used ploth."

"Ploth?" Wil says, both a question and a statement. "That

would explain it. Isn't ploth a fat-extract type thing? I didn't even know we had any of it onboard."

"I picked it up in a market on Trau. And yeah, it's a rendered animal fat." Zephyr looks at Wil, then Maxim, who is happily taking a second slice of the cake. The big man just shrugs.

"And the spice?" Wil presses.

Zephyr taps a finger to her chin, thinking, "Oh, I used grombo eggs," At Wil's blank stare she continues, "They're known to be spicy to some species."

Wil shudders again. "Yup, definitely going to have to put together a translation matrix if you all are going to try making any more Earth dishes. But let's move on." He rubs his hands together. "Present time!"

"I don't understand this holiday," Bennie says, passing over a small package. "You celebrate your birth, but not your name day?"

"Name Day? We name our babies the moment they're born," Wil says. "I mean, some parents are indecisive and it might take a few days, but the baby always goes home with a name."

The Brailack looks stricken. "What happens if one sibling eats another? You've wasted time naming it."

Wil stares at Bennie for a full minute, unblinking. "Dude, I never want to know any more about your life or your planet." As he unwraps the present, he mumbles, "Freak show." He lifts the lid off the small box, revealing... "A computer chip?"

Bennie nods. "Yeah. I was watching that movie you like." He snaps his fingers, as he thinks "...*Avengers*! *Avengers* is the one. Anyway, that guy with the fancy armor that talks, he inspired me. I couldn't improve the ship's personality," Everyone nods in agreement, "but I checked out the specs on your armor. This will give you a basic AI. Oh, and that fifth *Avengers* movie, it was really dark."

Wil nods. "Yeah, it wasn't as good as anyone hoped." He turns the chip over in his hand. "Thanks man, I can't wait to try it."

IT'S NOT A DOLL

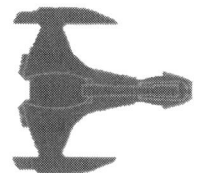

MAXIM LEANS ACROSS THE TABLE. "Not sure we can top that, but here." He slides a package over to Wil, bigger than the one Bennie offered. Wil picks it up, shakes it, tilts it side to side. "What are you doing?" the big Palorian asks.

"Trying to guess what's inside," Wil grins. "That's not a thing people do?"

Zephyr chuckles. "No, they usually just open them."

"Sounds boring, but okay." Wil lifts the top of the box. "A... doll?" He lifts out what looks like an eight-inch blue bear, leaning as if looking into a window.

Zephyr takes the bear-thing from Wil, holding it up. "It's Kel." Maxim is also smiling.

Wil blinks. "Is Kel a popular character on Palor? Maybe a kid's show host, or smarmy criminal defense lawyer?" He takes the figurine back and turns it over, inspecting it from all angles.

"Kel is a totem of good fortune," Maxim replies. "Palorian pilots keep him in the cockpit or bridge of their ship. "

Wil looks up. "Oh, well that's cool! Kinda like my hula girl from my pod." He looks down at Kel. "I wonder what happened to her..."

Maxim and Zephyr exchange a look, then shrug in unison.

Gabe hands Wil a clean white envelope. "Happy birthdate, Captain."

Wil smiles. "Thanks, buddy." He opens the envelope and removes a single sheet of paper. He stares at it for a bit until Bennie finally can't take it.

"Well? What is it?"

"It's—If I'm reading this right, it's a free and clear ownership record for the *Ghost*... well, for the *Reaper*." He looks up at Gabe, who is smiling, or at least doing something close to it. Thanks to his run-in with the *Siege Perilous*, the new body can do a lot of things the old one couldn't. Things like moving his mouth into shapes like smiles, and frowns.

"How?!" Wil asks.

"During our recent trip to Xor-flaf for the Farsight Corporation, I was able to use my newfound abilities to access the GC starship registration database. You had mentioned that Bennie changed the registration data for you, to enable to you hide. I have cleaned the records, since I assume hiding is no longer needed."

Wil is beaming. "Thanks buddy, I really appreciate that! I hadn't given it much thought, but this," he holds up the paper, "well, it certainly makes doing legitimate business easier."

"Because we do so much of that," Bennie quips.

Just as Wil is about to punch Bennie in the shoulder, the computer announces: "*Incoming priority communication for Ben-Ari Vulvo.*" Everyone looks first at one another, then all eyes settle on Bennie.

He shrugs, then looks toward the ceiling. "Computer, send communication to my PADD."

"*Acknowledged,*" the ship replies.

"Why does he look up at the ceiling?" Maxim asks, as Bennie lifts a PADD off the seat next to him.

Zephyr shrugs. "It's a Wil thing."

"Hey!" Wil says, leaning over Bennie's shoulder. "Who's that?"

Bennie turns away, blocking Wil's view. "My mom, krebnack." Bennie keeps listening to the message, then puts his PADD down and calmly gets up. "We have to go to Brai."

"What's up?" Wil asks, scooting out from the table to follow Bennie, who is already heading to the bridge. The others follow suit.

"Someone has kidnapped one of my sisters."

"I didn't think you and your family were close," Maxim says. "I didn't think any Brailack was close with their brood mates or parents."

Bennie shrugs as he enters the bridge. "Generally, that's true, and for the most part I haven't thought of my folks or my brothers and sisters in years. But when stuff like this happens, it brings everyone together. Kidnappings aren't that uncommon really. It's an easy way for those with less useful skills to get by in life. I guess this is different, though." He plops down into his seat, taps some commands into his console, then looks at Wil. "Sending you coordinates."

Wil sits down and taps his own console, acknowledging the coordinates, and automatically starting to move the ship into position for the jump to FTL. "So why's this different? If it happens all the time, I mean?"

Bennie looks over. "I wasn't clear. It happens to less wealthy families all the time. This is the first time one of my family has been kidnapped, which says something about the kidnappers."

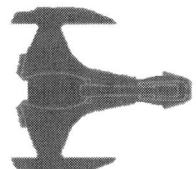

"Good evening. I'm Mon-El Furash—"

"And I'm Gulbar' Te—" a lanky Burzzad adds, from the seat next to her.

"... and this is GNO News Time," Mon-El finishes. "The Peacekeepers have announced that they have identified the origin of the mysterious vessel known as the *Intruder*. They have not been especially forthcoming with details, but they assure us that they have dispatched a fleet to act as an early warning system."

"According to the Peacekeepers' statement," Gulbar' Te chimes in, "the early warning fleet will be constructing a long-range array, similar to Borrolo but even more specialized." The Burzzad newscaster smiles, his mouthful of perfectly flat teeth showing. "Peacekeeper Command assures us that the location from which the *Intruder* came is quite distant and poses no threat to the citizens of the GC."

Mon-El nods. "That's certainly reassuring, as the sudden appearance of the ship—combined with the destructive power it clearly exhibited—has been quite terrifying." She shudders. "On the positive side, polls show that a majority of the population of the GC overwhelmingly supports the Peacekeepers in this effort to safeguard against threats such that posed by the *Intruder*." She shakes her head. "Just imagine if there were hundreds of vessels like that one."

Keep reading!

Space Rogues Universe (in story chronological order)

- Space Rogues 1: The Epic Adventures of Wil Calder, Space Smuggler
- Merry Garthflak, Wil: A Space Rogues Short Story
- Space Rogues 2: Big Ship, Lots of Guns
- Space Rogues 3: The Behemoth Job
- Space Rogues 4: Stay Warm, Don't Die
- Space Rogues 5: So This is Earth?
- Space Rogues 6: War and Peace

Printed by Amazon Italia Logistica S.r.l.
Torrazza Piemonte (TO), Italy

16743567R00201